Brown

Although some of the characters in this story have been drawn from people I've known, I would like to stress that the things they say and do are purely the stuff of fiction.

Cover by Nigel Chatfield

I feel trapped by a mutual affection.
(Mark E Smith)

And resentment rides high, but emotions won't grow.
(Ian Curtis)

Also, it takes much longer to get up North, the slow way.
(Ian Dury)

It was the very fag end of the Seventies and everything was brown.
So was Simone.

I first saw her in a student bar, skinny, faintly freckled, with hazel eyes and short dark hair.
She noticed me and came straight over with a tipsy smile.
"Hey, white boy," she said, "how about we get together and make beige?"
My immediate reaction was one of irritation.
But I got over it.
She was hard not to like. The kind of person who carries matches in case anyone needs a light.
Her father had recently died, leaving a pile of dated porn magazines. She brought them with her when she moved into my dark little flat in Longsight, and we used them as place mats.
She was sitting on the settee one day, watching me eat some home-made custard. I caught her eye, and the look on her face, one I had often mistaken for haughty, dissolved into a childlike grin, a narrow hand coming up to cover her slightly bucked teeth.
"Were you staring at me?" I asked.
"No! Just looking. D'you want more custard?"
"I couldn't."
"Don't you like my custard?"
"Of course I do."
But I didn't really. Nothing personal, I just never liked custard.
I should have said so from the start, but now I was stuck with it. A sort of Sunday afternoon tradition, like War, or 'Carry On' films on telly.
Sometimes she put bits of banana in it.
I didn't like bananas much either.

Monday.
I went round to the corner shop. The owner was an Irishman with a thin red face, blue nose and few teeth.
"How are you, Danny?" I said, as the bell above the door roused him from his newspaper.
"Ah, managing, Tim, managing. I do like to be managing. I'd fairly hate it if I couldn't manage. I have a little saying, 'if you're not managing, you won't manage.' Keeps me on me toes, that does."

He placed his hands into the large pockets of his off-white coat and scrutinised me with small blue eyes.

"You've run this place a fair few years," I remarked, picking up a box of farm fresh eggs.

"There, you've done it again, Tim, you're only after putting the proverbial finger on it! I think it's on account of all the learning you get at the University. I've managed this shop for nearly thirty years, seen them come and go, and all the time I've to be keeping an eye on my stock. Like it says in the window, 'from cans to candles.' I like to provide what the customer wants. Some of these Paki shops, sure they'll be open until ten at night, and Sundays, but can they get you a button, or a pair of laces? Fresh cut rashers at the counter? No sir, not on your nelly. Curry powder and intense sticks!"

Simone had been asleep when I came out, face pressed into the pillow. I wanted to have breakfast ready for her when she woke.

"Well, Danny," I said. "Good luck."

He peered at the betting pages, shaking his head.

"I'm going to bloody need it."

Simone's head appeared around the kitchen door, sleepy smile spreading. She breathed in deeply, scrambled eggs and toasting bread teasing her nose, and exhaled with a sigh.

"Do you have lectures today?" she asked.

"Tutorial. Metaphysical poets."

She laughed shortly.

"Fuck! And you *choose* to do this?"

"Why not?"

"I suppose. Maybe you can read me some physical poems some time?"

"Maybe not."

"You're mean!"

"And cruel, don't forget. Are you working today?"

"I work almost very day. And you never come to see me."

She was employed by the 'Glamour Cinema' to dance between porn films. They were actually projected videos, blown up images with blurred edges and distorted sound.

I saw one where a woman lay on a bed with an array of assorted vibrators arranged at her feet. She used the smallest first, and worked fairly laboriously up towards the biggest, a pale pink monster with knobbles and alarming girth.

Then, to a brash, treble-heavy tape of *'Je t'aime, moi non plus'*, Simone emerged from between purple velvet curtains, wearing a blouse, short stripy tie, grey pleated skirt, white socks and black plimsolls.

I didn't stay to watch her take them off.

"I don't particularly want to see you working," I said, turning off the grill on the dark brown gas cooker and handing her a plate of food.

"It's better than imagining stuff. It's just crap I do to help us live."

"There are old blokes in there wanking under their coats."

"What does their age have to do with it?"

"What?"

"Doesn't matter."

She put brown sauce on her grub.

Sage

Sunday again, already.

Simone's mother, Rose, was round for lunch. In fact she was cooking it, involving, among other ingredients, goat.

The air became heavy with simmering meat, condensation of emulsified fats steaming up the kitchen window.

"Mind if I nip out?" I asked.

Rose concentrated on stirring the pot.

"Would it make any difference if I did?" remarked Simone.

"Well I'll stay, if you prefer."

Rose turned, adjusting the strings on her apron.

"You'll just get under our feet if you do. You can bring me back a bottle of stout."

"But don't be too long," added Simone.

I usually went for a couple of pints when Rose was round. Gave her and Simone a chance to talk.

The fleur de lys flock wallpaper in the Coach and Horses, once maroon, was faded to a dull brown, the ceiling, nicotine ochre, criss crossed with mock Tudor beams.

I took a gulp from my pint of bitter before sinking, smiling, into a seat. Little opalescent shapes, like organisms under a microscope, floated across my field of vision in the hazy light.

Sage came in looking slightly sheepish. He was tall and wore a turban, the latter in deference to his faithful father, the former a genetic anomaly, both parents being barely five feet.

He spotted me quickly.

"Alright Tim, what are you having?"

Sage always addressed people as if they were at some distance from him on a windswept moor.

An old man's old West Highland terrier, startled, fired off a volley of high-pitched yaps.

"Stupid animal," boomed Sage.

"Go back where you belong," mumbled the man.

Sage laughed, flicked a peanut in the dog's face, and found himself a chair. He looked furtive.

"Something bothering you?" I asked.

"What do you think? It's easy for you, your family drinks. My Dad would go spare if he caught me in here."

"But he won't, will he? He's hardly likely to wander in mistaking it for a temple or something."

"He's cunning. He employs family to spy on me. Cousins snooping. I have to keep ahead of the game, out of sight."

"Sort of 'hide the Sikh', you mean?"

"Poor."

"Ka-poor, surely? Do you want to come for lunch?"

"Not Simone's custard?"

"No. Rose is round."

"Oh. Curry?"

"I think so."

"I'm supposed to be a vegetarian."

"You're supposed to be a lot of things."

"A tea total vegetarian virgin! My Dad's a hard man."

"He's sweet."

"To you, maybe, but not to his eldest son. He expects…"

He buried his upper lip in his pint and strained froth and stout through his moustache.

"Man, I can't even get a haircut! Everyone's getting crew cuts and I'm walking round like a fucking yeti."

"You're not supposed to swear either."

"Thanks, cunt."

Simone and Rose, looking frighteningly similar, were sitting at the kitchen table, plates and cutlery laid out before them.
"Nice of you to bother," said Rose.
"Yeah, and what's he doing here?" added Simone.
Sage hung back in the doorway.
"He was living off peanuts," I said.
"Wash down with beer," sniffed Rose. "You bring me that bottle of stout, boy?"
Luckily I had.
Simone opened it, and a bottle of 'Hirondelle'.
"Come on, Sage," she said, "there's plenty."
"This is really nice, Rose," said Sage, stuffing forkfuls fast.
"No need for you to shout, man, me not deaf you know."
"Sorry."
"So, boys," remarked Simone, "I suppose, having got pissed, and eaten all this food, you now intend sleeping in front of the telly?"
Before we could answer, Rose pointed a finger in the direction of the sink, then me, and handed a tea towel to Sage.
We listened to the women chat as we washed up.
"When you going to get a better job, girl?"
Simone had told Rose she worked as an usherette.
"There's not much about, Mum."
"Never mind, when Tim get his degree and start teaching, you can get married and you won't have to work no more. Especially when the babies come."
Sage grinned at me, whipping the corner of the tea towel at my groin.

Norman

He was a self-inviter, refugee from his sociology degree at Preston Poly. And there he was, shabby on the doormat.
"No welcome?" he asked.
"Come on Norman, get yourself in."
He was holding what looked like an empty carrier bag and had recently rather carelessly shaved his head.
"D'you fancy the rest of this pasty?" he asked, showing me the bag.
"Is that what the smell is?"
"What smell?"

"Never mind."
I nipped to the bathroom and turned on the taps.
"Tim, mate," yelled Norman, watching me from the hall, "there's no need to put yourself out."
"Oh, I think there is."
Ten minutes later Norman emerged from the bathroom surrounded by steam, a zombie in a graveyard mist.
He reached for his socks.
"You can't put those on," I said.
"Why?"
"They'll cancel out the bath. You can't wear any of it, ever. You can borrow some of my stuff and we'll go to Asda."

"Blimey," said Norman, looking down the aisles, "is there anything they don't sell?"
"Not a lot. But the main thing for us is the essentials, such as new socks and pants, deodorant, that sort of thing."
"You are one sardonic bastard."
"Thank you. Now, choose your underwear."
He did, but poorly.
"There's a fucking pony on these!" he yelled later from the bedroom.
"Just imagine it's a stallion."
"They're dead little an' all."
"Maybe they'll make your knob look big."
"What d'you mean, *look*?"
For some minutes the only sound from the bedroom was the twanging of elastic.

Simone came in later and found us in front of the box watching snooker.
"What is he doing here?" she demanded, before breaking into a benign smile and touching my cheek. "Your friends are all such disasters."
"Only the brown needed for the frame," announced the television commentator.
"We're watching the snooker," said Norman.
"Never."
"It's the semi-finals."
"Be still my heart. I'll make some custard."
Norman really appreciated Simone's custard.

"How can anyone make something so nice?" he asked, licking a coagulating remnant from the corner of his mouth.

"You should try her home-made yoghurt," I suggested.

"Should I?"

"Oh you should," said Simone, raising an eyebrow at me. "I use live fanny culture."

"He only missed the brown," said Norman.

He pulled off his plimsolls and stretched out on the settee, an ancient piece of furniture with worn upholstery sprouting horsehair like great tufts of pubes from a gusset.

And it was here, mostly prostrate, that he spent the best part of the following week, littering the worn carpet with take-away containers.

"How does he afford to eat?" Simone whispered one day on her way out to work. "I thought when we stopped feeding him he'd have slung his hook."

"He maybe gets tick at Danny's."

"And the take-outs?"

"Search me."

"I will. Bye."

I went in and prodded our guest in the ribs, and he rolled out from his sleeping bag, stood up, stretched, yawned, farted, and asked me if I was making toast.

Discovering I wasn't, he made his own, and I joined him in a cup of tea.

"So what's the deal with an English degree?" asked Norman, spreading Marmite like tar.

"What do you mean?"

"Well, what use is it?"

"Teaching, I suppose."

"You serious? You really want to be a teacher?"

We went into the living room and he lay down on the floor.

"I don't know what I want to be. And what are you doing on the floor?"

"Yoga," he said.

He started demonstrating.

"Old girl-friend taught me some positions."

"I bet she did."

He uncoiled his lower limbs and sat cross legged.

"Anyway," he said, "teachers are just school kids who never grew up."

I got down and tried one of the positions. It seemed quickly to restrict the flow of blood to my calves.

"Thing is," I said, getting up, "I don't particularly want to be anything. I mean why is it adults have to define themselves by what they do?"
"Come again?"
"You know, 'I am a Doctor', but are they still one when they retire?"
He pondered, picking at a sore on his upper lip.
"Yeah, I reckon so, coz they can still be called Doctor so-and-so instead of Mister."
"Ok, what about a fireman, when he's no longer wielding the hose? No! He did it once and now he plays golf or keeps tropical fish."
"I suppose some people like to impress. Depends what you do, really. I've heard there are people in France employed to go round picking up dog shit. That's a nice one at a party, 'I'm a shit collector', nice ice-breaker."
"Monsieur Merde."
"The turd policeman. There are some crap jobs, and I should know."
"How?"
"I had one."
"You had a job?"
"Once. And that was enough. It was in a chicken processing place and I had to cut 'em up. Some of 'em were still warm. Nice way to earn a living, cutting up the dead. I stuck it for a few days, and then I told the boss where he could stuff it."

Factory

Simone was working late.
For some reason I particularly disliked her evening sessions, even though, as she once pointed out, the 'Glamour' never saw daylight at any time.
"You could say the same about the clientele," I suggested.
"Don't be daft. And anyway, if anything, it's the afternoon punters you have to watch."
"You watching them watching you."
I went out to the Russel Club to see Joy Division.
Ian Curtis, corybantic on stage, starting like one repeatedly subjected to electric shocks, eyes rolling up into his skull.
"What's he on?" shouted Sage, stripping off his turban and stuffing it into a raincoat pocket.
Curtis was sporting a purple shirt, silk, or maybe viscose, sweat seeping through the thin fabric.
"She's lost control…"

A commotion suddenly broke out.

"Yes!" yelled Sage, clapping his hands together.

Peter Hook's bass had made its way into the audience.

"Did he throw it?" I shouted.

"I didn't see."

Hook stood rigid, legs akimbo, staring at the instrument being jostled among the crowd. Two bouncers stepped on stage, conferring with Curtis, while Hook stormed off, thrashing his impotent guitar lead across the face of his amp like a whip.

Stephen Morris played on throughout, a steady, repetitive rhythm, and was eventually joined by the remaining members of the band to complete a bass-less set.

"Excellent, fucking excellent!" exclaimed Sage, re-wrapping his head as we stumbled out.

The grey, crescent-shaped council blocks of Hulme curved around us like circling dinosaurs.

"How're we getting back?" I asked.

"Why don't you just stay with us?"

"Us?"

"Yeah, me and Hilary. She's got a flat in Charles Barry."

This was the first time he had mentioned Hilary, never mind having moved in with her.

I followed him up a pissy stairwell, down a concrete walkway, until we arrived at the purple door of a first floor flat.

Sage started searching through his pockets.

"Shit," he shouted. "Fuck this luck!"

"What?"

"You always say that. 'What?' I must've dropped my keys is what. You better get on my shoulders."

"What?"

"Just get up there will you? See that window? That's Hilary's room. Tap on the glass with a coin or something."

"Why don't you do it?"

"Ok, fine, I'll get on your shoulders. Firm yourself!"

I glanced at him. Tall, bulky.

"No, you firm *your* self."

After about ten pence worth of tapping, the sleepy face of a woman I supposed to be Hilary appeared between cautiously parted curtains. When I opened my mouth to explain, Sage's voice emerged.
"It's ok, Hil, it's me, and that's Tim. The bloke on my shoulders. I told you about Tim, didn't I?"
I felt like a ventriloquist's dummy.
Without replying, Hilary opened the window a little. A toothy smile split her broad face.
"Nice to meet you, Tim."
"Let us in, Hil!"
"Sage, can you stop yelling? Here's some keys, Tim. See you in the morning."
The light went out, and as I scrambled down the bunch of keys slipped noiselessly from my fingers.
"Did you see where they landed?" I asked.
Sage pointed solemnly at his turban.
I slept downstairs in a damp room with no light bulb, a restless night of dreams in which a bass guitar with a beard kept telling me I was a 'twat out of order'.
After several false awakenings, I heard somebody trying as quietly as possible to fill a kettle.
Hilary was standing with her back to me in the small kitchen that adjoined the room where I lay. Sensing she was being observed, she turned with an apologetic smile.
"Sorry if I woke you. I have to have tea first thing or I'm good for nothing. Speaking of which, I doubt you'll be seeing Sage this side of noon. Will you have a cup?"
She brought one through.
"I'd make you some toast, but I'm afraid someone scoffed all the bread. How's the tea? Not too strong for you?"
"Just right thanks."
"Excellent, a man who appreciates a proper cuppa! Sage barely lets the teabag see the water. Me, I think I'm addicted. Couldn't face class without it."
She told me she was in the early stages of her teaching practice.
"I'm not really sure if I'm cut out for it," she added, producing a small mirror from her bag. She applied some lipstick, brushed her fine, strawberry blonde hair, polished her glasses, and turned to face me.

"Well, Tim, do I look like a teacher?"

"Not like the ones I remember."

"That's what I thought."

"You wouldn't want to."

"No, I don't suppose I would. Hey, it's great to finally meet one of Sage's friends. I was beginning to think he was making them up."

"Why would he do that?"

"Oh, I don't know. Quite a lot of what he comes out with sounds a bit made up. It's probably just me. Sorry, going on about myself."

"Not really."

"Oh, you should try me! Luckily for you, though, I have to run."

We went out together, and after leaving her at the bus stop, I set off for home.

Simone opened the door before I could get the keys in.

"Nice night?" she said.

"It was ok. I stayed at Sage's girlfriend's place."

"Sage has a girlfriend?"

"Yeah. She's called Hilary."

"And what's she like?"

"Nice."

"And?"

"Kind."

She snorted.

"Nice, and kind. I feel almost like I know her."

"Well, you know."

"Except that I don't, do I? I mean is she black, white, what does she do?"

"I didn't ask."

"Do you have to ask someone what colour they are?"

"What difference does it make?"

"Well, none, to you, obviously."

"Are you annoyed because I didn't come home?"

"Not really, though you could have 'phoned."

"The 'phone's cut off."

"Always an excuse! Typical. No sense of curiosity either. Why is it men are so lacking in that department?"

"Never thought about it."

"No! Still, I'm happy for Sage to have found someone nice and kind. It'll be good for him. I was starting to think he might be gay."

"What?"
"You heard."
"Why?"
"Never mind, I have my reasons."
"What reasons?"
"Oh, I've seen the way he looks at you sometimes."
"What way?"
She started laughing, delighted.
"So you *can* be curious!"
She glanced at her watch.
"Shit, I'm on again tonight, I better grab some sleep."
She kissed my cheek.
"Maybe I could join you?" I ventured.
She folded her fingers round my hand.
"I really have to try and sleep."

Hands On

I was supplementing my grant by doing home care work, shopping or cleaning for housebound people, whatever they needed.
'Enabling the less able', as the agency put it. They took me on because I told them I had looked after my poorly grandma. In fact, all I'd ever really done, and only when her legs were playing her up, was to fetch her a quarter of wine gums.
I checked in one day, and they sent me to a flat in Didsbury occupied by a man named Mr Battyball.
"Come in, it's open," he called.
He was sitting in an old armchair, a very pale, round man, with fingers like raw chipolatas.
"Hello, son," he greeted me. "Fill my water jug, will you?"
It was a plastic container with tulip motif, stained with nicotine. I set it on the small table beside his chair.
"I don't drink as a rule," he said, half-filling a small tumbler from a bottle of Famous Grouse.
He was a former nightclub manager who had become accustomed, after many years, to the anti-social hours he worked. Now, retired, he found he was unwilling to go out of his flat.
"I'm not used to the daylight," he said. "Touch of the Count Draculas."
Also he had recently fractured his collarbone.

He raised the glass to his Charles Laughton lips, wincing with pain.

"I don't know how I managed this," he said, indicating with his chin the site of his injury. "Must have tripped over something, I suppose. I've never been particularly house-proud. Never spent enough time at home, only sleeping, and not always alone I might add. But no, that was me, up, shower and shave, cup of coffee and a fag, and off to work just when most people were settling down to watch the news. Make me one of them boil-in-the-bag, will you, and one potato? I don't eat a lot."

While I went to look in the fridge, he continued to chat.

"Here, did I tell you about Danny? He was a regular booking at the club. Lovely man. Not a pouf, you know. Class act. When he came on that stage, wig perfect, lovely legs…"

It took me a moment to realise he was referring to La Roue, and not O'Dowd of the corner shop.

"Don't over do that fish, will you son?"

While I attended to the meal, I heard Mr B. scrabbling about among his collection of long players, lifting the plastic lid of his music centre, and setting the stylus down on crackly Bobby Darin singing 'Beyond the sea.' The cod, in parsley sauce, bobbed about to the tune, steam gathering around the bare forty watt bulb that hung from the low, stained ceiling of the cramped kitchen.

"Beautiful singer," called Mr B. "Underrated. Charming, too. Generous! He used to give a guinea to every one of the cloakroom girls. Star quality. 'My love will wait on golden sands-ah…' Marvellous."

Serving the fish, I scalded my fingers cutting open the polythene bag, the sauce rushing precipitately onto the plate like the waters breaking before the birth of the greyish cod. Add to this one slightly flaky potato, all washed down with a lukewarm whisky and water.

After a couple of mouthfuls, Mr B pushed the food aside.

"Thanks, son, lovely," he said. "Here, see this ring?"

He indicated with a fish-flecked fork a monster cygnet affair on his left little finger.

"Very nice," I said.

"Nah, nothing much, not a bad bit of gold I suppose. No, what I wanted to tell you, that particular item of tomfoolery caused me quite a little problem some years ago. Thing is, I sleep heavy, see, and this night I had a lady friend stopping, and I must have had a bad dream or something, coz when I wake up she's only out cold! Terrific bruise over the eye. I must have made

some sudden movement, and that's a heavy ring. The ambulance men were very nice, very understanding…
Last I saw of the bird though. Cherchez la femme. Shame really…"
He removed the ring and held it up to the light, slowly shaking his head from side to side.
"Don't know why I still wear it."
"Brings back memories?"
"It does that, my old son, it does that… Still, this isn't getting us far is it? Can you fetch me a bit of shopping? There's a little off licence on Palatine road, I've got an arrangement. Two bottles of 'Grouse', son, tell 'em to ring me, they'll be all right. And maybe get me another of these fish things while you're out. I don't eat a lot."

Saa-m!

The television sitcom 'Bewitched' was responsible for me growing up believing cigars to be green. Larry Tate's always seemed to be.
When I first saw a real, brown one, I realised, either that 'Bewitched' must have been filmed using a poor colour process, or that our rented set had been crap.
At least we finally had colour. I still remember the day the new one arrived. The T.V. man switched on, and a familiar monochrome picture appeared, dashing my hopeful anticipation. Then he slowly *turned up the colour*. He must have pulled that trick a thousand times, but it was magic to me.
Before that I used to deny to the other kids at school that we still had black and white, a pretence they soon sussed by mentioning the hue of Shaggy's shirt on 'Scooby Do', and laughing with glee when I fell into the trap of confirming their fabrication.
But greatest contempt was reserved for my best friend Peter, whose parents had purchased a tinted screen that you attached to the front of your black and white. This was supposed to simulate colour telly, but the chief effect was one of watching programmes through an aquarium.
Simone and I now had a portable black and white with a bent coat hanger for an aerial. She kept urging me to get on the roof and try fixing a proper one.
One day I took her outside to show her how high up the roof was.
"We don't even have a ladder," I said.
She squinted skyward.
"Couldn't you shin up a drainpipe or something?"

"What?"

"Well, you could use the ledges."

"Are you really that tired of me?"

Leaving her obstinately scrutinising the façade of the building for footholds, I went in and turned on the T.V.

By coincidence, a Laurel and Hardy happened to be showing, 'Hog Wild', in which the pair were attempting to erect a rooftop aerial so Mrs Hardy could listen to her new radio.

Simone came in just as a brick fell onto Hardy's head.

"Look at it," she said.

"I am."

The picture was snowy, ghost images of the actors following them around the screen.

Simone sighed.

"When I watch my Mum's, the picture's so clear it takes me about ten minutes to get used to it."

"Of course. I mean everything's so much better at your Mum's."

"I didn't say that."

"You didn't need to. Just coz we've got a shitty black and white…"

"Is that supposed to be some kind of a joke?"

"You tell me. I'm sure everything's much more colourful away from here."

"Tim, how did we get into this?"

"You started it."

"Oh, for Christ's sake! How?"

"Going on about stuff."

"Going on? It was a stupid joke about the T.V. aerial!"

"And not an excuse to have a go at me?"

"Tim, I don't even know what you're talking about. I can't believe what's happening here."

"Well that makes two of us."

"So what can we do about it?"

"Why don't you just go and watch your Mum's nice colour television?"

She did.

Academic

Simone's seemingly indefinite absence afforded me some quiet moments of contemplation not even Norman could disturb, and I realised I had been neglecting my studies.

In fact I hadn't been near a lecture or tutorial for over a week, a circumstance reinforced by the arrival of a 'concerned' letter from my personal tutor Doctor Brooks.
Time to pull my socks up.
I got my satchel, containing an unfinished essay on Malory's 'Morte D'Arthur', pocketed my pen, and struck out for the library.
I got as far as the Union building, where I decided to nip into the bar for a quick spot of lunch.
I bought a half of Guinness and some chips, ferreted out my essay, and pretended to be reading it through.
"You've got that upside down!" came a mocking voice at my shoulder.
It was Imelda, who, despite being the only student around who was both Irish and named Imelda, was generally known as 'Irish Imelda.' This was technically a misnomer as she was from Derry, but it was a brave soul who would point this out to her.
She stole several chips from my plate, stuffed them in her mouth and asked if I felt like taking her to a Stiff Little Fingers gig.
"I'd rather break my fingers."
"Charming! My brother would do that for you, so he would, no problem."
"Except that he's in Derry."
"How d'you know, smarty pants? He may be over, for all you know."
"I doubt he'd even get across Belfast."
"He would so."
"No."
"Listen, our Roland goes wherever he wants, so he does."
"No he doesn't."
"Does too! Anyway, how did we start this discussion?"
"I'm not having a discussion."
"So you won't take me to a wee gig?"
"I don't think so. Wouldn't like to rile Roland."
"I thought you said he was in Derry?"
"What the fuck do I know, actually? Keep the rest of the chips, you look like you need them."
"I'll take that as a compliment."
"Take it how you like."
"Aw, Tim, touchy! I reckon you fancy me."
"Reckon on, sweetheart."
"You're weird."

"Am I?"

"Definitely, but in a good way. So how about we go and see The Fall? They're playing the Poly tonight, and I have a spare ticket."

I usually went to see bands on my own.

Simone wouldn't go.

"All that standing around, plastic glasses, smelly students."

"I'm a student."

"Not a smelly one."

"Cheers. Anyway, I reckon you're missing out. What about if Bob Marley was playing?"

"I think that's pretty unlikely."

"You know what I mean."

"But do I? And why Bob Marley? Why not the massed steel drummers of Saint Lucia?"

"Do they exist?"

"How should I know? Remind me, Tim, what's my favourite record?"

"The best of Andy Williams?"

"I rest my case."

Anyway she was still at her Mum's.

Imelda jabbed my hand with a plastic fork.

"Are you still with us?"

"Yeah. Ok, let's go for a drink somewhere, and then we'll see about The Fall."

"What's wrong with here?"

"It's full of students."

"That is very weird logic, so it is. Ok, we'll go to the 'Bowling Green.'"

This was a darkish little pub off the beaten track.

Imelda sat down while I fetched us halves of Guinness, and when I brought them over, I found her sniggering.

"I was just remembering Ian Anscombe," she said.

"What?"

"This lad at school, Ian Ronald Anscombe. Poor bastard, initials I.R.A."

"Parents can't have been thinking."

"Or maybe were."

"Did he have a sister called Ursula Diana?"

"No, I think her name was Bobby."

She stuck a forefinger in the head of her stout, sucked it, and started laughing again.

"Oh, God," she said, "I'd forgotten this. There was this lass by the name of Lesley Behan."

I looked blank.

"Les Behan, get it? Poor cow."

She held her drink up to a shaft of hazy, dust-flecked sunlight that had broken suddenly through the window.

"Jesus, I wish to God I could afford a proper drink, so I do."

"What's a proper drink?"

"Oh, I dunno. Something different, like a port and lemon maybe."

"That's proper?"

"Improper, actually. Like all alcohol. The devil's brew."

"So that's who makes the stuff."

"Keeps him busy on a wet weekend in Hell."

She giggled behind her hand, cheeks reddening.

"You look nice when you're flushed," I said.

"Like a toilet?"

She leaned across the table and fixed me with her pale blue eyes. There were red tints shining in her auburn hair, a pulse visible under the pale skin of her neck.

"I suppose you are kind of cute," she whispered, and suddenly we were kissing, until the landlord advised us to stop or leave, so we went out blinking into the light, limpid afternoon.

Between us we had enough left for a half bottle of cheap vodka, so we headed off to the Moss Side shopping centre. As we came out, Imelda unscrewed the cap and took a swig. She shuddered, banging a fist on her chest, and swinging the bottle towards me.

After the initial throat-stripping burn, the stuff seemed to settle nicely. I pointed at the Harp lager building that stood before us, gleaming corrugated façade against a sky of watery, unbroken blue.

I smiled and took another nip.

"It's actually quite beautiful really."

Imelda laughed.

"That place? It's a hideous shite-lager factory!"

"It's a brewery."

"Well, whatever. Just pass me the hooch will you?"

"If your folks could see you now."

"My Da would thrash the hide off me."

She swung a skinny arm round my neck, drew me near, and looked closely at me with her forget-me-not eyes.

"What are we doing, Tim?"

"We're on the road to perdition, Immers, and there aint no turning back."

Her face turned ash-pale.

"Hey, Imelda, I'm kidding!"

She swung sideways to her knees, shoulders hunching, and all the liquid I had seen her swallow rushed out of her in a single, spectacular spew.

Another lonesome gig.

I sold Imelda's ticket at the door and made my way through the sparse crowd towards the stage. Mark E Smith, wearing a brown V-neck jumper with gold pattern, was hunched over a mike. The band was still tuning up behind him, but he was ready to go.

"Hiya!" he shouted, "we are The Fall, the most hated band in Britain! Right, that's the end of the guitar practice, start the fucking song."

The Don

Another morning scramble, another chilly day. Missed the alarm again, and all my clothes seemed to be in the wash, so I went out wearing one of Simone's T-shirts. It had 'The Jam' screen-printed on it repeatedly in a style meant to resemble graffiti.

"Do you think he likes The Jam?" muttered a passing student.

His mate sniggered, but quickly glanced away when he caught my malicious fail-to-take-a-joke glare.

I felt bloody-minded, bloody-brained, as if some sluggish liquid was creeping across my cerebellum. Octopus ink clouding around my organ of control.

I skipped my lecture in favour of a morning pint, and the minute I sat down a small squadron of tiny beer-coloured flies gathered around the aromatic ale, vying with one another for a landing place on the rim of the glass.

"Try this," said a man at the next table, holding out a pack of cigarettes. "I think you'll find they don't like the smoke."

I accepted a fag and puffed inexpertly at the hovering insects.

The cigarette donor laughed loudly. He was familiar. A lecturer, I couldn't recall the name. He tossed off his whisky, shook the few remaining drips into his beer, and beamed at me through his beard.

"Name's Drummond," he said, extending his hand.

Dr Drummond, that was it. He was wearing a 'Glad to be Gay' badge, which, recalling as I did this man's reputation regarding female freshers, I took to be an example of his brand of irony.

"But do call me Donald," he added. "And, now, don't tell me, I taught you, didn't I, a couple of years back?"

"I'm just in my first year."

"Philosophy though, right?"

"English."

"English. Yeah, right. English. Want another?"

I didn't particularly, but found myself nodding none the less, and soon he was back, balancing pints and shots in his large hands.

He plonked them down, and stood looking at me, scratching his beard.

"I'm sure I know you from somewhere. Didn't you crash that field trip in '78? Bunch of girls. Biology students. Took me along because I had the camping gear. Could have sworn you were there. Or was it Stratford?"

"I don't think it was me."

"Well, you know what they say, 'if you can remember it you weren't really there', something like that. Could have sworn... We had that heated chat about Nietzsche, remember?"

"Not really."

"Me neither."

He closed his eyes, pinched the skin on the bridge of his nose, and fell silent.

After a few minutes, just as I was beginning to wonder if he had dropped off, his head suddenly jerked head up, eyes wide behind his glasses.

"What was that?" he asked.

"Nothing."

He smiled, nodding.

"Ah! Nothing. The big N."

He finished his scotch, lit a cigarette, and tossed over the pack.

"And yet can we really believe there *is* such a thing? Surely there's always something, even if we don't see it?"

"You mean the cow in the field thing?"

He slapped his hand on the table.

"Exactly! When we look away, the cow remains in the field. But does it? What if it only appears, as it were, when we're looking?"

"Doesn't that go against what you were saying? I mean, that would suggest there actually can be nothing."

He laughed.

"Know what? You're on the wrong course. You should seriously consider changing."

He pressed me.

"Would you consider changing?"

"I might. If I was forced to."

A grin broke through his whiskers.

"Forced to. Pun on Forster, right?"

I smiled evasively, and he whacked a hand on my shoulder and urged me to drink up and make room for more.

After the next round the bell was rung for time, and Dr Drummond gave a rueful smile as we stood to leave.

"Shame," he said. "Bloody silly licencing laws. Ah well, it's been an enlightening session just the same. Seems like I've known you for ages. Really could have sworn…Still, looks like it's auf wiedersehen for now, old chum. I'd invite you over, but the place is a mess. See you in school."

I watched him for a moment weaving his way down Oxford Road, a large shambolic figure, his grey checked overcoat flapping in the wind.

I turned and set off for home, and as I trotted along, the air hit me, and my head felt like it was expanding.

I felt reckless, cutting rashly across the busy roads, and didn't pause for breath until I was at my door.

Fumbling for my keys, I found they had developed a curious life of their own, wriggling through my fingers and refusing to enter the lock.

I buzzed, and eventually Norman let me in, and I pushed past him, bounced down the hallway and stumbled up the stairs.

"Looks like somebody's been hard at study," he observed.

"I might switch to philosophy."

"Eh?"

"I said I think I should have something to eat."

He looked shifty.

"Thing is," he said, "there ain't a lot left. As in not really anything."

I looked in the cupboard. A tin of processed peas and an empty Jaffa Cakes box.

"Right," I said, "this calls for a big shop."

"Are you sure that's wise in your condition?"

"Not really, but I'm not asking you to do it because I want at least some of the stuff to make it home. Have a think, meanwhile, about whether or not you still want to be here when I get back."

Two old women sat opposite me on the bus, upper lips pleated, as if gathered by drawstrings, revealing over-large dentures. The nearest, wearing a wool overcoat of dusty lilac, tutted over her tabloid.
"I don't hold with it," she remarked, glancing at her companion for her reaction.
"Don't hold with what?"
"Us having a lady P.M. Not right, some woman running the country."
"She'll not last. I can't see folk voting for the likes of her again."
They both nodded, origami upper lips stretching into thin smiles.

Asda again.
A wonky coaster led me astray from the start, massed shelves of multicoloured stock ranging repetitively past like the background to the 'Wacky Races.'
Tinsel versions of pop songs shimmered around the aisles, taunting me as I tried to bring my trolley to heel.
I took a sneaky turn and pulled up beside a tower block of biscuits, but everything around me seemed to carry on moving, colours and shapes whizzing past, slogans, product names, details blurring.
'Buy one, set one free', 'fornicated with vitamins and minerals', 'beanz meanz hymenz…'
I felt my trolley rolling away, so I climbed aboard and free-wheeled until I collided with a pyramid of soup cans, sending them clattering, spinning and rolling on the shiny floor.
Everything was going out of focus.
I grabbed at the nearest support, realised it was a child's head, and collapsed among some boxes of Quaker Oats.
'Security' arrived, two men sporting maroon peaked caps that made their heads look too small for their bodies.
As they drew closer, their faces merged into one giant mutant head.
"Was you intending to pay for those cans?" it asked.
"I hadn't…I mean I didn't mean to cause any damage."
They separated somewhat as I got my breath, and one of them started picking up boxes.

The other carried on staring at me.
"Never mind damage," he said. "An accident can be overlooked. We was referring to the cans of beer."
I realised I was clutching a four pack.
"Oh, these, paying for these? Absolutely."
"Well we don't reckon you had any intention of paying," they both said, slightly out of synch like a strange echo.
I felt a bolt of pain behind my eyes, opened one of the cans and took a sip.
"I don't now, fuckers."
Which was what led to my first experience of being escorted out of a shop. It wasn't done particularly roughly, and if I hadn't lost my footing and crashed into a row of parked trolleys, I might have come through it unscathed.

It was unlucky that I should run into Simone as I walked to the bus stop. If it hadn't been for my appearance, dishevelled and bruised, I don't think she would have stopped. As it was, she merely raised an eyebrow slightly, before moving on.
After watching her walk away, and wondering if she would look back, I headed off to Danny's corner shop.
He started to scrutinise my face the moment I walked in.
"Danny, it's a short story, but a dull one."
"No, no, not the shiner, the whiskers."
I had been tentatively allowing a beard to grow.
"Now who is it you remind me of? You know, he does that multiple swap shop. My nephew watches it. Wears a nice jumper. Edmonds, that's it. Noel Edmonds."
"Danny, please tell me you sell razor blades."
"Middle shelf, left. Disposables too, they're very popular."
He watched me fetch the rest of my shopping.
"Ah, you like that Nescafe do you? I'm told it's the best. More of a Mellow Birds man meself. D'you think I should stock some of the decapitated stuff? Don't see the point of it, personally, but if customers want it…"
On my way home I noticed a banner for the Evening News that read, 'RUBBER MAN SEEN ON CAMPUS.'
Back at the flat I mentioned it to Norman, who was, of course, still there.

"Do you think it's the same thing as Elastic Man?" he said, and without waiting for an answer, grabbed the jar of coffee and headed straight for the kettle.
I followed him, made myself a sandwich, and collapsed onto the settee.

There were three large circles painted on the playground wall, probably intended as ball targets.
My friend Peter and I were pretending they were those creeping rings of light associated with the Mysterons on 'Captain Scarlet.' Peter was quite good at the deep and creepy voice, while I mimed being caught in their power and transformed into an evil version of myself.
Those body-snatcher B-movies. A benign character, accompanied by an 'unearthly' high-pitched chorus, wanders through some mist, and returns to his family with a hard, fixed expression on his face. Frustratingly, nobody believes the son when he twigs his Dad has become the host to a malevolent alien intent on world domination. To make it worse, even those one might reasonably expect to be helpful in such circumstances start exhibiting the same signs. The police chief turns with a vacant stare.
"You don't know what you're saying, son…"

I woke just in time to see Norman finishing my sandwich.
"I was eating that," I said.
He shrugged.
"Not from where I was looking. Your mouth was open, but nothing was going in. And then you started mumbling some old shite about science fiction and aliens. I was never into any of that witless crap."
"Not much you weren't!"
"I wasn't! Star Trek and all that, a load of shite. Doctor fucking Spock and his stupid plastic ears."
"*Mister* Spock."
"Like I care."
"You just didn't get it."
"Too right, hombre. But you know what? *It* got you."
"William Shatner was quite good."
"Come off it, Tim. He always looked like he was gagging for a drink."
"My Mum fancied him."
"That doesn't make it great television."
"So how come you know so much about it if you never watched it?"

"My kid brother did. Some of it must have seeped in."

"Passive viewing."

Simone came in and dumped her bag in the middle of the room. She held out her arms.

"Are you back?" I asked.

"What does it look like?"

She tried to smile, but there were tears in her eyes.

I approached her, hoping Norman might make himself scarce.

"It wasn't your fault," I said. "It's me should be in tears."

She shook her head and sniffed.

"It's not that, it's Jordan."

This was her elder brother, who worked as a sort of bouncer at 'the Glamour.'

"I think he's getting mixed up in something."

"Like what?"

"I don't know. Someone in the audience shouted something at me today during my act."

"What, 'Get 'em off' was it?" asked Norman.

She regarded him with the expressionless gaze of one inhabited by an alien.

"Right, I'll, er, I'll go and, er..." he mumbled, shuffling out.

Simone sat down.

"Tim, it sounded like a threat. About Jordan. Why would they do that?"

"What kind of threat?"

"I don't know, it was the way he..."

Norman came back in.

"Forgot my glasses."

Simone kicked a chair over, and while we waited for the dust to settle, I grabbed a can of lager from the fridge. Simone snatched it and took a long swallow.

"I'll leave you to it, then," said Norman.

Simone waited for the door to close behind him.

"I don't know, Tim, I'm maybe just being...I can't believe he would be so stupid. Actually, what am I saying? Of course I can believe it."

"So what happened exactly?"

"It was this guy, in the audience. I noticed him staring at me, but in a different way from the others. And then he shouted, 'Jordan owes us', pointed at me, and walked out."

"That's it?"

"Isn't it enough?"

She lit a cigarette, inhaled, and shot me a defiant glance.

"And, yes, I've started smoking again, ok?"

"I didn't say anything."

"You didn't have to. Look, I know I'm probably overreacting, but I just have this feeling."

"Maybe you need to speak to Jordan."

"Oh, believe me, I intend to."

Harold Eastwood.

He was an ex ballet dancer who lived in a smart block in Chorlton.

"Harry, do call me Harry, dear boy."

My job was to try to get him used to being alone in his flat. He had been in hospital a long time with what he called 'a nervous disposition' and, despite having been deemed fit for discharge, had developed a horror of being home alone.

The plan was for me to accompany him on regular trips to his flat in order to boost his confidence about moving back.

We would go together in a cab, and, as we got near, he would become increasingly agitated, causing him involuntarily to move his false teeth around. Too large for his lean face, they sloshed and clicked unnervingly. Arriving, he would rush to the door, panicking over the lock, and run in to the bedroom to check his wardrobe. For some reason, despite there being no sign of a break-in, he always thought something would be missing.

His flat had the faded look of a colour photograph left too long in the sun. There was a living area overlooked by a little kitchenette, a petrified pot plant, silted with dust, a leatherette-covered wireless wafting radio 2.

I sat there one sunny afternoon being serenaded by Matt Munro, as Harry, cigarette in hand, made coffee, tinkering nervously with teaspoon and china, and clinking instant unsteadily into little cups. They rattled on a small tray as he shuffled through towards the low coffee table.

"Here we are," he announced, setting down the trembling tray.

His cigarette remained balanced on the edge of the Formica kitchen worktop, slowly burning itself out. Another smouldered in the pedestal ashtray beside his armchair.

Harry lit a third.

"Sit tight, old chap," he murmured, "I think I've got it. Sugar?"

"No thanks, just milk"

"Ah. Drat! I've only got powdered."
"Powdered's fine."
By the time he found the Coffee Mate, my drink had gone cold.
"That alright?" he asked, watching me stir.
I nodded.
"No it isn't. You don't have to be polite."
He sipped his in silence for a moment, looking around the room.
"You see that nude study?" he remarked, pointing a long, arthritic forefinger. It was a watercolour of a pale, slim young man with reddish hair and a middle parting.
"Very nice," I said. "Someone you know?"
"I should hope so! Yours' truly. Didn't usually let Bunny do me sans apparel, but he could be so charming, very persuasive."
This was a reference to his artist friend, Bunny Atkinson, who had bequeathed to him several paintings. Everything else had gone to his two young nephews, referred to by Harry as 'the boys.' They sometimes came to see him in hospital, and occasionally, so they said, went in and tidied the flat for him.
"The boys love that picture. Love all of 'em actually, always saying so. Reminds me, better 'phone."
This was another ritual on each home visit, the 'phoning of the boys. And, finally, the re-checking of the wardrobe.
"I've got some rather nice stuff in there," he told me. "Bound to be interfered with."
After that, we returned to the hospital.
I dropped Harold off, and went straight to the White Horse in Hulme. For some reason I was drawn to the place, even though I didn't like it. The crowd that hung around there irritated me. Young students, self-consciously eccentric, confidant, clannish.
I wanted to run home to Simone, but she was out working.
Two spotty young men with spiky quiffs were sitting opposite me, and I became increasingly aware they were looking over. Every time I glanced up, I caught the eye of one or the other. They started sniggering, so I decided to stare at them directly and see what they would do.
They did nothing, so I got up and left.
I wandered over to the office of Salmon Cabs to get a ride home. Rumour had it that the name had been coined in error. It was supposed to have been Solomon Cabs, but the sign writer got it wrong.

The car I climbed into was full of smoke, and as the driver started the engine, he handed me a joint. I took a quick puff and nursed it until he had a free hand.

He smoked steadily as he drove, one hand relaxed on the wheel, and after a few moments I became aware, in his mirror, that he was scrutinising me through the haze.

"You knocking around with Simone, right?"

"You know her?"

"We're second cousins. How she doing?"

"Ok, I think."

"Working?"

"Yeah."

"She's a good girl, you know. But don't get mixed up with her brother."

He pulled up at the flat.

Hit Parade

Simone and I were watching Top of the Pops one evening. I had lost the toss and was missing Star Trek on two, so I was mostly sneering and laughing my way through it.

Ungrateful, really, since it was on this programme that I first saw David Bowie. He was performing 'Starman', with make-up that made his ears look like plastic. When he pointed at the camera, and sang 'I picked on you', you really did think he meant you.

Unless you were my Dad. He used to turn the sound down.

"Don't look so clever now, do they?"

I badly wanted to do the same to him during 'Songs of Praise'. All those pious goldfish gobs...

Mum was a little more tolerant of the flamboyancy of pop stars. She particularly approved of Gary Glitter.

"At least he looks clean."

This evening 'Madness' were on.

"I might get the album," said Simone.

"Why bother? Its just re-cycled ska."

"So what? You always have to witter on about the old stuff."

"I'm not wittering. You should listen to a bit of Prince Buster."

"Do I tell you what to listen to? Look, you've made me miss them now."

"They are better than most of the shit that's on, I suppose. It's a mystery to me any one buys any of it."

"And its an even bigger mystery," said Simone, "that you are still here."
I went to the Poly bar, where I found Sage lurking in a corner. He told me he was working on a 'one-man show.' His idea was to combine comedy, social comment and tap dancing.
"Since when could you tap dance?"
"I can't. My plan is to dance with actual taps attached to my boots. It's a visual gag." "Faucets for the feet."
"Yeah, not bad that."
"And you think you'll get bookings?"
"Absolutely, man. I'm working on some great one-liners."
"Such as?"
"Like I said, I'm working on them."
He went to the bar.
Pinned above it was a hand-written notice on day-glo orange card.
'DRUG-FREE ZONE. ANYONE USING OR SUPPLYING ILLEGAL DRUGS WILL BE BARED.'
That would show them.
Sage came back, grinning.
"Anyway," he said, "if the cabaret fails, I've got a cracking money-spinning idea up my sleeve."
"Conjuring?"
"Nah, it's an invention. A motorcycle helmet that's solid and protective but looks like a turban. Moulded from fibreglass. I just need a snappy product name."
"Safer Sikhs?"
"Not bad, Tim, not bad."
He produced a blunt pencil and jotted it down on a crumpled take-away menu.
I patted his shoulder.
"You're serious, aren't you?"
But he was deep in thought.
I recalled his last business venture, an after-hours alcohol and cigarettes delivery service called 'Party On.' The idea was for him to buy up stock and be available on-call through the night for people wanting to continue their revelry after hours. Three factors had hampered the success of this scheme. One, it was illegal, two, Sage couldn't drive, and three, he got so bored waiting for calls that he drank and smoked most of his supplies.

An uncle, who had put up the cash as a starter loan, had soon joined the growing body of individuals from whom Sage strove to keep his distance. "Got it," said Sage. "The Turbo."

Fad

There was a rumour going round about pies containing kangaroo meat. I couldn't see why that was so much worse than chicken or cow, but it had prompted Simone to instigate a new food regime. That and stories about eggs being full of poisonous bacteria. Go to hospital on an egg.
Simone was talking about 'going veggie.' She started buying stuff from 'On The Eight Day', a health food place on the Oxford Road.
Brown rice you had to boil for days. Bolus-defying bread. Pale, sweaty-looking chunks of a substance called Tofu, almost devoid of flavour. Nettle salad.
I thought she was joking when she mentioned that last one, but there, later, lay the faintly hairy leaves on my supper plate.
"Are you trying to tell me something?" I asked.
"Baby, I've been trying for so long," she replied, stirring soya milk custard.
"Did you speak to Jordan?"
"I told you, no one has seen him."
"Did you?"
"Did I what?"
"Tell me"
She sighed.
"I don't know why I bother."
"Do you want me to have a go?"
"What do you mean, have a go?"
"At looking for him."
"Oh. No, I don't think so. Thanks anyway, but best leave this to me."

Big Little Man

Imelda, I had soon learned, was a person unusually at home with her bodily functions. She would break wind without breaking her conversation. A forerunner in all forms of flatulence and a great burper, to boot. She would even discuss fanny farts, though I had yet to be privileged with a demonstration. Other emissions, though, she had unstintingly shared, from silent seepage, presaged by a cock-eyed grin, to lifting a buttock and letting rip at full pelt with a cry of 'Geronimo.'

The product of a Catholic school.

She could also do a good line in belch speak, maintaining control long enough to complete, as she once proudly croaked, a 'three-word sentence.' Sneezing also a speciality, never spraying anything less than four or five in a row.

Blowing the nose? Maximum volume, industrial output.

In the absence of anything naturally occurring, she liked to demonstrate her artful trick of creating squelching farts by squishing a damp palm in her arm-pit.

I was walking into a lecture one morning, musing on these phenomena, when I noticed her waving and shouting on the other side of the road. I couldn't hear for the traffic, so she weaved her way over.

"Hi Tim, sorry I boked the other day."

"What?"

"You always say that! I puked, remember?"

"I'm trying not to, thanks."

"So how was the gig?"

"It was…difficult."

"Surprise, surprise. Come on, then, where's the money?"

"What money?"

"From my ticket."

"How do you know I sold it?"

We went in to the union and Imelda made me buy her a pie.

"That's just for starters," she commented, stuffing her face.

"As you wish."

"I do. Hey, Tim, did you hear about that girl on my course?"

"What girl?"

"Geraldine Tonks. She was walking home from midnight mass and some bloke jumped out at her, and he was dressed form head to toe in a rubber outfit."

"Where from?"

"I don't know! Are you wanting to buy one?"

"No, I mean where did he jump out from?"

"What's the difference?"

"I think it's pretty crucial. Like, was it shrubbery, a doorway?"

"I don't bloody know."

"So how do you know he jumped out?"

"Jesus, Tim! She told me."

"But you didn't ask where from?"

"Sorry Tim, no, I neglected to cross-examine her. I didn't really think she was in the mood."

"So how does she know it was a man?"

"His voice, I suppose. He said something to her."

"What?"

"Something unrepeatable."

"It can't be unrepeatable if you know what it was. Unless you were there."

"Of course I wasn't bloody there!"

"So what was it?"

She lowered her voice.

"He said he wanted to lick her knickers."

"Is that it?"

"Isn't it enough? And then he made a grab at her, but Brian Eames ran over and scared him off."

"Who's Brian Eames?"

"Just some lad on our course. Get me another pie will you?"

I did, and left her to eat it, as I was already late for Doctor Spragg on 'Beowulf.'

In fact, I realised, I was so late it wasn't really worth turning up, so I went to see what was on at Studio One to Five cinema. It was a dull-sounding horror called 'Saw Point' about yet another maniac picking off young Americans. I went instead to the 'Shady Lady' and I got myself a shandy so I could kid myself I wasn't really drinking.

I was half way down the glass when Stan Bardolino entered the bar.

He was a very small Geordie with a big presence.

"You bloody alcoholic, Tim," he growled, extending a square mitt. I steeled myself for his customarily firm grip of greeting.

"Alright?" he asked, and without waiting for a reply, he turned to the barmaid.

"Give us a Newcy brown, love, and whatever this reprobate's having."

I had bitter this time, without the tang of cheap lemonade.

Stan lit a pungent cigar, snapped shut his stormproof, and swivelled his shaven, bullet head towards me.

"So, how've you been?"

"I'm alright, I suppose."

"That's the stuff, man, nice and positive."

It was odd, because I didn't really know how I came to be numbered among Stan's acquaintances. Yet it was the same for everyone. Many knew him, but few knew why.

He puffed smoke in my face.

"Since when did you smoke those?" I asked.

"Since when did you ask those sort of silly bastard questions?"

"About five seconds ago."

"Fair enough. Fact is, I decided to give up the tabs for a spell and try something that gives *me* pleasure but causes maximum discomfort to others."

He smiled, foul emissions seeping through the gaps in his teeth.

"I've smelled worse," I remarked.

"What, Simone's mother's farts after one of those goat curries of hers?"

"When have you smelled one of them?"

"Ah, that would be telling, Tim. I get about. Anyway, if this cigar is, as you claim, not up to the mark, I shall have to buy cheaper."

As far as I knew, Stan had never hurt or even upset anyone unless provoked, but he liked to appear cynical. Hardening his shell.

The one thing he wouldn't let go, however, was when strangers commented on his height.

I saw an example of this one afternoon when he and I were ordering drinks at a bar.

Two wags standing beside us started nudging and grinning.

"I'd buy a round," said one, "but I'm a bit short."

"Go to the bank then," replied the other, "and take the short cut."

Stan turned to them, clapping his hands very slowly, and suddenly punched the nearest so hard in the stomach he was bent double.

"Sorry," said Stan, "I'm short tempered."

He then kicked the winded man out of the way, climbed onto a barstool, and gripped the other by the neck with both hands.

"What's the matter, mate," he hissed, "short of breath?"

I smiled, recalling the incident.

"Stop grinning like an idiot, Tim," said Stan, prodding me in the ribs. "It's your round, and mine's another bottle of brown."

"Would you like a short with it?"

He narrowed his eyes and gave me smoke-in-the-face laughter.

"Droll, Tim, very droll. I generally prefer to punish such comments, but for you I'll make an exception."

"Thank you."
"De rien, man. Anyway, how's it really going? Drinking beer in school time! What would Simone say?"
"Plenty."
"Exactly. You should watch it, count your lucky stars. Not bad-looking, on course for a degree, and going steady with a bonny girl."
"Not sure about steady."
"See? Look to the lady, man, before it's too late."
"Do you think I'm making a mess of things?"
"I wouldn't go that far. I was just inferring you might take a look at yourself."
"Implying."
"Well pardon my shit, Sherlock."
"Sorry."
"There you go, apologising. Don't put yourself in the wrong all the time."
"Do I?"
He stubbed out his dying cigar.
"I dunno. All I'm saying is it's what I used to do, your age, until I learned better. Not anymore. No one pushes me around."
"I don't suppose they do."
He smiled and lit another cigar.

But if...

I was about fourteen, and my Mum had picked me up from school. The car smelled of vinyl seats and lipstick.
"I won't be a minute," she said, stopping in the village. "Couple of errands. You may as well stay here."
There was a fly lying on its back on the dashboard, feebly moving its legs, and as I stared at it, I suddenly felt like I was going to cry, not in sympathy for the insect, but due to the un-anticipated recollection of an incident that afternoon at school.
A girl I'd been noticing a lot, without knowing why, was walking by in the playground with some friends. Amy Philips, small, blonde and neat, with brown eyes that sometimes caught mine and flickered away without scorn. One of her girlfriends said something like, "she fancies you," and pushed her forward. She shrugged off the jostling, but sent me a shy smile.
If ever there was a moment…but I felt myself getting red, so I turned and walked away, and I couldn't look back.

And now, sitting in the stuffy car, I was fighting back tears of self-pity. There was no way I could turn back the clock, too late to try to talk to her, even if I thought I could.

The blurry shape of my mother appeared at the window, and I managed a smile as she opened the door.

"You all right, love?" she asked, easing into the driving seat, and putting her hand on my knee.

I nodded, swallowing dryly, and in that moment I realised all that kind of stuff was down to nobody else but me.

Side by side on my piano

Simone and I seemed to be increasingly at odds with one another, so much so that I

could hardly remember the times when we weren't. I put it down to the stress caused

by her brother's apparent disappearance, but since I wasn't allowed to mention him, there wasn't much chance of talking it through.

"I'll kill him," muttered Simone, from time to time.

It didn't seem to cross her mind that some one may already have saved her the trouble.

One evening we went out for a drink together for the first time in ages, and we managed to get to closing time without mentioning the subject. Simone was more like her old easy-going self, sinking a couple of lagers, and laughing at my exaggerated stories about my home care clients.

"If you don't make it as a teacher," she said, "you'd be a great social worker." Neither prospect struck me as appealing.

Later, as we were walking home, Simone put one hand in mine, and stifled a yawn with the other.

"I don't know how you can get through so much beer, it makes me really sleepy."

As we turned a corner, we saw there was a bunch of lads coming towards us. The one at the front had a scarf tied round his head, and kept bellowing, "We are the Sultans!"

"Of swing!" the others chanted in response.

Fresh from the Dire Straits gig at the union, and probably on their way to a hall of residence.

As we passed among them, the group reluctantly broke to allow us through, apart from the leader, who deliberately brushed against Simone.

"Nice sun tan," he murmured.
I stopped and sensed him also slowing to a halt.
Simone closed her eyes.
"Leave it, Tim."
But I couldn't.
"What did you just say, scarf head?"
He looked down his handsome nose at me.
"Oh, just remarking on how nice the weather's been."
"Well if I hear another word, I'll shove that fucking scarf so far down your throat it'll keep your arse warm, whatever the weather."
He smiled, coming very close to me, nostrils flared, nicotine breath.
"Oh really? Why not just use it to lynch me from the nearest tree?"
His companions exchanged uneasy glances, while Simone stood with her back to us, rigid, staring at her feet.
I fingered the fringe of the scarf.
"Know what, old fruit? It would be a pity to spoil the tree."
He whipped the scarf from my hand.
"You really are quite an objectionable little bugger aren't you? Look, I can't be bothered to punch you, so why don't you just take your little piccaninny and…"
His sentence was cut short by an astonishing sound, something between a scream and a roar, as Simone swung her body, jumped, and hammered a kick to his groin.
He remained completely motionless for about thirty seconds before listing slowly forwards, the rosy tint of his outdoor cheeks turning sixty-a-day grey. One of his cohorts, having edged closer, stopped short at Simone's keen, scrutinising glare.
"Listen," he said, "no offence, right?"
Simone very slowly shook her head, a strange taut-lipped smile on her face, and then she started walking.
I took a parting look at the Sultan. He was still stooping as he turned to go, but he had recovered his voice.
"Fucking scum," he said.
Quietly.
Simone didn't say anything to me the whole walk home, and when we arrived I went straight to the kitchen, made her a hot drink, and brought it through to our bedroom.
"What's this for?" she asked.

"What?"
"Why are you doing this for me?"
"I thought you might still be upset."
"Still?"
"Well, it was a bad situation back there."
"It was a crap situation that you had to go and make worse."
The hot drink went cold.

By the time I woke the next day, she was gone.
Norman wasn't.
"All right, Tim? Nice morning. Simone seemed a bit off today. She on the rag or something?"
Ignoring him, I went to fill the kettle.
"Oh, you and all, eh?"
"Don't push it, Norman."
"All right, all right. Just asking."
There was a load of dirty dishes piled precariously high in the sink.
"What's this," I asked, "some sort of sculpture?"
"It could be," said Norman. "I've seen worse."
"Have you? Christ, just for once it'd be nice to be able to make a cup of tea in a clean mug. It's not much to ask, is it?"
"Suppose not. Here, there's some footy on the box this afternoon, I'll nip over to Danny's, get a few cans."
"Make sure you pay for them."
I sat in the quiet kitchen, faint sound of next door's transistor tuned to Piccadilly radio, and ate a slice of cold toast somehow overlooked by Norman.
Later, still sitting there, I was roused from daydreams by Norman calling out that the match had started.
"Not really in the mood," I shouted.
But I could only sit for so long, especially once Norman got into the game.
"Come on, come on. Come on, come on. Come on, come on, come on," he chanted, roar of the crowd behind him.
I went in.
Norman was on the edge of his seat.
"Come on you irons!"
"Calm down," I said, "they can't hear you."

"How can you be sure? Anyway, I'm enjoying this. I don't have a T.V. remember?"

"You don't have anything."

"Thanks for reminding me."

He kept his eyes on the little figures racing up and down the screen.

"Oh, here we go, yes, go on, shoot, yes, yes!"

He started to jump up and down on the settee, causing surprising amounts of dust to billow out, swirling in the hazy living room light. Then his foot went through and became trapped in coils of springs.

We managed to free it, at the expense of the sock.

"No, surely not," he lamented. "One less possession! My best pair and all."

"You mean your only pair?"

He nodded ruefully.

"Now I don't even have two socks to rub together. I suppose I'll have to walk barefoot, like a monk, or Tarzan."

Marmalade-coloured sunlight came through the window, shredded by the shadows of breeze-shaken branches.

"It's getting dark earlier," I murmured.

"It's only half-time," said Norman. "Did I hear you say you were making a brew?"

"I thought you were on beer?"

"Not in the interval."

Through the kitchen window was a different sky, thunderously dark, with a tinge of iodine.

I poured tea the colour of resin, saw it swirl in the milk and become liverish.

"They're coming back on," shouted Norman.

I found him examining the spaces between his toes, picking at little coils of moist mixed fibres.

"It's weird," he mused. "I only ever get athlete's foot on the left one."

I noticed, as I set down the mugs, that he had arranged a series of scraps of dry skin along the edge of the smoked glass coffee table. These post-pedicure peelings he brushed onto the floor to make space for the tea.

"Did you sugar it?" he asked.

"We haven't got any. Simone says it's deadly. I think we might have some brown."

"That'll do, it's all the same."

"So go and find it. And while you're at it, why not bring some scissors so you can cut your toenails in front of me?"

"Sound idea! They could do with a trim."
Fortunately he found only the sugar.
I watched him stir it in, three teaspoonfuls, and then he extracted a fresh Embassy from the pack.
"I thought you were a roll-up man," I said.
"Only if I'm skint, which is, admittedly, a lot of the time. These were a special deal."
"Knock-off, you mean?"
"That would be telling."
He lit a match.
"All the fun of the flare," he said.
"What?"
"You know, roll up, roll up…never mind."
"But I do mind, Norman. We need something to do. Somewhere to go."
"What's wrong with what we're doing here?"
"You really are content to just sit and stink aren't you?"
"Steady on, I had a bath."
"When?"
"Quite recently."
"And I suppose it's you been nicking the shampoo?"
"Not me, I don't wash my hair. It's more natural; after a while it just stops being dirty."
"Are you kidding? Take that to its' logical conclusion and we all might as well stop washing at all."
"Nah, tried that, it only really works with hair."
By the time Simone came home it was dark, and Norman was asleep on the settee, head back, mouth open.
I was sitting beside him in the gloom.
Simone came over, hand on hip, chewing her lip.
"State of you," she said. "You're hopeless, you know that? Are you coming?"
"Coming where?"
"To bed, you idiot. Unless you prefer to cuddle up with Normski."
We both woke early the next morning.
"I'm sorry about the other day, those lads. I was an idiot," I said.
She yawned.
"Let's forget it."
"Actually there's something I've been meaning to tell you."
"What, is you black?"

"Don't be daft. Although it does…it's a bit awkward. I feel a bit guilty about it, but I don't know if I should."
"So what is it?"
"Well, years ago, my Mum used to drive me and my mate Peter up from Kent to London, and me and him made up this silly game."
"What was it?"
"We were in the back, right, and as we came into the suburbs, each would have his side of the road and we'd start spotting black people."
"That's it?"
"Yeah. Whoever saw the most was the winner."
"And did this involve any name-calling, rude gestures?"
"No! That's just it. It wasn't a kind of comment, we just weren't used to seeing black people."
"Says a lot about where you lived. I don't see why you should feel guilty about it."
"I hope not. Stupid game, really."
"Could have been worse."
"And there really wasn't anything pejorative, trust me."
"I do, though I don't know what pejorative is, coz I's jess a paw coloured gal."
"With no education."
"Don't push it."
"To top it, on the way back when we stopped for petrol, it was a hot afternoon, and my Mum said to this West Indian guy at the pump, 'this weather must suit you?' I
wanted to hide under the seat."
"Crickey! What did *he* say?"
"Just laughed."
"Probably used to a lot worse nonsense than that."
"Probably. So you don't think the game was wrong?"
She shook her head and started to smile.
"Nothin' like a little 'spot-the -coloured-folks' to pass the time."
"We probably should have stuck to I-spy."
"Yeah. I spy with my little eye something beginning with N."
"Are you allowed to say that?"
"Yes, but you're not. And if you played your little game in Lewisham these days, it'd probably be spot the white person."
"And you're allowed to say that too?"

She laughed.

"Tim, I'm allowed to say all kinds of things."

Nice

Simone's nephew, Jackson, came to stay for a few days while his Mum had a rest. His father, Jordan, was still missing.

The four-and-a-bit kid came into the kitchen from the back yard.

"Know what I seed?" he kept repeating, gradually raising his voice until one of us responded.

"What did you see, sweetie?" smiled Simone.

He faltered, as if momentarily forgetting.

"Er, er, I seed, I seed...I seed a massive ant what had black and red bits on its body and on its face. It was giant it was, a giant ant."

"Wow," said Simone. "And you know what? The word 'giant' has the word 'ant' in it!"

Jackson frowned, perplexed, before continuing with his observations.

"Know what? There are ants in the jungle what are called solder ants."

"Soldier," I murmured.

"Giant solder ants," he went on, "Grandpa Royston told me, he seed 'em he did."

Simone rolled her eyes.

"Your Grandpa Royston, him see a lot of things."

Annoyed at Simone's scepticism, and not fully understanding, Jackson stamped his foot.

"I KNOW! Anyways, he seed way more fings than you."

She patted his arm.

"Alright. You want to have some lunch?"

He pursed his lips.

"I don't like those kind of fings you have."

"What things?"

"EVERYFINK! It's yuck."

"You tell her, boy," I said.

She sucked her teeth and looked awfully like Rose.

"Come on, Jackson. Tim's teasing. It's nice if you really try it. You have to give it a chance."

To be fair, for a child who lived on spaghetti hoops, it was a tough call to expect him to enjoy the sort of stuff we were having. But I think the real root of his aversion to Simone's cuisine stemmed from the time she had offered him some Tofu. Mistaking it for another, sweeter confection, the boy had pushed a large chunk in his mouth, and as he chewed, an immediate expression of doubt had flickered in his eyes, followed by a disgusted downturn of the lips, and the rapid expulsion of the unwanted pulp onto the floor.

From that day he regarded anything she offered him with suspicion. Today it was chickpeas and couscous.

"Come on," said Simone, tasting a forkful, "mmm, really yummy."

Jackson pushed his plate away with the back of his hand, averting his head as though the very sight of the food offended him.

"Ok," said Simone, "maybe I'll make some custard, how about that?"

"Hate it."

Simone turned to the window and leaned on the draining board.

"Give me strength," she muttered. "Child needs his father."

I liked Jackson for short periods of time, but it didn't make me want my own.

Simone would sometimes give coy, suggestive glances from him to me. I could only manage a weak smile, and what she inferred from my feeble responses I couldn't tell.

"Look, Jackson," said Simone, "what's Daddy going to say if you won't eat?"

"Daddy aint home."

"Well, I know, but..."

"When's he comin' home?"

Simone took the boy's hand and led him to the door.

"Put your coat on," she said, "and let's go and get some chips."

Later, when Jackson had finally gone to sleep, Simone came over and sat next to me on the settee.

"Thanks," she said.

"What for?"

"Well, the boy and everything."

"He's a doddle compared with Norman."

"Mmm. Where is Norman, anyway?"

"Oh, he'll be back."

"You're too nice, you know?"

"What?"

"It's true. People really like you."

"What people?"

"I don't know. Everyone. They all think you're really nice."

For some reason this irritated me.
"Nice."
I took to noisily chewing gum and ignoring people. Blanking folk on the Hulme walkways.
I also started regularly frequenting the White Horse. I would sit right next to the man who spun records on an old turntable, and pretend to ignore everyone, frowning into my beer. Yet inside I was fighting a little imp urging me to approach so-and-so and look for some fun.
One evening a girl called Dawn, whom I knew by sight, seemed to be taking every opportunity to pass near me on her frequent visits to the ladies. Maybe she just had a weak bladder.
"Up at the crack of Dawn!" whispered my little imp of the perverse.
I tried to drown him with a stinging shot of rum, chased down with a gulp of Guinness.
Sage appeared, looking like he had just performed the Indian rope trick and actually succeeded in entering some wonderful other world above.
"Whoa, man, whoa," he yelled, "slow this thing down while I get off!"
I grudgingly acknowledged his gurning guru grin.
"Of course, Sage. Anything else?"
"Yea, yea, plenty else. Funny faces, funny faces, funny faces everywhere!"
A few heads turned. What could I do to Sage to prove to them what a sour-minded git I was?
Just let him carry on.
"Tim!" he blathered, pointing in my face. "Tim, gentlemen, please. Tim-Timothy, Tim-Timothy, Tim-Tim-Teroo."
He broke off, giggling incontinently.
I bought him a double Pernod, with no water, and he knocked it back, and began to sing,
"Where do they go, those nose flutes we blow at night? What do they do, those…"
He broke off, choking, banging his fist on the table, eyes red and bulging, turban awry.
I pushed the rest of my drink towards him and walked out.

I thought about going to the Glamour and pulling Simone off stage.
No more erotic revue for you, baby.
As if…

I didn't fancy Norman and telly, so I wandered into some nameless pub instead.

Decided to stick to Guinness, having started on it.

Some body told me once, never drink beer on top of stout, sure fire route to a headache. Stan Bardolino, that was it. He knew about such things.

"Go on drinking like that," came a voice, "and you'll end up like me."

It was Dr Drummond, sitting in a corner, beer and scotch in front of him.

I didn't feel like chatting, so I stayed at the bar, but he ambled over anyway, spilling a little beer on his shoes.

"With me," he said, leaning close, "it's a Dorian Gray sort of scenario. You're studying English, right? Or was it Philosophy? Doesn't matter. Point is, my liver represents the portrait in the attic. Thus, though outwardly I remain relatively unchanged, the old inner organ absorbs all the sinful behaviour, and gets all raddled and twisted and so on. One day during my post mortem they'll uncover it, and be amazed to see how smooth it becomes, while my face suddenly takes on the thousand natural shocks that flesh is heir to, and a few more besides, do you see what I mean?"

"I think so. Sort of Hamlet walking on the Wilde side."

He levelled an index finger in front of my nose, a smile spreading on his face.

"I like that. D'you know what? I think that deserves a prize."

He made a sweeping gesture towards the optics.

"Go on," he said, "have what you want. Try them, try them all!"

I wished, next morning, that I could remember which ones I did try, if only so I could avoid them in future.

Simone was sitting up reading, and when I finally got my eyes to stay open, she gave me her practised 'no-sympathy' look, closed her book, and went off to the bathroom.

Minutes later, the door opened and Norman peered cautiously in.

"You alone?" he whispered.

"No, Simone's hiding under the bed."

He was about to reply, when we heard Simone humming a tune as she returned, so he hid under the bed.

"You look worse than ever," she said, getting clothes from the wardrobe.

"Actually, you look sort of odd. Shifty."

I yawned as convincingly as I could.

"Don't know why you think that."

"Neither do I. We can discuss this later, I'm off shopping with Mum."

Always shopping. Still, she earned the money.

Norman surfaced, flicking hairy dust from his jumper, sat on the end of the bed, and produced a small paper bag from his pocket. He started to grin like Liberace, holding up the bag and shaking it.

"Look at these beauties!"

I looked in the bag.

"What are they supposed to be?"

"Supposed to be? What do you think they are?"

"They look like thin toadstools."

He shot me a look of pity.

"Ye Gods, Tim, where've you been hiding?"

"Not under the bed at least."

"Tim these are only magic mushrooms. Got them on the moors, what a coup! All nicely dried and ready to go."

"So what do they do?"

"Do?"

"Yeah, do. I mean if they're magic, pull a rabbit from a hat?"

He closed his eyes and shook his head.

"You are not worthy. Winding me up. I was gonna share these, but now I'm going off the idea."

"Didn't Perry Como do a song about them? Oh no, that was moments."

"Seriously, Tim."

"Ok, ok. But aren't they a bit dangerous?"

"How? A little trip can't hurt you."

"It can if it's off a big building. I heard about a bloke who thought he was superman and ended up in a wheelchair."

"Ok, then let's not take 'em on any big buildings. Or motorways."

"What if I become convinced your body has been taken over by an alien being?"

"Not body snatching again? You're obsessed, mate."

"Maybe. But if that did happen, I might feel compelled to destroy you for the good of humanity."

"You're not taking this seriously."

"Au contraire, that's exactly what I am doing."

"Know what, I'm starting to regret letting you in on this."

"Wonder if one can cook them? We could conjour up an enchanted omelette."

"Definitely regretting it."
He put the bag in his pocket and got up.
"Hang on," I said, "I'm free today as it happens."
"And Simone?"
"You heard. Out to the shops with her Mum. She'll be ages."
But I was wrong.
She returned to find me grinning at the television. It wasn't on, but I could see Norman's reflection. He was standing on the back of the sofa, arms outstretched, walking back and forth as if on a tight rope. It seemed to me that Norman was actually performing on television, and I kept applauding.
"Christ!" said Simone, her head growing two or three times its' normal size.
I tried to say something but could only laugh.
"Roll up, roll up!" shouted Norman.
I thought he meant for a spliff, but my attempts to make one disintegrated. Simone and her expanded head had left the room.

Kids can be cruel

"Silly Bill, he fell ill,
had a drink and took a pill,
maybe he was off his head,
we'll never know
coz now he's DEAD!"

Thus went our playground chant. Me, my mate Peter, and my brother Dan. I used to feel something that I now recognise as guilt when we sang that about Bill. Peter must surely have done. After all, Bill was his late Dad. Nevertheless, we all laughed ourselves sick over it. Peter, a red head, would turn puce, hiccoughing and belching through his asthmatic chuckle.
One day we were at it and Peter's Mum, Beryl, overheard us. We were in her garden. Bill's garden.
There was the greenhouse he had built from old window frames, never used, standing empty beyond the unmown lawn.
Nothing of his on the washing line, just some tea towels and a flesh-coloured bra, sunken cups, straps and catches.
Beryl stood at the kitchen door staring at us. Her mouth was tight with indignation, and her fury suddenly exploded in an almost incoherent stream of scream, shot through with words like 'ungrateful', 'beastly' and 'bastards.'
Peter went completely silent, staring wide-eyed.

Dan and I looked at our feet. My black slip-on plimsolls. His beige desert boots.

Simone, noisily brushing knots out of her hair, roused me from my reverie. "Oh, you're with us, then?" she said, tying her headscarf. She checked her lipstick in the mirror and addressed my reflection.
"You aren't going to be much use today, are you?"
"Why?"
"After whatever you and Norman were on?"
She turned and looked at me properly.
"You look awful, actually."
And, with a short smile, she was off.
For the rest of the morning I drifted in and out of dreams that were mixed up with the radio left on by the bed. In one of them, Simone and I were getting married, and the priest was Simon Bates.
That woke me.
I needed coffee, but the jar was empty, so I dragged on some garments and slipped out.
Leaving our door on the latch, I walked down the communal hallway to the front door, only to find it double locked. Realising my keys weren't in my pocket, I turned back to fetch them, but as I approached the stairs to the flat, I heard our door click shut.
So now I was trapped in a fusty oblong space with only a faded poster of Gary Numan on the wall of for company.
In an episode of 'Kung Fu', Kwai Chang Caine, incarcerated in a confined space, slows down his metabolism by meditating, calmly sitting it out cross-legged.
Fine, if you're not desperate for a crap.
All I could do, until someone came along, was concentrate on other things. The cracked, brown lino floor, a supermarket flyer offering jumbo sausages at a rock-bottom price…
No, this wasn't working.
I tried calling out, but the tight-lipped letterbox gagged me.
Numan, meanwhile, seemed to look down at me with an expression of gloating superiority. This from a man who extolled the virtues of living in cars and wondered whether friends might be electric.
Cold outside? Well I wouldn't know, would I?

No use, I couldn't hold it any longer. I crouched in a corner and ripped down the poster.

That'll wipe the sneer off his face.

Almost as soon as I was done, another tenant came in, carrying a carton of chicken and chips. I pretended I was on my way out and stood back to let him pass. He acknowledged me with a nod, paused, sniffed his food, and went into his flat.

I dumped the soiled poster in a bin on my way to the shop.

Danny's lips were pursed into a thin blue line.

"I'll tell you something Tim," he said, "either I'm getting older, or policemen are getting younger. And shorter."

"Are they?"

"Well obviously I don't mean existing members of the force have somehow reversed the ageing process, or that they're shrinking. I'm talking about the new ones. They're definitely smaller. I think it has to do with getting more Asian recruits. Can you see that? In Manchester? It'll be officers in turbans next. Where's the authority in that, tell me? I can't cope with it. I've nothing against them, don't get me wrong, but how are they supposed to understand the law enforcement in this country?"

I concentrated on a small tin, baked beans with bangers.

"Half of them don't even speak the language," he added.

By now I had wandered behind one of his well-stocked shop units, but it was his habit to carry on talking while you shopped. It didn't seem to concern him whether or not you actually listened.

"I can't understand all this multi-racist business. Bloody liberalism, that's what I call it."

Often he would continue his monologue even after you had left the shop. You could see him through the window, jawing away as he wiped a surface, or stacked cereal boxes.

I brought my wire basket to the counter, and he went quiet, momentarily, in order to check out the items. When he came to the beans he raised an eyebrow.

"These have sausages in, you realise? I thought you'd converted to vegetarianism."

"That's all Simone's idea. She thinks it's healthier."

"If you're a rabbit, maybe."

"I think they're omnivorous."

"You don't say? Them little fellows eating other little beasties! You learn something new every day. Any how, what's Simone going to make of you buying this sort of stuff?"

"Nothing, because she's not going to see it."

An annoyingly coy smile played around his sparse teeth, and he slightly inclined his head, and slanted his eyes at me.

I checked my cash.

"Cut me some of that bacon too will you Danny?"

He looked fairly astounded.

"Great God in Heaven, Tim, you might get away with a sly feed of bangers and beans, but you're a smart man if you can conceal the smell of fried rashers. That sort of thing lingers."

"I appreciate the advice…"

"But it's none of my beeswax? No, you're right, fair play. A man needs a bit of flesh on his plate. It's not a meal without it."

As he sliced it, he drew my attention to a few out of date items on the counter. He would often have an assortment there in the hope of still making a sale. Today there were three small sponge cakes.

"Can I tempt you to one of them?" he said. "They've a lovely moist constituency."

I shook my head.

"Sorry, Danny, but they don't get my vote."

"Oh well, to each his own. Not the sweet tooth is it?"

"More a savoury one."

"There now, I've some nice individual pork pies that'll be right up your street."

"Better not, I've already gone for the bacon. Any more pig would be pushing it."

He gave me a tart smile.

"Tim, are you not your own man?"

"I don't really know."

"Then you're not," he concluded.

I hastened back to the flat, cheered by the anticipation of an indulgent breakfast.

Then I remembered I didn't have my keys.

Bad Moon

Sage appeared at our door one evening with his entire head swathed in bandages, small slits for the eyes.

"Christ, Sage, what's happened to you?" I asked.

"Don't be a tosser, it's that party, remember? Fancy dress."

"What?"

"Am I not talking English? Party. Fancy dress."

"Oh, yeah, fancy dress party. So what are you supposed to be?"

"Take a wild guess."

"The mummy?"

"Wrong, you pillock. Since when does the mummy wear a suit? It's the invisible man, obviously. Fucking genius or what?"

"I wouldn't go that far. Pretty good though. The gloves are a nice touch. One slight thing, your turban does make your head look a bit long."

"I'm not wearing it."

"Oh."

He slapped me on the back as he barged in.

"Glad to see you've thrown yourself into the spirit of it. Let me guess, an under achieving undergraduate, right? Is Simone coming?"

"Working."

"Oh, right. Fancy un-dress."

"Carry on like that and you'll be needing those bandages."

He laughed loudly.

"Yeah, right, I'm really bricking it. Got any beers in?"

He seemed quite coherent, probably ran out of dope.

"Look, Sage," I said, as we shared a can. "Sorry about that trick the other day with the Pernod."

"You did a trick with some Pernod?"

"Not exactly."

"So why the apology? Look, we should get moving, so you better decide what you're wearing."

"I don't know, Sage, I'm not sure about this dressing up lark."

A muffled sigh of exasperation escaped through his bandages.

"Too late, Tim, I'm not going out on my own like this."

"You must have done to get here."

"Stop being evasive and get your fucking costume."

"I haven't got one."

"That we can get round. You're about the same size as Simone, right?"

"No. I mean, yes, but I am not dragging up."
"Pity. As my old man would say, you'd look rather fetching, old boy. Everyone knows you're a closet poof anyway."
I snatched the can away from him.
"Touchy, aren't we?" he said, laughing. "Ok, how about a toga? Sling a sheet round you, brush your hair forward, bit of Simone's make-up, you're one of those degenerate fucking Romans, Caligula, or Nero, how's that?"
So, a wet night in Wilmslow, and I'm walking the streets in a bed sheet and pair of Simone's flip-flops.
Sage started ripping a hedge apart.
"You could do with some of these on," he said, attempting to attach dripping laurels to my head.
"This party better be worth it," I muttered, as another passing vehicle's hooter parped derision.
"Sad cunts," observed Sage.
"Them, or us?"
My toga was starting to stick to my shoulders.
I prodded Sage.
"I thought you said it wasn't far from the bus?"
"Keep your leaves on, we're nearly there, I think."
We tramped on to the irritating slap of my footwear on sole, and the gurgle of rain down drain, until at last one property on the terrace stood out as the likely venue.
There were low lights behind the curtains, and we could hear that familiar cacophony of chattering laughter and throbbing music.
The door was opened by Count Dracula, and we insinuated our damp forms among the costumed company.
"Fucking stuffy inside this," came Sage's muffled voice. Steam was starting to rise from his head.
A werewolf came sidling up to me.
"Tim, what the hell are you supposed to be?"
"Imelda?"
"Well it's not Lon Chaney. You look ridiculous, Tim."
"Look who's talking."
"I know, but at least people can recognise who I'm supposed to be. What are you, a ghost that's been dragged through a hedge backwards?'
"Funny."

"I know, and what's also quite amusing is, I can see your nipples through that sheet."

"Thanks for noticing. I'll probably get the flu."

"You can cuddle up with me, I'm all furry."

"I don't think so."

"Oh, come on, don't play games with me. I take it that wasn't Simone you arrived with?"

I nodded, and a leaf fell from my hair.

"Thought not. So why the stuffed shirt? Or should I say sheet?"

She put her hairy hand in mine, a wolf in wolf's clothing, and led me into the kitchen. On the way I spotted Sage scoring some grass from Superman. I found two plastic glasses and poured shots of vodka.

Imelda had to take off her wolf mask to drink. Her hair was pinned up, and she looked warm and slightly damp.

"Were you expecting an orgy?" she said.

"What?"

"Well, dressed like you are, you know…"

"This was Sage's idea."

"Who the hell is Sage?"

"Can you hear that laughter?"

"You'd have to be deaf not to."

"That's Sage."

"Is he always that noisy?"

"Most of the time. Especially when he's smoking."

"Herb, you mean? Hey, that's quite funny, Sage, herb, get it?"

I took a peek down the hallway.

Sage was wandering from room to room, big spliff in his hand, bandages unfurling from his face and trailing behind him.

The party wasn't very crowded, but there were one or two notable costumes. One man had actually blacked up and was wearing a sort of raffia skirt. He was with a uniformed woman with a great stick-on Stalin moustache.

Sage came stumbling into the kitchen looking for a drink.

"Hey, Tim, howdy, howdy doodle do," he said, squeezing Imelda's thigh.

She pushed him away and he fell back among some empty cans on the table.

"I don't understand why you would hand around with the likes of him," she remarked, replacing her mask.

Her leering wolfish grin covered her indignation.

"He can't help it," I said. "He knows not what he do-eth."

"Well he can bloody do-eth it somewhere else. D'you fancy a dance?"
We shuffled around to 'Psycho Killer', a song never easy to dance to, made harder by the prone presence of Sage in the middle of the carpet conducting the music with a sausage.
The next song was 'Hotel California.'
"That does it," said Imelda. "We're going."
"What about Sage?"
"What about him? Are you his bloody minder?"
I glanced back at him as we left. He had the sausage in his mouth now and was trying to light it.

We had a bit of trouble getting a cab, until Imelda took her mask off. She directed the driver to her place.
"Come in for a cup of tea," she suggested.
"I don't know…"
"Ah, come on, I don't bite. Unless it's a full moon."
We sat on the bed in her room, sipping tea.
"God, will you look at the time," said Imelda, putting her cup down beside the alarm clock on her bedside cupboard.
She stretched, arching her back and yawned.
"I'm getting awful hot in this bloody suit, Tim. Will you undo me?"
The zip went from the nape of her neck to the base of her spine, fur peeling back to reveal pale, naked skin.
"I'm only in me knickers," she said, giggling. As if to corroborate this, she stepped out of the crumpled outfit and turned to me for a moment, before jumping into bed.
I hastily swallowed the rest of my tea.
"Well, I suppose I'd better be on my way."
She smiled.
"I've got a better idea. Why don't you get out of that sheet of yours and come under mine?"

Next morning I was woken by the persistent drumming of rain on the skylight, a monotonous tattoo to a dreary day.
I was alone.
Getting out of bed to dress, I quickly remembered what I'd been wearing the night before. Not ideal garb for the hours of daylight.

Imelda was taller than me, but a pair of her jeans, turned up, fitted tolerably well, and she had a fair selection of T-shirts. I went for an orange one with 'Roxy Music' printed across the front, which Imelda had customised with a marker pen, changing the R to a P.

I slipped downstairs, conscious of my flimsy flapping footwear, but the house appeared to be empty. All good students, off to their studies.

I made tea and switched on the TV. A schools programme about different types of energy, of which I didn't seem to have any. On the other side was the test card, with dispiriting light music that eventually drove me out of the house into the tipping rain.

I had no money and it was quite a walk, but it gave me time to think. Not such a good thing, as it also gave me time to worry about what I was going to say to Simone.

Back home, I was relieved to find only Norman was in. He glanced up at me from the TV.

"Simone's been mithering."

"Oh."

"*Oh?*"

"OH!"

"Oh."

He resumed his viewing of Worzel Gummidge on the telly, so I joined him.

"In my opinion," he observed, "Una Stubbs is the quintessential Aunt Sally. Quite sexy too."

"I suppose so, but she's not very nice to Worzel."

"Course not. That's what makes it. She is, in fact, actually cruel to him, and he's too stupid to see it."

"The Crow Man's his only friend."

"Not so much friend, as creator. He looks out for Worzel, but he can destroy him just as he made him. Note his references to the compost heap, a concept so terrifying to Worzel he can't even pronounce those words. And as for the bonfire…You know, in my view, Anglia TV have, in this show, produced the ultimate condensed New English Bible. The All New Old Testament Show."

"Remind me, are you on a media studies course?"

"Never heard of it."

Barbara Windsor had a cameo role as a ship's figurehead.

Leaving Norman to his critical viewing, I went out and ducked into the student union. There was someone at the bar who looked familiar, yet I couldn't quite place her. She smiled and beckoned me over.

"Timmy, baby," she said, kissing me on both cheeks, "don't you know me?"

"William?"

"No, Mae bloody West, who d'ya think?"

William. Fruity as Carmen Miranda's hat stand.

I looked him over.

"Suits you."

"Suits me? Listen to it! What you mean is, William you look absolutely gorgeous."

He flashed me a flirtful of dark pupils and eyeliner.

"William you look…"

"Oh, skip it, I'm only jerking your chain, I should be so lucky. You don't think it's a bit OTT? The wig's only temporary while I grow the hair. Get me a drink will you, my usual."

"You don't have a usual."

"Campari and soda then."

"Seriously?"

"Well, I can hardly sup pints of bitter in this gear, can I? Plenty of ice, please, I don't want to get tipsy. Still getting used to these heels."

He lit a long cigarette with a gold band around it.

"Frock's nice, don't you think?"

"Lovely."

"I know. My colour."

He sniffed his wrist.

"Shame about the perfume though. I was trying out the samplers in Lewis's, you know, see what suited, and they only asked me to leave! Dozy orange-faced shop girl called security. I said I'll take my custom elsewhere, thank you very much. Last time I go there! Nice drink, thanks. Nice long drink. You should try it, all that beer you keep swilling, you'll put on weight. Have you seen the state of my cousin Shane? No you wouldn't have. He's out here, I swear. If it wasn't for the beard, you'd think he had a bun in the oven."

When William got past the starting post you had to listen to the finish.

"Do you know, have you any idea what I've been through to achieve this?" he asked, standing up and giving me a twirl. "No, of course you haven't, but

I am here to educate you, Timothy. Prepare to become familiar with the process of gender reassignment."
But my education on the subject was sidelined by the arrival of one of William's cronies.
"Get you!" he began, and once they got going I was out of the picture.
On the way home I had a burger, thus adding to the growing store of secrets I was keeping from Simone.
She didn't say anything as I entered the living room.
"Norman not here?" I asked.
"I told him to go for a walk. I can't stand the TV on all the time, and I don't see why I should have to hide in our room. He's made the sitting room into his bedroom. Look at the state of his sleeping bag."
"That's ours."
"Not any more, it isn't."
"I'll wash it."
"Too little, too late. And why should you? It's time Norman started pulling his weight. Or better still, slinging his hook."
"I'm going to have a word."
She sighed.
"So you keep saying."
"Promise."
"Never mind. How was the party, by the way?"
"Alright."
"Stay at Sage and Hilary's?"
"Yeah."
Now I would have to square Sage and Hilary.

I got the chance to have a chat with Hilary sooner than I expected when a letter arrived from her expressing concern about Sage.
'He's been a bit weird lately,' she wrote. 'I mean, really odd, not just his usual nonsense. I wondered if you and me could meet up, because I don't know who to talk to about it, and you know him better than me.'
I found a working 'phone box in Daisy Bank road, called, and we arranged to meet in Whitworth Park.
I found her sitting on a bench reading 'In cold blood'.
Her hair was braided and looked gold in the sunlight.
She looked up and gave me a big, slightly nervous smile.
"I hope you didn't mind me writing. Your 'phone wasn't working."

"We were cut off."

"Oh."

She closed her book and got up, and we strolled across the grass to the children's play area, where we sat on a roundabout.

Hilary started telling me about her teaching practice in a secondary school in Gorton.

"God, Tim, there are some hooligans in 2C."

She obviously felt uncomfortable about launching straight into a discussion about Sage, so we both avoided the issue for a while.

The roundabout oscillated extremely slowly, giving the impression that, while we remained static, objects before us were moving. The swings, climbing frame, trees, subtly shifting like dissolves in a film.

Then I noticed a tear roll down her cheek.

"Am I being silly?" she said, blowing her nose. "I mean, do you think I'm over reacting?"

"Sage can be a bit of a handful, I imagine."

She laughed.

"I don't mind that. He's fun. He was. Sometimes now it's like I can't even understand what he's talking about."

I wondered how much he smoked at home.

"I don't know. I'm not sure he even cares if I'm there. It's like he's a different person or something. God, I'm not explaining this very well am I?"

"Have you talked about it?"

"With Sage? No, not really. To be honest, I don't know how. All my other relationships have been uncomplicated. Boring, but uncomplicated."

"Maybe I could have a go, sound him out a bit?"

"Would you? I'd really appreciate it, Tim. But don't tell him I've been going behind his back will you?"

"Don't worry."

"I'll try not to."

It didn't seem appropriate to raise the issue of my supposedly having stayed the night at her flat, so I left that one down to fate.

When I got home, Norman was re-installed in front of the television.

"Alright?" he said. "I found some money."

"Where?"

"Cheetham Hill, on the pavement"

"How much?"

"Dunno. What do you reckon?"
He showed me a brown note of some foreign currency that I didn't recognise any more than he did.
"What are you going to do with it?"
"What do you reckon?"
"I reckon, go to a bank and get it changed, see how much you get."
"I'll see you later."
A few moments after he went, the intercom crackled but failed to admit the caller.
It was Simone's brother Jordan. He hastened inside, glancing over his shoulder into the street, and went up into the kitchen.
"Simone in?" he asked.
I shook my head.
He lit a cigarette, smoked rapidly.
"Anyone else in?"
"Not at the moment."
"I saw someone come out. White geezer with a stoop."
"That would be Norman."
"He coming back?"
"He's sort of staying."
"Yeah? Well, that's funny as it happens, coz that's what I need to do, for a bit. Lie low, if you know what I mean. Can this Norman be trusted?"
"Not by shop keepers."
"He sounds alright. You gonna make me a brew?"
I filled the kettle.
"So, little sister's working I suppose? Yeah, don't worry, I'm aware of what she does. I work there too, remember, though in a different capacity."
I poured the tea.
"She needs to get out of that shithole," he said, lighting another cigarette. "All those old geezers ogling her. Midweek, it's half price for senior citizens. You know what she calls it?"
"Wank Wednesday."
"Correct, brother. Used to be Masturbation Monday. If you had a proper job she wouldn't have to do that shit."
He had never really taken to me. Nothing had been said, but I could tell from the first time we met that he didn't think I was suitable for his sister.
"Listen, man," he said, I have to get in the tub."

He left his smouldering cigarette, and as I stubbed it out, Simone came bundling in with a lot of shopping bags.

"I've been spoiling myself," she said, kissing me. "Got something for you too. Hey, can I hear taps running, don't tell me you've persuaded Norman to have a bath?"

Before I could answer, Jordan's voice boomed out.

"Were do you hide the shampoo, brother?"

Simone dropped her bags and headed for the bathroom.

I listened to her shouting. She sounded scary, even from a distance.

"What are you playing at, J? Mum and me haven't heard nothing from you, she's been worrying herself sick. Me, I'm past caring what happens to you since you obviously don't give a toss what anyone thinks. But for her sake, what's been going on, and don't be giving me none of your bullshit!"

At this point the bathroom door closed, and I couldn't make out their muted exchange.

When Simone returned to the kitchen she was still yelling.

"You better be on the level, J, coz if you put me or Mum in any danger…"

She sat opposite me at the table and lit one of Jordan's cigarettes. After a few drags she became calm, and smiled, shoving a carrier bag across the table to me.

"For you."

I pulled out a tiny, dusty-pink T-shirt with a heart motif that had the word 'LUV' printed on it.

"You shouldn't have."

She laughed.

"Sorry, wrong bag, here."

This time it was a v-neck sweater that seemed to have been teaselled together from a mixture of horse and goat hair, with an aroma redolent of the nether regions of beasts.

"It's all natural, made by indigenous peoples. I thought it would suit you. Go on, try it on."

As I pulled it over my head, shuddering as the hairy sleeves clung to my arms, I was suddenly reminded of Imelda's wolf costume.

"It's great," I said.

She walked round me, tweaking the hem.

"Looks nice!"

"Thanks, I've never had one quite like it."

"Each one's different, hand-made."

Not for the first time, I felt within me a response of ingratitude to her generosity and sincerity. But I was unable to express it.

At times like this I wanted sometimes to simply walk and keep walking. No preparation or explanation.

Sheer hit-the-road mode, destination unknown.

I tried it once. Got as far as Chorlton and came back in tears.

Maybe, like the werewolf, I was seeking to destroy the thing I loved most. That werewolf again.

Simone came over and put her face very close to mine.

"You know I love you?" she whispered.

Jordan came in wrapped in a steamy towel.

"Touching scene," he remarked. "Bung us a fag, sis."

So now we were four.

Simone allowed Jordan to have the small back room that was supposed to be a sort of study.

"But this is strictly temporary," she told him. "You sort yourself out, and you get out."

He had apparently displeased certain people over some 'business matters' and didn't want them to know where he was.

As he put it,

"Anyone asks, you aint seen me."

Much as her brother infuriated her, Simone didn't want him hurt.

He grinned.

"Yeah, nice one, Simone. Trust me, I'll be out of here before you know it."

"Same as with everything you do. I'll believe it when I see it."

She later found me writing an essay at the kitchen table.

"I'm sorry, Tim, it won't be for long."

"It's all right. Quite like working here."

"We'll talk later, ok? I have an evening show"

"I thought you were off tonight."

"Swapped with one of the girls so I could go shopping. Love you in that sweater."

She paused in the doorway.

"When you see Norman, can you make sure he understands about J? Better still, see if you can persuade him to leave."

"Jordan?"

"Norman, silly. He's been here for years!"

When Norman came in, I was alone in the living room.
I tried to explain to him about the J situation, but he just kept laughing at my new jumper.
"You're turning into a llama," he said, grinning goofily.
"It isn't all that amusing."
"It is after a couple of these."
He pulled several small bottles from a paper bag, opened two and handed one to me. 'Gold Label Barley Wine.'
I'd never had it before and drank most of mine in one go. Norman sat there watching, grinning inanely as I drained the sweet liquid.
"Not bad," I began.
Then the high-octane aftertaste kicked in.
Norman was delighted.
"Fucking rocket fuel or what!"
"Lift off."
"You just watch, that jumper of yours is going to get funnier and funnier."
"It's a present from Simone. Hand made"
He doubled over in silent mirth and came up swigging and singing.
"Fly me to the Mars, I wanna play among those stars!"
"The Mars? I take it that drink isn't your first?"
He shook his head, raising the bottle towards the bare light bulb like it was a satellite.
"I've had one or two."
"Or three. Look, before you go into orbit, can you just listen a minute about Simone's brother?"
"Go ahead, mission control."
"It's not a joke, Norman."
"All right, calm down. Keep your hair-shirt on."
I gave in and cracked another bottle.
Norman was enjoying himself so much he hadn't even switched on the TV.
"Taking on fuel!" he yelled. "Star trekkin' where no man trekked before. Da-da-da-da-dar-dar, da-da-da-da-daar...oh, hang on, that's 'Hawaii Five-O', oh, hello Simone, fancy a bevvy?"
As she came in an empty bottle rolled under her feet. She picked it up and examined the label.
"Mmm, nice vintage."
"You're back early," I said.

"Your powers of observation will never fail to astound. The cinema was shut, ok? And don't be asking me why. In fact, don't ask me anything. I'm off to bed."

Norman regarded me in silence for a moment, mock-turtle mouthed, and twiddled his narrow stripy tie.

"What?" I said.

He offered me another bottle, but I couldn't focus, and it slipped from my fingers.

"Whoops," said Norman. "That one's gonna be lively."

"Which is more than I am. Why d'you have to keep forcing it onto me? You're not exactly knocking it back yourself, so why expect me to?"

He smiled, breathed in deeply, and exhaled.

"One, I am not forcing it onto you, and two, you're right, I'm *not* exactly knocking it back. What I *am* doing is drinking subtly."

"What?"

"That note I found was worth nearly twenty quid. I've been on this stuff all afternoon, ever since I came out of the pub. So I don't need to knock it back. I'm topping up, that's all."

"I don't know how you can stomach it."

"I enjoy rude health. Iron guts they used to call me at school. Kids would set me challenges. Drinking vinegar. Eating chillies. I won a few bets that way. Come on, what you need is solids, you can take me for a curry."

So off we went to Rusholme.

He dragged me into one of those places that prey on the masochistic machismo of the undergraduate. If you could finish their hottest dish, they gave you a free T-shirt with 'I survived the Prakash vindaloo' printed on it.

"This place keeps me in T-shirts," said Norman. "Never had to buy one."

"You've never paid for any of your clothes anyway."

He nodded, rubbing his hands together as the food arrived.

He was a freeloader par excellence, and an even better thief. Never-nabbed-Norm. He would nick stuff just for the sake of lifting.

He once turned up with a copy of Webster's Dictionary under his coat.

"Present for you," he said, handing me the volume.

"It's American," I remarked.

"Is it? Oh well, you can use it to learn Yankee, in case you ever go there."

"It's not another language, you idiot. Just some different spellings."

"Well you live and learn. Never mind, if you don't want it, somebody will."

He put his hand in his pocket and pulled out some pens and a notepad.

"I got you these an' all," he said, tossing them over.
"How many times have I told you? I don't need you to nick stuff for me. I'm on a grant, remember?"
He laughed.
"Yeah, so am I, sort of. Barely enough to keep me in beer. Rather than call it nicking, just think of it as subsidising your education. Supporting a future pillar of society."
"And what sort of pillar goes about nicking stuff?"
"A better-off pillar. They don't miss the odd notebook."
"They would if everyone robbed them."
"Exactly! Then the state would have to provide. Anyway, I don't rob a lot."
"Ha!"
"I don't! Besides, there's loads worse than me. Perverts, for instance, like that bloke skulking about in a rubber suit. I mean, what kind of person does that?"
"Someone with a bouncy personality?"
"What? Oh, yeah, I get it. And it's so bad I'm gonna pretend you never said it. Anyway, have a look at this calculator I picked up. It's got musical keys as well as numbers. You can play a tune on it."
"Go on then."
"Can't. Batteries not included. Fucking rip off!"
Returning from the Indian, I found I was unsteady on my feet. The waiter's first words to us echoed in my head, "anything to drink, please?"
Norman was weaving along pretty confidently. He hooked his arm under mine.
"Come on soldier, what you need is a night cap."

I woke the next morning beneath Norman's malodorous sleeping bag, most of my face pressed into the corner of the settee. No sign of Norm.
I sat up, blinking in the early light. My mouth was dry, tainted with the tang of stale garlic, and there were saffron-yellow stains on my T-shirt.
Empty bottles all around me told the tale, especially the one with the rolled-up piece of paper stuck in its' neck.
It was a message from Simone, unsigned.
'Sort this mess out.'

I arrived tired at Mr Battyball's flat.
"Come in, son, it's open," he called.

He was practising putting a golf ball into an empty glass. He had his back to me and was so used to my visits he didn't even turn round.

"Hello, son, look, I must be on the mend. Couldn't have tried this a month ago. My stroke's not up to much though. Put one of those boiled fish on, will you, and one potato? I don't eat a lot. Oh and fill my water jug…"

Nothing else to do there, so I went on to Harold Eastwood's.

He was much more settled now, in an unsettled sort of way. No longer residing at the hospital.

"Hello there," he said. "You must have smelled the coffee."

He poured boiling water on the soluble solids and gave me an apologetic smile.

"I'm afraid the milk's turned, and I know you prefer it white."

"I could nip out for some."

"Oh, don't bother, I've still got some of that Coffee-Mate, if that'll do."

"Fine for me, but that still leaves you with no milk."

He gave a modest smile.

"Not necessarily. I'm, well, you see, I'm shopping again."

"That's great, great to hear you're getting out and about."

"Kind of you to say so. It's hardly an earth-shattering achievement for a mature adult, but it is a start."

"You'll be down the launderette next."

"Oh, no. Not yet. The noise, those awful machines. It would be such a help if you could still take the washing. For the time being. It's all ready, oh, except a coat in the wardrobe that wants dry cleaning."

"I'll fetch it shall I?" I said, heading for the bedroom.

"No!" he shouted, hurrying before me. "Keep back, I'm perfectly capable."

He stood in front of the bedroom door, breathing heavily.

"Sorry," I said, returning to my seat. "I didn't mean to interfere."

"No, no, it's me who should be apologising. I shouldn't have yelled at you like that. It's just that I'm rather private about my things. Silly, really. I'll find the coat myself after we've had coffee."

He brought through the tinkling tray of china, moving cautiously as if he were proceeding down the aisle of a train. The cups trembled and the sugar bowl slid, but he managed to get them to the table without spillages. It was a low coffee table, with a glass top beneath which were neatly laid out a series of cigarette cards, illustrated with the signs and names of English pubs. I tapped the glass.

"Been to all of these have you?"

He smiled, and an expression of something like regret passed over his taut features.

"Lovely idea, lovely. But I've never really been much of a pub man. Smoked all the cigarettes though, I'm sure you can believe that. And it seemed a shame to discard the cards. Some of them are quite striking in their way. 'The Bull', for instance, pretty fierce, is he not? Do you know, I lived near the village where that sign hung? And some ridiculous petition was got up, presumably by women, for it to be altered, in case it frightened the children! Can you imagine? I mean what did they expect? Bulls *are* fearsome creatures. Some people have no bloody imagination."

He took a long drag on his fag, and a sip of the bitter instant.

"Sorry, dear chap, I don't mean to rant. I'll just fetch that coat while I think of it."

He was careful to keep the bedroom door closed while he sought out the garment.

My last visit of the day was to a new client, an Irishman who had recently been discharged from hospital following treatment for drink-related complications.

His pub signs were etched on his liver.

A sallow-faced chap of forty, going-on-sixty, answered my knock.

"Mr Bennett?" I asked.

He shook his head, turned, and called into the flat.

"Francis, it's the social."

He led me in to a cold room, with floorboards carpeted only with dog-ends. The sole item of furniture seemed to be a cheap, garishly patterned divan mattress, no sheets.

Mr Bennett was sitting on it.

He was a squat, round-shouldered man, with a ruddy face and grey stubble, wearing tracksuit bottoms and a string vest.

He raised his head from his chest and regarded me through red-rimmed, watery eyes, before pointing a pink fur-apple of a forefinger around the room.

"I trust you don't object to company?"

I became aware of the shapes of several men hunkered down in the shadows, cradling cans of Special Brew.

Mr B gave a down-turned smile and patted the space next to him on the mattress.

"Why don't you take the weight off?"

After scrutinising my face for a few moments, he lightly punched my upper arm.

"Will you take a drink?" he said, indicating some cans at his feet. He was wearing slippers, with sticky patches on them that resembled tar.

"Not for me thanks," I said.

"On duty, eh? Pity, you look like you could do with one."

"Maybe later."

He took a sip of his.

"Ah, you're all right, son. I want you to know I appreciate what you're doing. Sure, it's great work that you do."

There was a low murmur of assent from the squatters.

Looking around, though, I realised I had no idea what I *was* supposed to be doing. Neither, it seemed, did they.

We all sat nodding at one another for a while, an uneasy silence that was suddenly broken by a squeal of pain from Mr Bennett.

"Watch it!" he shouted, grabbing my arm with one hand and yanking at the waistband of his pants with the other. One of his guests, apparently understanding, hurried over with a plastic bucket, only seconds too late to catch a jet of urine, which spurted up through Mr Bennett's fingers, and fell, a treacle-coloured fountain, onto my shoes.

"Jesus, God, sorry son," said Mr B, fumbling with his drawstrings.

The man who had answered the door earlier offered me a slightly damp, greyish handkerchief, which, after I had given my footwear a perfunctory wipe, he took back and stuffed in his trouser pocket.

"Well," I said, "is there anything you want, Mr Bennett?"

He frowned and scratched his neck.

"No, no, I don't think there's anything I want."

I sensed that he and his cronies were more or less waiting for me to leave. It reminded me of times when my Dad would try to stay up beyond his usual bedtime and accompany me in front of the TV. It was well-meant, but I could never really settle until he had gone.

Similarly, the moment I left Mr Bennett's, I guessed there would probably be a collective sigh, and an outbreak of relieved badinage.

"Well then," I said, "I suppose I'll be on my way."

"Thanks for coming," said Mr Bennett. "Sorry if I don't get up."

"You're all right. I'll see myself out."

"Thanks again, son. I'll see you when you're older."

Two headlines on the way home.
Local rag, 'ABUSED DOG MAY HAVE BEEN USED FOR GAMBLING.'
Manchester Evening News, 'RUBBER MAN STILL AT LARGE.'

Fun

Simone emerged naked from the bath, as most do, and flipped her fingers around for me to hand her a towel.
As it happens I was also undressed, and had been examining myself in the mirror.
"I'm convinced there's something wrong with my arse," I said.
She squeezed water from her hair, scrunching it up in her hands, and shaking drips onto the floor.
"For somebody who farts as often and at such volume as you, it seems a reasonable conclusion. I'm only surprised it's taken you so long to realise."
She attempted to snatch the towel I was holding just out of her reach, and I eventually let it go. She cracked it like a whip at my buttocks.
"Farty pants!"
"Yeah, well I'm not joking actually. It's sort of been sore."
She slipped on her mules. Why mules? Wear them with a donkey jacket.
By now she was in the bedroom. I could hear her rummaging for matching socks.
"It's nice of you to share all this with me," she shouted, "but I don't know all that much about arses, and I think a doctor might be more helpful."
"I can't get my arse out for a doctor."
She came back in, trying to look serious in socks and knickers.
"Don't be such a twat. You might have cancer or something. If you don't let a doctor see your rectum, you could end up minus one. You'll be shitting in a polythene bag."
"Thanks a lot."
She gave me a very quick kiss on the cheek.
"Sort it out, baby. Oh, and remember Mum's coming for lunch. You and Jordan start getting it ready, I'll be back as quick as I can."
"Me and Jordan? That's a laugh. He'd need a map just to find the cooker."
"Well you can be his guide."
By the time Rose arrived I had made some kind of a salad, and Jordan had made himself a cup of tea.
"Hello Ma," he said, lighting a cigarette.

"Don't you Ma me! What bloody game you think you're playing at, boy?"
"Don't start, Ma."
"Start? I don't even know where to begin…"
I shut the door on it and found Norman in the living room.
"Still here, then," I observed.
"Don't be sarcy, it doesn't suit you. If you've got something to say to me, just say it."
"Ok, when are you going?"
"Anything except that."
"I'm surprised they haven't chucked you off your course. You're hardly ever there."
"I'm on a sort of sabbatical."
"My arse!"
"Oh, yeah, how is it, by the way?"
"What?"
"Your rear end. Any improvement?"
"How d'you know about that?"
"You told me, remember? The other day, in the Indian."
"I talked about it in the restaurant?"
"You did indeed. Pretty loudly, as I recall, and in considerable detail. Much speculation about the effects of spicy food. Or should that be speculumation?"
"I hate to think. Simone reckons I should get it looked at."
"Then do it. That her Mum I can hear in the kitchen?"
"Yeah. I better get back to lunch."
"Don't you mean *we* better?"
"No."
I went back to find Jordan leaning over the sink smoking, and Rose sitting at the table, wiping her eyes with a tiny lace handkerchief.
Simone came in and stood staring at the three of us.
"This is jolly," she said, unwrapping some solid-looking veggie pasties.
Jordan stubbed out his fag on the drainer.
"Aint it just?" he said, opening a bottle.
The meal was begun in silence, Rose the first to break it.
"And you," she began, stabbing a fork at me, "you're spending far too much time with undesirable company."
Good thing I had excluded Norman.
Simone nodded, sipping wine.

"Oh really?" I remarked, letting go of my fork, which remained upright in a speared pasty. "And what company would that be?"
Rose scoffed.
"What company? You hear, girl? What bloody company? I'll tell you what! It's your skanky so-called friends. Don't think I don't know. And that blasted agency, sending you out to all those dirty old people. It's not natural. If you must work, and interrupt your studies, you should find yourself a nice suitable job, like Simone."
"I see," I replied. "And you consider the clientele at Simone's workplace to be suitable?"
Rose frowned and licked a flake of pastry from her lip.
"What's that supposed to mean? People giving you trouble, Simone?"
"I wouldn't let 'em," murmured Jordan.
Rose looked confused.
"Don't listen, Mum," said Simone.
"That's right, Rose," I said. "No need to worry. Everyone at the Cinema keeps a very close eye on Simone."
"She the best damn usherette they could want for."
"Oh, the best. Everyone's always very happy with her performance."
Rose was lost for words, which pleased me, despite a spring of remorse that rose in my gut.
"Steady, bro," said Jordan, shooting me a look.
Simone trod on my foot under the table.
"So, Mum, what do you think of the pasties?" she asked.
Rose rearranged the food on her plate.
"Different," she said. "Novel, if you like that sort of thing. But I reckon you need a proper bit of meat, and a bit of spice, to stay healthy. Me and your father worry about you, girl."
Simone laughed.
"If he's so worried, let him tell me to my face."
"Meaning what?"
"You know. Clearly a case of concern by proxy."
"Come again? You been too long in the company of bookworms. And it's below the belt, taking a poke at your father when he's not here to defend himself."
"Exactly! He never is here, to defend himself or for any other damn reason."
Jordan got up.
"I'm fed up with this, going out to get something I can eat."

Rose sucked air through her teeth.

"Now are you satisfied?"

She got her hat and coat, and I held open the door to avoid her slamming it. Simone remained sitting at the kitchen table, fighting back tears and staring at the remains of her pasty.

"Anyway," she murmured. "He isn't my Dad."

Sometimes there is nothing for it but to leave Simone to her thoughts, especially when Norman has come in sniffing around the leftovers.

I dragged him and his furtively gathered scraps into the living room, where he put 'Dragnet' by The Fall on the turntable and used the record sleeve as a tray for his scavenged meal.

"I don't get this at all," he commented, pointing at the loudspeakers. "What made you buy it?"

"And not nick it, you mean?"

"No, I mean this particular album. Hark at it! I'll tell you what it is, there's a distinct lack of Karl Burns going on here. Listen to that drumming, sounds like the crash cymbal's sitting on the mike."

"That's his name, funnily enough."

"Eh?"

"The drummer. His name's Mike."

"Give me strength, Tim, what difference does it make what his fucking name is? Still sounds crap."

"You can't blame it all on the drummer."

"I don't. The whole thing sounds like it was recorded inside a fucking washing machine. On a wool cycle. Nah, I reckon this album will be to The Fall what 'White Light' was to the Velvets. Commercial fucking suicide."

"And after such an accessible debut."

"Again with the sarcasm."

He blew crumbs from the cardboard sleeve, flipped it like a frisbee towards the record player, and started rifling through my vinyl.

"Haven't you got any Skids?" he mumbled. "Let's see, Joy Division, Leonard Cohen, Joan Armatrading... Christ, if I ever feel like topping myself I'll know where to come. Hang on, Dennis Brown, more like it. 'Wolves and Leopards', great stuff. Excellent singer. Funny title though, I mean I get the wolves, but why the leopards?"

"So it rhymes."

"Ah, shepherds!"

He put the needle to the disc.

"Come to think of it," he said, "are there still such things as shepherds?"
"Course there are. How else would the sheep get rounded up?"
"Oh yeah. Or be kept safe from wolves and leopards."
"I shouldn't think leopards are a frequent issue."
"Or wolves these days. That's what I mean, you wouldn't think shepherds were really needed any more. Farming's all machines now."
"So you reckon there must be some kind of combine sheep rounder-upper?"
"Why not?"
"You don't think it might be a tad risky?"
"Even better! Cut out the middle man with combined harvest and butchery."
"Not a pretty picture. And what about the telly programme? 'One man and his mechanised sheep herder' doesn't have quite the same ring somehow."
"Suppose so. And if a bloke had to drive it, he'd still be a shepherd. Anyway, that programme has to be the all time most boring thing on the box. Some twat in a cap whistling at a dog. Never watched it."
"And yet you seem quite familiar with it."
"I'm familiar with Idi Amin, but it don't mean I'm doing him."
"Another rumour disappointingly scotched."
I went and checked on Simone.
She was in bed with the curtains drawn, so I let her lie and went out for some air.
I took a bus into town, and found myself drawn into the looming, biscuity-tiled presence of the Arndale shopping centre.
To supplement the wholesome food of home, I got myself a take-away meat and potato pasty, but when I bit into it there was a warm apple filling.
A bad pasty day.
I dumped it and went outside to find crowds of people lining the streets, come, I thought, to jeer at me, and my hapless choice of confectionary.
Almost obscured by waving flags, I thought I recognised the Queen, smiling, and shaking people's hands.
"Bring down the Monarchy!" someone shouted.
Sounded like Sage, but I couldn't see him.
I hurried away from the melee to the quiet of the canal, and sat watching the dank water moving slowly, impotently, between the man-made banks.
The quiet waters by. Hymns at Sunday school. I used to murmur the words, too shy to sing, my tummy grumbling in anticipation of the dinner waiting

for me when I got home. Mum in her apron, turning with a smile, oven gloves patterned with sunflowers and singe marks.

I wanted to go home, but not to the flat.

So I went to the Thompson's Arms and got a half.

A man sitting nearby was eating a mince-based meal that smelled exactly like a fart. The food seemed to regard me reproachfully.

"That's right, *assume it's me*."

I downed my beer fast and skedaddled.

Wandering, day-dreaming into evening, I heard a thumping racket coming from a building next to the University known as The Squat. Semi-abandoned, it was sometimes used as a venue for gigs, usually chaotic affairs with unknown bands and mediocre beer. Nevertheless I stumped up my fifty pence and was in.

The lead singer was just announcing their last number, 'Cancer Ward'. She was wearing a black leather peaked cap with chains on it, and stood stock still, delivering the lyrics in a clipped, monotonous fashion intended, judging from her stony gaze, to convey indifference. I thought of Simone, also on stage, exposing her self to a handful of hand jobs.

'CAN-cer ward, CAN-cer ward,' came the chorus of the song, shrill emphasis on the first syllable, sub-Siouxsie style, followed by a clumsy climax of crashing cymbals.

There was a smattering of applause mixed in with some half-hearted heckling. I clapped automatically, and the singer gave me a familiar smile. William.

Suddenly I felt a lot happier.

He came straight over to me after the set.

"Fancy seeing you here! Actually, it's a bit embarrassing you turning up when I'm doing my Eva Braun. The band's strictly a stopgap, get some stage confidence, then I'm going solo. I can feel it my water, Tim, the pop world is about to be rocked by cross-dressers and trannies, and I intend to be in the vanguard. Or in the van with the guard. Ooh yes, I like the sound of that, nice burly bodyguard to keep the fans from ripping me clothes off. Don't laugh, I'm gonna be mega, me. Strapping lads on building sites'll be whistling my tunes."

"Hasn't David Bowie already been there?"

"Bowie? Strictly panto, Timothy. Vaudeville. I'm talking about living it, being it. Bowie minces on wearing a load of slap, like a kimono dragon, or whatever they are, and then the next thing you know he's a fucking pirate, and after that a skeleton in a zoot suit. I mean, don't get me wrong, I love the bones on him, no pun intended, but what I've got in mind is gonna blow the likes of Mr Bowie, nee Jones, out of the fucking water and onto the beach."

He broke off for a quick sip.

"So, what do you think of the get up? The chains are a bit O.T.T. right? I thought about PVC but it sweats…Know what I really wanted? Jackboots. But how does a girl ask for something like that? The looks you'd get. So I settled for stilettos…"

He paused to light a cigarette.

"The hair is definitely too long though. I'm thinking of having it all off. Then again, it might make me look dyke-ish, which would kind of defeat the object, if you know what I mean. I'm telling you, it's norr-easy being different. Anyway, that's enough about me, what the heck have you been up to? Still living in sin? Simone, wasn't it? Coloured girl. Here, I once went out with a black man, and if he was anything to go by, I'll tell you one thing, don't believe the hype, know what I mean?"

"Did he like reggae?"

"What? How would I know? It was a one-off, and probing his musical preferences was not exactly the first thing on my mind."

"Simone doesn't. She's an easy listening kind of girl."

"And why not? You can't beat a bit of Perry Comatose. Look, Tim, I'd love to stop and chat, but you'll have to forgive me, just remembered I've got a date, so I'll have to love you and leave you, ta-ra…"

He made for the exit as fast as his heels would carry him.

To Hulme it may concern

Next morning, Simone was gazing out the bedroom window at clusters of pigeons huddled under the eaves, sheltering from the drizzle.

"Tim," she asked, "do you think the rain is like the world being sad and crying?"

"No."

"Didn't think you would."

"So why ask?"

She turned up the radio. Simon Bates, presenting 'Our Tune.'

'Ok, let's name names, let's tell it like it was…'

Mawkish tales to maudlin music.

Simone liked it though. She would lie on her front, head resting on her palms, legs crossed aloft, and go dreamy.

'They followed different paths, which love conspired to cross in years to come…'

Simone sighed.

"That's so *sweet*."

'But it was bitter-sweet, for Jay was to discover he was dangerously ill…'

As I left the room I swung the door and it banged against the dressing table. I decided to go and visit Hilary and Sage, and as I arrived in Hulme two unexpected things happened. The sun came out, and a child threw a lump of concrete at me.

Actually, the second wasn't all that unexpected, and then the sun went in again.

There was no answer at Hilary's, so I went to the chippie and bought some mushy peas and a steak pie, and ate them out of a carton that became soggy in the rain.

I hadn't brought a coat but was quite enjoying the feeling of moisture soaking through my jumper and t-shirt, clammy on my shoulders, trickling down my neck.

A mongrel sauntered over, flinching lest I shout or throw something, and settled when I didn't. Such was the yearning in his dark eyes, I fed him part of my pie, which he hardly chewed before hastily swallowing. He continued to stare at me while I ate the rest of it. Getting up, I put the remains of the peas on the ground and left him sniffing at them disappointedly.

Nearby, the landlord of The Iron Duke was standing outside staring up at his pub sign. Somebody had altered it to read 'Dyke.'

I went in, and he followed, re-installing himself behind the bar, a baffled look on his face.

"Who'd do a thing like that?" he said.

"Probably students," I suggested.

He tutted.

"And they're supposed to be the ones with brains. What can I get you?"

I thought at first I was the only customer, but then I heard mumbling from the other end of the bar. There was a figure leaning there that resembled Sage, and as my eyes adjusted, I realised it was him, looking smaller, somehow, and thinner.

I went over, but he kept his eyes ahead, and continued to talk at the wall. His gaze was fixed on a piece of card pinned up behind the bar that had packets of peanuts on it, overhanging one another like roof tiles. Partially visible behind the thatch of snacks was a photograph of a young, tanned woman wearing a bikini, and it was this that had evidently caught Sage's eye. Nearing him, I could now make out his low mantra.

"Somebody buy some nuts, somebody buy some nuts."

I thought of my promise to Hilary that I'd 'sound Sage out.' Somehow, this didn't seem like the ideal opportunity.

"Buy some nuts, buy some nuts."

"There's nobody here," I said.

He gave a little start and broke off.

"Oh, er, alright?" he said.

He offered me a peanut.

Then he told me he had spent the whole morning smoking Mary J, before murdering Hilary.

She was lying in the strangest position I have seen since the time Norman, on the way home from a party, had tried to settle down to sleep on the bonnet of a parked car.

One of the lenses of her glasses was starred, and a brownish halo of drying fluid surrounded her cranky head. A bowl of cornflakes lay upset in a corner.

"What do you reckon?" asked Sage.

"Reckon?"

There was an odd lack of urgency.

"Funny," murmured Sage, "they do say the kitchen is the most dangerous room."

"Seems they are right. Especially when it contains you."

"Christ, Tim."

I tried to think.

When I was a child, whenever I was 'off colour', my Mum always used to put her palm on my forehead. I crouched down and put mine on Hilary's. Her skin felt damp, and cool.

I pointed towards the 'phone.

"Call an ambulance."

"I don't know the number."

I stared at him.

"Oh, yeah," he said.

Spirit

From time to time, Simone would claim she was being spooked by the ghost of one of her uncles. She woke me one night, moaning and writhing, and I knew he was there.
"Uncle Winston?" I asked.
She switched on the bedside lamp and sat blinking at me.
"You know perfectly well his name's Wilfred."
"*Was*."
"Look, just coz he died, it doesn't mean he's not still with us. Like tonight. He comes to my bed."
"Just like old times then."
"Thanks Tim."
"Sorry."
She pulled the blanket up to her neck.
"I can smell him, that brand of rum he drank, Cockspur."
"That figures."
"What do you mean, that figures?"
"Nothing."
"It might be a joke to you…"
"No. No it's not. I just wish there was some way of exorcising him. It's bad enough what he put you through when he was alive."
"May God rest his soul."
"No rest for the wicked."
"Good riddance. No, I don't mean that. He wasn't all bad."
"No? I would gladly have killed him myself if the number 53 to Gorton hadn't got in there before me."
"You see, it is all a joke to you, isn't it?"
It wasn't, though.
When Uncle Wilf went West, I thought that was the end of it. I didn't expect a spectre.
Yet here he was, with his Cockspur breath, perving from beyond the grave. I could just about handle Simone being leered at by lookers at the Glamour, but to be interfered with by a phantom?
Phuck!
Wilfred having murdered sleep, I went to the kitchen to make tea, and as the kettle began to whistle, I thought of Hilary. She was in hospital in a coma, and so far I hadn't mentioned it to Simone.
I sat in the grey early light, sipping tea and wondering what best to do.

Sage was like a snail on a razor blade.

The police had quizzed him and had so far reluctantly accepted his claim that he couldn't remember much about what had happened. They were hoping to get Hilary's side of the story, and for Sage, there was talk of a psychiatric assessment.

I went up to check on Simone, and as soon as she got up, she lit up.

She had really got into her stride with the fags, and it annoyed me. Sitting there on the end of the bed in her dressing gown, hair all frizzed out, ash on the counterpane.

It was the way she relied on them. If she needed to make a 'phone call, scratch of a match before dialling. Someone at the door? Puff puff, "Oh, hi there!"

"Did you sleep?" I asked.

"Not really."

She crouched down and dragged her old cassette player from under the bed.

"I'm starting today," she announced.

"Again?"

She rummaged in the dust, scraps of loo roll and odd socks, until she found the set of Spanish-for-beginners tapes her mother had lent her.

She claimed some Spanish ancestry. Port of Spain, maybe. Her great-grandmother had run a sort of flamenco flophouse, the kind of place where you got the clap, clap, clap.

Simone often told me she wanted to be a proper dancer.

"You mean one who keeps her clothes on?"

"Ha ha."

She pressed play.

'No revuelva todo, por favor.'

Concentrating, she clenched her left hand into a fist and repeated the phrase. She had a small thumb on that side, like a conker, with narrow crescent nail.

"Don't stare at me," she complained, "you're putting me off. Go and get me some cigarettes will you?"

"If you ask me in Spanish, I might."

She paused the tape.

"Er, por favor quiero cigarillos... Oh, just get them, will you?"

Danny was standing behind his counter looking unusually thoughtful.

"No luck on the gee-gees?" I asked.

He seemed to become slowly aware of me, as if from a trance.

"Ah, Tim. No, nothing like that. I'll tell you the truth, it's family matters. My eldest boy Gavin is a worry, I don't mind telling you. Where we went wrong with that lad, I don't know. I've no idea what it is he does for a living, and you can be sure he won't discuss it. I can't cope with it. And on top of that he expects his room to be kept how it is and I could do with that for extra storage. The mess in there! Stuff strewn everywhere. And he shows no interest in the shop, not unless he wants money. He's up to no good. If I could just put my finger on it. But there's no talking to him. Oh no, he'll only bite me head off if I try. And you know the pity of it? If he could just tidy himself up he could be quite the illegible bachelor. Was there something in particular you wanted?"

"Fags for Simone."

"Back on them, is she? I can't cope with the things. Gavin, he smokes like a bloody chimney, and there you are, see? How can he afford it? God knows, the bloody things aren't cheap. My prices are lower than Ayub's mind you. Twenty was it?"

When I got back to the flat I could hear a male voice from our room. No way Norman would be up yet, and it was not a recording.

"Morning, brother," said Jordan. "Those for me are they?"

Lunch for me was usually a half of Guinness and a packet of peanuts in the union bar, and I was joined today by Norman.

"Can't stand it when he's around," he said, referring to Jordan. "I mean, how can a sound lass like Simone have a brother like that?"

"Half brother."

"Half wit, more like. Bloke's a wanker."

"He won't be staying long."

"Glad to hear it. Some people have no idea when they've out-stayed their welcome. You getting me a drink or what?"

Bardolino came in.

"Hello boys, did I hear Tim's buying? I'll have a bottle of brown and a steak pie, hold the gravy."

"Haven't seen you about much," I remarked, for the sake of conversation.

"Ah, well, I've been away on a little job down in London. Quite a good earner. I might buy you a pint if you're nice to me. I met this bloke in a pub, Rotherhithe I think it was, Irish fellah by the name of Dermot, or Declan. Anyway, he had this idea of setting up some sort of community house, where you all muck in, like, and nobody needs to work. A communal squat, he called it."

He negotiated part of his pie before continuing through flakes of pastry. "Well my first thought was, ditch this fucking head case, but actually some of what he was saying made sense. You could do it down there, alternative lifestyle and that. I don't think I could bunk up with a bunch of squatters mind."

"The great unwashed," commented Norman.

Bardolino laughed

"Unlike your fragrant self. You really must tell me the name of that perfume you're wearing."

"It's aftershave. I nicked some of Jordan's."

"Do you ever actually pay for anything?"

"Not if I can help it."

"You should nick yourself some decent stuff. Paco Rabane, for instance."

"Who's that, some Dago?"

"Ye Gods!"

"Simone's been playing her Spanish tapes," I interjected.

"Thanks, Tim," said Bardolino. "Now I can sleep easy."

"I can get her any of those language tapes," said Norman. "Or any kind of tapes. A C120 is good, coz you can get a lot more on it. The draw back is, to fit all that tape into the cassette, it has to be thinner."

"The tape or the cassette?" I asked.

"The tape, obviously. Which makes it prone to jamming."

Bardolino shook his head, eyes closed.

"Hark at the two of you! There's only so much excitement I can take, man."

"You'll thank me," said Norman, "next time you get a jammed cassette."

"The fuck I will, because I can't stand all that personal stereo stuff. I listen to my music at home and on vinyl."

"Prone to scratching, and a martyr to static."

The pros and cons of recording media thus summed up, we sat for some moments in silence.

"Why Bardolino?" Norman suddenly enquired.

"Me Dad's Dad was from Italy."

"That's interesting. Have you looked into your ancestry?"

"Nah."

"Surprising. You're as bad as Sage. What's it he says, Tim?"

I didn't really want to get into Sage.

"Something like, a long line of Bangladeshi bandits."
Bardolino scoffed.
"Don't talk to me about Sage! Where is he, by the way? Haven't seen him for yonks. Not that I'm complaining. You know what I think? He takes Hilary for granted. He's unworthy of her. Mind you, he's unworthy of just about anyone, but Hilary's a bit special, like."
"You mean you fancy her?" I suggested.
"Watch it, watch it! I was talking about Sage."
"You mean you fancy *him*, then?" asked Norman.
"Keep this up and you'll both be riding for a hiding. I was only saying that your turban toting pal doesn't, in my view, appreciate the lass with whom he cohabitates, and I'd hate to see her hurt."
He scrutinised the butt of his cigar for a second, then ground it into an ashtray.
"No. That I would not like."

Wake your ideas up

'Oh Sagey, oh Sagey, oh baby,' I was singing, in a tremulous falsetto.
Glad I woke from that one.
Then I kept drifting back to sleep, each time having a short dream where I got up, dressed, went to the kitchen to make tea, and always woke before drinking any.
Deja brew.
Eventually I actually made it to the kitchen and was pouring tea when the intercom buzzed.
It was Sage.
'Oh Sagey, oh Sagey, oh baby,' I sang to him.
Then I woke up.
Simone was smiling through the steam rising from the cup of tea she had brought me.
"What's funny?" I asked.
"You were making strange noises."
"Strange dreams."
"What about?"
"Well, not being able to wake up, mostly."
"Oh yeah, really strange that! Beats the one I had about trying to resurrect my dead grandmother by attaching electrodes to her nipples."
"When did you dream that?"

"Wake up, baby!"

She handed me the tea. It was in a cheap 1977 Silver Jubilee souvenir mug, gold rim and a black and white Queen that looked like a poor zerox.

Simone had been given it by her mother, with the exhortation that it should be looked after as it would one day be valuable.

It irritated Simone when I pointed out how similar the image on the mug was to that on the sleeve of the Sex Pistols single 'God save the Queen.' Funnily enough, the record was probably already more collectable than the cup.

"You're quiet," remarked Simone.

"I'm drinking tea."

She picked at my pyjama sleeve.

"Are you ok with Jordan being here?"

"I suppose."

"Ok, drink your tea. And after that, are you going in to Uni?"

"Why?"

"Nothing. You just seem to be skipping quite a few lectures and stuff."

"And that's nothing? Has Rose been poking her nose in again?"

"Let's leave Mum out of this."

"I wish."

"What's that supposed to mean?"

"Would you prefer it in Spanish?"

"Don't be facetious. Anyway, at least I try to broaden my mind. My Mum's right, you keep too much dodgy company. It's interfering with your studies."

I got abruptly out of bed, banging my mug down on the floor.

Simone flinched slightly.

"Now you've spilled it on the carpet."

"Big deal, it's brown anyway."

"That's not the point…" she began, but I was already on my way to the bathroom.

I put soap on my face and started to shave, saw the mask in the mirror, and something inside me cracked.

I found Simone in the kitchen setting out bowls and spoons. I went up behind her and put my arms around her shoulders.

She turned.

"It's only because I care," she murmured.

"I know."

"Do you? Do you like me, Tim?"

"What makes you say that?"
Her brow crumpled.
"That's a politician's answer, evasive."
"I'm a space evader."
"Come on, less Bowie parody, more straight answer."
"Of course I like you, you know I do…"
"But do I?"
"Maybe I don't show it enough."
"Show what?"
"It."
She smiled sardonically.
"You show *that* often enough. I just need a little love and affection."
I stifled a Joan Armatrading quip and nodded.
"You won't regret it," she said, "and you've got soap on your face."
I went off to finish shaving, but the bathroom door was locked, and the sound of Jordan flatly singing 'You Can't Hurry Love' echoed from within. Pointless to knock, so I went back to the kitchen, and was trying to wipe my face with a tea towel when Simone brought the post.
There was a post-card from my Mum who was on holiday in Tenerife with Arthur.
He had managed to force in a comment at the bottom.
'Can't keep your mum off the wine!!!'
'Can't keep yourself off my Mum', I thought.
Foreign holidays. We never used to go further than the seaside, South Coast. Mum swam, but Dad was not fond of the water.
"Just let me feel that sun playing on my back," he would say. Rolled-up trousers, and maybe a pale-legged paddle before retiring to his deck chair and the Daily Mirror.
And always there would be a moment when Mum would complain of his inactivity, commenting with some resentment, 'he's in one of his quiet moods.'
I didn't mind. I didn't want him to be one of those bronzed buggers, charging into the sea in tight trunks and flip-flops. Maybe Mum did.
Simone put her hand on my shoulder.
"What's that?" she said.
I tossed her the card.
It showed a massive hotel, and there was an arrow scratched in ballpoint above one of the many balconies.

At least they hadn't said 'wish you were here.'
"Wonder if they sent one to Dad?"
Simone tried to lighten the mood.
"Looks lovely and sunny."
"Looks crap."
"Tim, Arthur's not going to go away! I know how you feel, but…"
"Do you? You always know! Doesn't anything ever piss you off?"
"Of course it does. Tim, look at my parents. They say they're together, but when they are, they hardly ever speak to one another without shouting. Sometimes people need to face the fact that it's time to call it a day."
"Do they?"
"I think so."
"Do you want to?"
"What?"
"Call it a day."
She stirred her muesli.
"Why do you say that?"
"Because maybe you do."
"Well I don't."
I couldn't even muster a smile.
"Well," she said, "I'm off."
Her muesli went soggy.
I was scraping the remains of it in the bin when Norman came shuffling in.
"Hey," he protested, "I could have had that. There are millions of starving people in the world."
"And there are millions of annoying people."
I pointed at the bin.
"Help yourself."
"Nah, I'm not *that* into muesli."
I tore the post-card into narrow shreds and tossed them on the table.
"There you go, Norman, a little picture puzzle for you."
He looked nonplussed, but continued, as usual, to hang around like a dog hoping for scraps.
But the cupboard was bare.
"Have you ever actually made yourself a meal?" I asked.
He considered, then smiled.
"I did try one of them Vesta things once, but I burned the noodles."
"You could manage cheese on toast, couldn't you?"

"Dunno, can you do it in a toaster?"
"What do you think?"
"You could put it on its' side. Might work."
"The toaster wouldn't, not after that. So if you do try it, hands off our toaster."
He looked slightly offended.
"Come on, I don't have a toaster. Mind you, I'm sure I could lay my hands on one."
"Why not just nick a meal?"
"Now that really would be a take-away."
"There's no such thing as a conscience-free lunch."
And then Jordan came in, smelling of Brut.
He lit a cigarette, sat down opposite us, and blew smoke into Norman's face. Sensing they were about to kick off, I decided it was time for a walk.
Too much crap was piling up, like the uncollected refuse in the streets. I broke into a trot, hoping to leave it all a few paces behind me, but it kept up. So I returned, doggedly, to what had become an arena of conflict, namely the kitchen. For some time now Jordan had been trying to freeze Norman out, unaware that he was dealing with a T-shirt man for all seasons. Lately, a more verbal strategy had been adopted, and it was starting to produce results. Norman, though a pachyderm in many respects, would rise to the barbed comment like the next man, and by the time I got back, a comment of that nature had clearly been issued, and Norman had risen.
"Yeah, well I've known Tim for years," he was saying.
"So what?" countered Jordan. "I'm family. Remind me, what are you still doing here?"
"I'm a guest."
"That's a laugh! Know what? Simone would kick you out like that," he said, clicking his fingers.
"Is that right? And I suppose she's loving it having you holed up here?"
They noticed me in the doorway and went into surly, stern-breathing mode. I headed for the study, remembered it was currently Jordan's bedroom, and went looking elsewhere for my satchel.
Simone was right, I had been skipping lectures. The last one I went to Imelda had insisted on joining me. We talked and laughed so much that Doctor Skilbeck suggested we either be quiet or leave, and to the barely suppressed amusement of the other students, we took the second option. So much for vowel shifts.

The thing to do was to get myself off to the library and do some work. So I got a train to Stockport, and straight in for a pint of Robinson's. A man opposite me was tapping his fingers on a beer mat with no apparent regard for tempo. Maybe it helped him relax, but not me. I felt gritty minded, and stared at him until he noticed, at which he let the coaster alone.
I felt at once relieved and ashamed.
And then, Satan only knows why, out from the jukebox came 'Alone again, naturally' by Gilbert O'Sullivan, and what's more the man began to whistle along.
Meanwhile a dog had appeared at my feet and was gazing up at me with eyes that craved attention. It was a small terrier of some kind, and most of the hair on it's back had fallen out to reveal a suppurating rash.
"He'll not harm you," said the whistling mat tapper.
"Not contagious?"
"Eh?"
"Nothing."
The air outside seemed full of cold rain, yet none was falling, and a dispiriting squall cut across the street, giving the lie to my windcheater jacket.
I sheltered briefly in a second hand bookshop, and came out with 'Thank you, Jeeves' in paperback. There was a black and white photograph on the cover of Ian Carmichael and Dennis Price, 'now a popular television serial.' As I read it on the return train, the thin, dry pages, brown with age, began to come loose from the dried-up spine of the book, falling at my feet.
"Your book's moulting," came a voice. Sitting across from me was a young woman with matted blonde hair and an orange rucksack. She smiled, eased off one of her boots, and propped a bare foot onto the seat beside me. It was almost black on the sole, otherwise very pale. I thought of Simone, who had soles lighter than her uppers.
She went on with her own book, 'Mister Johnson' by Joyce Cary, twisting and arching her foot as she read.
"Joyce," I said stupidly, "unusual name for a man."
She smiled.
"It's an Anglo/Irish thing. Taking your grandmother's surname as your first one, something like that."
New Zealand accent.

"Really? So, if your grandmother's family name was Pratt, it would have to be your Christian name?"
"That's not very likely is it? My name's Ginny, by the way."
Out the window, trees, backs of terraces, stations, seemed to whiz past us, though it was us that whizzed past them.
Ginny tossed her book on the space next to her.
"Aren't you going to tell me yours?"
"Leopold."
"Ok, Leopold, you don't have a cigarette, do you?"
I wished I had.
"No sweat, I can get some in a moment. I'm staying in Levenshulme."
"That's where I get off."
"Is that right? You fancy buying me a beer or something?"
Full of poorly focussed expectation, I followed her into a dark bar.
"Get me a whisky, will you, double? I'll get some smokes."
I had just enough for her drink, and a half for me. She took a gulp, and it caught in her throat, making her cough and splutter.
"Jeeze!" she hissed, "maybe I should lay off the hard stuff. Fancy swapping?"
She took a gulp of beer.
"Nice and tepid, just the way I like it."
I swallowed half of the remains of the scotch.
"You know what?" she said, "if the grandmother of James Joyce had had the surname Joyce, then he would be called Joyce Joyce. Oh, Jesus, I cannot believe I just said that! Here, you better finish both the drinks, I really should go."
"You don't have to rush off."
"I think I better. So long."
She hauled her rucksack onto her shoulders and walked steadily out.

"You're drunk," averred Simone. "Where have you been, anyway? Sage came round, seemed keen to see you."
"What did he say?"
"Not a lot. What are you two cooking up? He's not trying to get you in on the act is he?"
"What?"
"You know, that stupid comedy thing he said he was going to do."
"Oh. I don't think so."

"Well don't let him, you've got enough on. I don't suppose you've been to school?"
"I've been reading."
"Well that's something, I suppose. Sit down and I'll make you a sandwich."
Peanut butter in bread that had big seeds in.
"Make sure you eat it all. I have to get to work, I'll try not to be late back."
I had a long overdue essay, and this seemed like a good time to tackle it. I made a strong coffee from the jar of proper instant that I kept stashed away and went to our bedroom.
The subject I needed to address was 'Dramatic unity in James Joyce's Ulysses', but the minute I picked up my biro, the intercom buzzed. It was a cheap device that made callers sound like they were speaking through a mouthful of dry cornflakes. Distorted, impossible to understand. Also the mechanism for opening the front door had finally completely broken.
I went down, opened up, and Imelda oozed into the vestibule like oil on brackish water. She held out her arms to me, then, in a fit of giggles, let them drop. The alcohol smelled sweet on her, but I wasn't in the mood.
"Listen," I said, "this isn't such a good time. I have this essay that I really need to get on with."
"That's nice," she replied, smiling loosely. "I'd love to watch you write your wee essay. I'll be quiet as a mouse, so I will."
"You'll be bored."
"Won't."
She followed me unsteadily up the stairs, wobbled into the sitting room and flopped on the couch, just missing Norman.
"How do?" he asked.
"Who's asking?"
"Good," I said. "You two can get to know one another, I'll do my essay, and we're all happy."
Imelda shook her head and wagged a finger at me.
"No, no, no. You're not leaving me with him He's got no socks on."
I made for the bedroom and she followed.
"Changed your mind about the essay, Timmy?"
"No, this is where I'm trying to do it."
"Oh."
She climbed onto the bed and lay on her front watching me, head propped unsteadily on her forearms.
I picked up a pen.

"What's it about?" she asked.
"Can't you just let me get on with it?"
"Touchy!" she said, turning onto her back and shaking with silent mirth.
"I missed the deadline."
"Breadline?"
"Yes."
My mind was locked blank, and my breathing short.
"You look funny," she said, and then suddenly she broke into song.
"Do you want your ould lobby washed down, conshine?
Do you want your oul' lobby wash down?"
"Imelda, please," I begged. "I love you dearly, but can't you just keep it down?"
"That would be more than you could the other night," she replied, and rolled laughing on the bed, until she fell off, which amused her even more.
"Do you?" she asked, catching her breath, and looking up at me.
"Want my ould lobby washed down? Sure, if it gets you off my back."
"No, love me. You just said, 'I love you dearly'."
"And so I will if you just shut up for a bit."
"Ok, ok, won't say a word."
She remained on the carpet, and, hoping she would fall asleep, I started to read what I had written.
'The crux of the novel is where Joyce draws the strands together in the meeting of Dedalus and Bloom...'
'Puede usted recomendarme un buen vino?'
She had found Simone's language tapes.
"Imelda," I shouted, screwing up the paper and throwing it at her. "For fuck's sake!"
She got onto her knees and shuffled over to me, putting her head on my lap.
"Tim, I wanna be with you, and you have to be with me. I wan'us to get wed, Tim, come on, you have to marry me, because you do, you have to..."
I felt a frost in my guts.
"Have to?"
"Yes! You have to be with me, and it's no good between you and Simone, so you can't marry her coz you're gonna to marry me, and we're gonna be together for ever, and, oh, Jesus, I think I'm gonna throw..."
Reader, she did.

Later that week I had to attend a meeting with my personal tutor, Doctor Brooks.

I sat in her study watching her read through my slightly stained essay, and when she finished she regarded me over invisible glasses.

"It's, how can I put this, somewhat *sparse*, Tim, don't you think?"

"I wanted to be concise."

"Ah. Well there is concise, and there is short, and I'm afraid this falls into the latter category. I can't grade this, Tim, and I don't think that comes to you as any great surprise, does it?"

She didn't expect an answer.

"Exactly. Now, take what you have here, think about your thesis, and expound for me at greater length."

"Thank you," I said, taking the sheets and making for the door.

"Oh, and Tim," she called.

"Yes?"

"There's a word you've used that I'm not familiar with. 'Conshine.' Is it a quote? I don't recall it from Ulysses, but then Joyce does use an awful lot of words."

"I think it's Irish slang."

"Really? Well that would make sense, I suppose. We'll meet again next week."

I went out, and as I was heading up Oxford road I spotted Imelda sitting on a bench. She pretended not to have seen me, so I walked over and sat next to her.

"Oh, it's you," she said, staring at the pavement.

"Yes, and I've just been interviewed by my tutor because of you. She was not impressed."

"What's she got to do with it?"

"Er, my essay, remember? Frequently interrupted, and lightly pebble dashed?"

"Oh, sorry about that. Sorry about it all, I was a bit far gone."

"Don't worry about it, you went spark out after the throwing up episode."

She scratched her nose.

"I think I said a bit much. You don't want to pay too much heed to me when I've had a few."

"I didn't."

"Oh. Well, better get to my lecture, see you later."

"See you."

Went back to the flat, only to hear it reverberating with verbal jousting between Norman and Jordan.

I didn't want to go in, and anyway it was high time I sought Sage.

It took some doing.

Knocking at Hilary's and calling in vain through the letterbox, 'phone boxes that stank of piss and fag butts, an endlessly engaged tone, until, at last, the crackly sound of his voice.

He sounded like he had been asleep for years.

"How do I know it's you?" he croaked.

"Isn't it obvious?"

"It could be an impersonation."

"You're right, it's Mike Yarwood."

This seemed to reassure him, and he agreed to meet me, insisting for some reason it should be in the bar on Stalybridge railway station.

He was late, of course, and when he did arrive, glancing covertly here and there, I didn't immediately recognise him. He had shaved off his beard, and his hair was uncovered, tied back in a ponytail.

He came over with a glass of whisky, spilling a little as he sat down, and taking a few edgy sips before speaking.

"This is murder, Tim."

"What?"

"No, not that. At least I don't think so. You know I haven't been to see her. I mean this is killing *me*. I can't even face going to see her. I don't know if she's said anything, remembers anything..."

"Well surely the only way to find out is to go?"

"Figure it out, man! I might not be the ideal person to wake up to, know what I mean?"

"What happened, Sage? I mean, how did it get to be like this?"

He re-lit a skinny roll-up and took a drag.

"That's what I keep asking myself. And I keep drawing blanks."

"You must have some idea."

"I've got a few, but nothing clear. I was in the pub, you came in, and all of a sudden I realised what I must have done."

"Did you have an argument with her?"

He smiled.

"That's the thing, we were getting on really well. Maybe I am just some sort of psycho."

He drained his glass, held it up, and peered through it at the refracted light from the window, turning the vessel like a camera lens. A train pulled in and a few people ambled past, looking for the exit, or wandering into the bar.

"Tim," said Sage, still examining his kaleidoscope world, "I was wondering. I mean, I was wondering if, maybe you could go and see her?"

"I don't know…"

I could already smell the surgical spirit.

"Come on, Tim, this is doing me in, man. Maybe I should just hand myself over to the cops, actually."

"No, Sage, I don't think that's a very good plan. Look, all right, I'll go."

He was close to tears.

How be yer?

The flat was at least quiet when I got back, apart from a blaring television. I went into the living room to berate Norman and found him lying on his back on the floor. Nothing particularly unusual in that, but then I noticed blood oozing from his nostrils, some of it dried on his face.

Slap his face, or throw water on it?

Neither. I found a little bottle of Grappa that Simone had brought back from some forgotten foreign holiday and eased the neck between Norman's swollen lips. He started to cough and splutter, some of the liquor, now tinged with pink, dribbling onto his chin as I propped him up against the settee.

I realised the T.V. was still cranking away, an advert for 'the brush-o-matic' interrupting the Friday matinee. I went over and switched it off.

"I was watching that," murmured Norman, coughing and trying to laugh.

"What happened?"

"Jordan…"

"Shit! I knew you pissed him off, but I didn't think he'd go this far."

Norman shook his head. He was clearly in pain, and having trouble speaking.

"Don't excite yourself," I said, and the idea of him doing so suddenly struck me as grotesquely comical.

"Sorry," I said, suppressing a smile. "I can't believe he's done this. Simone won't have him in the house after this."

Norman took a slug from the bottle and spat some bloody saliva onto his chest.

"Tim, will you shut up for a minute? They've got him."

"What?"

"Why do you always say that? What do you think? They came for Jordan, and like some fucking cretin unworthy to sweep the streets of Twatsville, I tried to stop them."

He had his voice back.

"Those bozos wanted to take him and didn't take kindly to my intervention. Got any more of this medicine?"

"That's all there is. I should call an ambulance."

"Nah, I hate hospitals. I'll live."

He wasn't bleeding much, and the gunge around his nose seemed to be settling, like lava crusting over. Surprisingly, a smile crept across his face.

"Rub up against me and you pay the price," he murmured, feeling in his trouser pocket. He brought out a wallet, flipped it open, and nodded approvingly at the wad of notes it contained.

"Not bad," he remarked.

"Please tell me you didn't lift that?" I said.

He patted my arm.

"How could I lie to my best friend? Here," he handed me a twenty, "bring more medicine."

For some reason I didn't want to spend stolen cash at Danny's, so I went to Ayub's and got a bottle of brandy.

I felt guilty, because I couldn't muster any genuine concern about Jordan. Norman was dabbing his face with a dishcloth when I came back in.

"Shouldn't you at least see a doctor?" I asked.

"You are the doctor," he replied, grabbing the bottle.

I tried to have as little of the brandy as I could, given Norman's sharing nature, so he went on whacking it back for both of us, bemused and bruised. One of Norman's qualities, if that's the word, is his memory for trivia. About a third into the bottle he reminded me of this by exhorting me to test him on sit-com theme tunes. He could hum them all, and did.

'Love thy neighbour', 'On the buses', 'Bless this house', 'The Liver birds', 'Man about the house', 'George and Mildred', 'Whatever happened to the likely lads?', 'Terry and June', 'It aint half hot Mum', he even knew the words,

"Meet the gang, coz the boys are here, the boys..."

He stopped abruptly. Simone was standing in the doorway.
"What's going on?" she demanded.
"Don't mind me," said Norman. "I am becoming comfortably numb."
Simone stared at me.
"Our room, now," she said.
Later, in the wee hours, the light clicked on and Simone started scrabbling for her cigarettes.
"I don't know how you can sleep after what's happened to Jordan," she said.
"What's he done, Tim, and what'll happen now?"
"He never lets on about anything, so how can we know?"
"He doesn't 'let on' because he thinks what I don't know won't hurt me. He's trying to protect me."
I couldn't help laughing.
"In that case, I wonder why he came here."
"If you don't know that, then I can't begin to tell you."

Trauma

On my way to visit Hilary, I was reminded of a time when my brother was kept in hospital because of a particularly relentless asthma attack. Mum had taken me to see him, and it was shocking to see how pale he was, and all the tubes. I was used to him wheezing away at home, or in the playground, and would often accuse him of exaggerating, but this was different. This time I started thinking he was going to die, and it would somehow be my fault. Noticing my anxiety, he leaned close.
"Wait till I get home," he whispered. "you can thrash me at Monopoly."
I think he said it to make me feel better; he was much more skilful at the game than I was, we both knew that. He would spread his assets, buy medium price properties, a few utilities. I always aimed for the dark blue areas and ended up with the brown.
I got to the infirmary at two-thirty in the afternoon. The sky was almost dark, and the building looked sombre, even the windows.
I half-hoped they wouldn't allow me to see her.
But I went in anyway and loitered, expecting someone to come and ask me what I wanted. Various white coats and aprons flitted to and fro, doggedly going about their business, none of them seeming to notice me. Eventually I simply wandered off down a corridor.
There were signs with various ward names, and others indicating specific areas of the hospital. It was ridiculously easy for me to locate Hilary.

Apparently anyone could stray in off the street and have access to patients. No need even to don a stethoscope, nor air of confidence.

There were several beds, all penned in by curtains on rails. I peered gingerly in at the first. A very thin old man lay asleep, mouth wide open, breathing stertorously. I walked slowly and quietly on the shiny linoleum to the next bed and eased aside the curtain. It was Hilary, though I didn't recognise her at first because of the bruising and dressings. There was nothing by her bed, no books or fruit, just a little cupboard that had a disc-shaped vent on the door. Not even any flowers, and I soon realised why. Hilary was in no condition to appreciate them. It looked like she was being fed through a tube, although that might have been to help her breathe. What did I know? There didn't seem to be anyone I could ask.

People in these situations on television, in films, always hold the patient's hand, and talk reassuringly. They look for a sign, which usually turns out to be a flicker of the eyelids. Hilary's were still. I looked at her pale hand, palm up. Her arm was dangling over the side of the mattress, a plastic bracelet on her wrist. I didn't want to touch her.

"Well, Hilary, I don't know if you remember me? Friend of Sage's," I began, quietly. "He was wondering how you were."

I felt like it was some body else speaking.

"I don't know if you can hear what I'm saying. Sorry, I haven't had much experience of this. Not any, actually."

Then her eyelids did start to flicker, and she sighed, turned her head and peered at me.

"Oh, hello. Sorry, I must've been asleep. Can you hand me my glasses?"

She put them on.

"Ah, I think I know you. Friend of Sage's, right? Can't remember your name, I'm afraid. Having a bit of trouble with the old memory. Sage hasn't been to see me, has he?"

"I'm not sure."

"I'll take that as a no. Didn't think so. If he knows where I am, why doesn't he visit? Ever since I regained consciousness they've been trying to get hold of him, see if he can shed any light on what happened to me. Has he said any thing to you?"

"Not really."

She yawned.

"God, I'm sorry. Seem to be tired all the time. Hey, it's nice of you to visit. Come to think of it, why have you?"

"Well, actually, Sage asked me. He's sort of been afraid to come in. Squeamish or something."
She smiled.
"That doesn't sound like my Sage!"
She looked closely at me.
"Now, hold on, don't tell me. You're the one who was going to help me because I was worried about him, right?"
I nodded, wondering what she would remember next.
"Yes. Steve, isn't it?"
"Tim."
"Tim." She laughed. "Now all I have to do is try to remember why I was worried about Sage. Tell him not to be so daft and to just get his arse in here will you?"
"Ok."
"You know what, Tim, I really appreciate you coming to see me. I feel like it's all really starting to come back."

Outside, a gap in the clouds allowed a glaring beam of sunlight to assault my eyes. I sat on a wet bench to think a while.
"Cheer up, man, it may never happen!"
It was Stan Bardolino, standing beside a large van. He came over.
"What brings you here? I saw you coming out of the hossie. Nothing wrong, I hope?"
"No, no I was just visiting."
"Relative?"
"Er, no, Hilary, you know, Hilary."
Why did I tell him?
He frowned.
"What's the matter with her?"
"Oh, some sort of accident, I think."
"Sounds a bit vague, that, Tim. What happened? Car?"
"She was at home, I think. What are you doing here, anyway?"
"Delivery, supplies. You can give me a hand if you like. Then I might go in and see the lass. Nothing serious, I hope?"
"She took a bump. Actually, no, I don't know much about it."
He brushed the bench and sat down, looking keenly into my face.
"I think you know a bit more than you're letting on, Tim."
"Well, it's possible, I mean, Sage…"

"Sage! If he's hurt her…"
He jumped up and paced in front of me, pointing a finger.
"I want a word with Sage."
"Stan, she can't remember what happened, and Sage wasn't exactly…"
"Wasn't exactly what?"
"Well, you know, he was a bit wiggy."
"Wiggy? A bit flaming wiggy? I'll give him wiggy if I see him!"
I helped him shift some boxes that had black skull and cross bones printed on them.

"Sage, is that you?"
"Oh, Tim, yeah it's me."
He had answered the 'phone in a falsetto voice.
"Are you all right, Sage?"
"Yeah, I'm ok. You never know who's calling. So, how did it go? I mean you did see her?"
"Yeah, it was ok. I mean, she seems to have recovered really well, but her memory's a bit dodgy. You should go and see her. She was asking why you haven't been."
"That's good, I think. We can maybe put this behind us."
The pips started, and I was out of change, but before we were cut off I just managed to tell him to watch out for Stan Bardolino.

I was in the library trying to pad out my Joyce essay, when movement outside a nearby window distracted me. It was Imelda, waving a long stripy scarf, and pulling ludicrous faces. Once she had my attention, she beckoned for me to join her, but I shook my head, pointing at the sheet of paper in front of me. Nevertheless, she continued with her scarf-waving, now holding it above her head in football supporter style and hopping from foot to foot. Other students were beginning to realize the distraction was connected with me, and I was getting some terse glances. Imelda's frisky capers in the bright December sun were hard to ignore, especially once she began to accompany the performance with some discordant chanting.
Ulysses would have to sail another day.
"At last," said Imelda, as I came out. "I've been trying to get your attention for ages. It's too nice to be stuck in the stuffy old library."

"It's the only place I can get any work done. Well, it was until you happened. You're my nemesis, do you know that? Doctor Brooks is going to go spare."

"Who cares? Boring old Brooks. Who is he anyway?"

"She. Doesn't matter. What do you want to do?"

"We could have a picnic."

"Too cold. Let's go in the refectory."

Imelda had her usual pie, and I started tackling a greasy sausage roll. Imelda seemed to find this amusing.

"I thought so," she said. "You're no more a veggie than I am!"

"Simone says it's better for me."

"And if Simone said it was better for you to jump in a lake, would you do it?"

"I did once."

"Liar!"

"How do you know? I might just be a natural lake-jumping kind of bloke."

She squashed her pie with a plastic fork, lumpy brown filling oozing, glistening, from the soggy pastry.

"It wouldn't surprise me. Would you jump for me, too, if I asked you?"

I was spared from answering by the arrival of William.

He looked very pale, almost translucent around the cheekbones.

"Tim, thank God I've found you, get me a cup of tea, lots of sugar, I've just had a nasty moment."

"What happened?"

"Tea first, I need to calm my nerves."

After a couple of sips, he told us he had had an encounter with the rubber man.

"Horrendous! He jumps right out, must have been lurking in the shrubbery, and he says, in this smutty sort of whisper, that he wants to lick my knickers."

He patted Imelda's hand.

"Sorry, dear, not very nice for mixed company, but I had to tell someone straight away, I'm that wound up."

He drank a little more tea.

"Are you ok?" asked Imelda.

"Oh, I'll be fine, tough as old boots, me! I'm Wendy, by the way."

"Wendy?" I said.

"Yes, Tim, Wendy. And who is this delightfully gamine creature?"

"Well if you mean me, I'm Imelda."

"Lovely name, charming. Love what you've done with your hair! Not everyone suits a fringe."

"Are you going to report the incident?" I asked.

"Are you kidding? I don't want some mucky minded bizzy probing me. Anyway, I dealt with it. That pervert picked on the wrong girl! I was quite promising in the boxing ring when I was a lad. A couple of good punches to the head and he was off, tail literally between his little legs. I'd have liked to get that mask off him though, dirty tosser."

"Good for you," said Imelda. "Can I ask you, what shade of eye shadow is that you have on?"

"Nice, isn't it? It's called 'lagoon', new on the market. Here, try a bit, I've got a mirror."

I left them to it and trolled off to the agency.

They sent me to a new client, Mister Khan. He stood about five feet in his slippers and wore an eye patch. His wife had recently died, and he was not used to fending for himself. He greeted me enthusiastically.

"Come in, come in, most kind, marvellous social work visiting programme!"

He was in textiles, he told me.

"I can get you very nice pullover. Man-made, most durable polyester, long lasting and superb in being moth proof. Cheap also."

All he wanted me to do was a bit of cleaning. I wiped over the work tops, which were greasy and had fluff adhering to them, scoured the cooker, and asked if he wanted any shopping.

"No, no, all taken care of, thank you most kindly, but if you will please get me fried fish from Fryer Tuck, which is the take-away chippie on corner. Fried fish, no chips."

Having delivered this rather spare meal, I headed off to see Mr Eastwood. He opened the door cautiously and peered out at me rather sheepishly from behind a large pair of dark glasses.

"Oh, hello, old chap," he said. "Sorry about the cheaters, sheer vanity really, only I took a bit of a tumble the other day and I'm a bit bruised. More the old ego than anything else, felt such a fool. Had to happen in public of course."

I followed him in, and he picked up a cup of coffee.

"Sorry, would have made you one, only I must have forgot you were coming."

He stirred his, clinked the spoon twice on the side of the cup, and placed it on the saucer.

"Are you all right, otherwise?" I asked.

"What d'you mean, otherwise?"

"Apart from the fall."

"Oh, that. Yes, I think so, nothing broken. More a bloody nuisance than anything. Rich tea?"

He handed me the plate of thin biscuits.

"Thanks. So, I suppose you won't be needing me for much longer?"

He set down his cup, removed his glasses, and regarded me through eyes surrounded by dark, greenish shadows.

"I hope they won't take you away just yet, old chap. I look forward to your visits. Helps get me through. But I'm a selfish old man, I know that. There are others far more in need of your excellent good offices than I."

"It's not up to me, anyway."

"Oh, I know, dear boy, I know. I've got that blasted social worker coming round tomorrow. Says she's going to 'assess' me. Maybe I should play up the injuries, what?"

"Well, good luck with it. Talking of those in need, I have to fit in another client."

"You busy bee. I do hope I'll see you again."

A sharp sleet set in as I made my way on foot to Mr Bennett's.

The door was usually opened by one of his cronies, but today there was no response.

I knocked harder, and the door budged, but as I pushed to go in, there seemed to be some kind of obstruction.

There was a gap, but not wide enough for me to squeeze through, so I peered through into the gloomy bed sit.

There, slumped on the floor, was Mr Bennett, unwittingly performing the combined functions of a doorstop and draught excluder.

The only way I could get in was for me to put my shoulder to the door and use it to shove the body out of the way. This proved to be easier than I thought, perhaps assisted by the malodorous lubricant in which he was lying.

"Mr Bennett," I said. "Francis!"

No reply. I leaned down near to his face, disturbing a dozy winter fly, presumably lured out of hibernation by the appealing aroma of Mr B.

With my ear close to his mouth, I was able to make out the faint but steady sound of breathing. The door had more or less rolled the man on to his side, so I decided there was no further need to move him. Fumbling for change, I set out to find a 'phone box.

Emergency call placed, I returned and sat on the floor beside Mr B to wait for the ambulance. Ten minutes has never seemed so long, except for when I was a kid, and my Mum would stop to chat to a friend when we were out shopping.

When it came, there was no siren, or screech of brakes.

Two men in green garb walked in, glanced at me, and crouched beside the patient.

"What's his name?" one of them asked.

"All right," he said, and began to shake Mr Bennett by the shoulders, shouting in his face. "Come on, Francis, wake up mate! What you been up to? Francis, can you hear me?"

Mr B let out a loud groan.

"Fuck off, you fucker," he grunted.

"Not much wrong with you," replied the medic.

Back home there was a strange sound coming from the flat. It turned out to be Jackson, marching around and shouting through a yellow plastic microphone that distorted his voice. Simone was laughing, pleased to see her nephew enjoying the cheap gift.

"Maybe he'll go into the music business?" she suggested.

Norman snorted.

"Why would anyone want to listen to some bloke strutting around shouting into a mike?"

"Well you never know," replied Simone.

"Heard anything from his Dad?" I asked.

Her smile faded, and she shook her head.

"YA, YA, YA, YA!" shouted Jackson.

I picked up the box the toy had been in. 'Echo mike' it was called. There was an illustration of a boy wearing a clown's wig, gleefully employing the instrument, with the following advice printed below,

'An enjoyable megaphone which needs not to use the power sauce, one's mouth makes close to its body for the exercise of sing songs. Shake the main body lightly and you get the magic voice to meet the occasional use. Mama, Papa, I and lady employees to play with it together!'

But Papa wasn't there to play.

Made in Taiwan. When I was a kid it was always Hong Kong. Those stocking fillers, plastic tool kits, garishly painted farm animals that smelled toxic…

"Let's have a go," begged Norman, reaching for the mike.

"NO, NO!" shouted Jackson, into it.

"Come on, Jackson, we share, remember?" said Simone. "Doesn't your Mum teach you anything? Let Norman have a go."

Jackson reluctantly relinquished the instrument, holding it limply at arm's length, and dropping it just before Norman could get a hold. It hit the floor, and we got the magic voice to meet the occasional use.

"You'll break it," admonished Norman, picking it up and proceeding to bellow the words of 'My Way'.

Jackson snatched the box from me and began kicking it around the floor.

"Have you done your essay?" asked Simone.

I walked over to the window, watching the rain.

"I haven't had time."

"Tim! Do you *want* to get chucked out or something? I can't believe you still haven't done it!"

"Well, it's true, so you might as well believe it."

Simone lit a fag, took a couple of fast drags, and turned to the still-performing Norman.

"And as for you," she said, "I think that's enough of Frank. Will you give it a rest?"

"I was doing Sid actually," he replied, setting the toy down on the windowsill.

Jackson carried on kicking the box.

Time for another attempt at the essay.

I got my satchel and headed for the Hot Pot, a small, modern pub beside some council blocks in Moss Side. Here, at least, I thought I would probably be left alone. The only people I ever saw in there were an unkempt man with the grey, depressed features of one expecting later to become a werewolf, and a gone-to-seed teddy boy wearing a faux leopard skin cap. The staff comprised of a lean, coiffed man of around forty-five, and a much larger, fatter fellow with a voice like he was gargling phlegm. They were a couple and referred to one another respectively as Gert and Floss.

Today it was Gert who looked up from his newspaper.

"Hello, handsome," he said, "what's your fancy? And don't worry, you don't have to say me."

The choice of ale was poor, so I ordered a pint of Stella.
Gert went over to the hatch that opened onto the cellar and shouted down, "You finished changing that barrel, Floss?"
There was a mangled growl from below.
"I think that was a yes," said Gert, and proceeded to pour my pint. The pump chugged a bit, like a tap when the water's been off, and a head of foam rose quickly in the glass.
"Lively!" remarked Gert.
Floss came up from the cellar, sweating.
"You've made a right dog's breakfast of that," he said, "here, let me finish it."
He moved the glass up so the tap was near the bottom, slopped off the excess head, and handed me the sparkling brew.
I sat in a corner, and, trying to ignore the loud, patterned carpet, which seemed to jump up at me, and the mutterings of wolf-man, got out my paper, pen and books.
"Look out," commented Gert, nudging Floss with his elbow, "Einstein's in."
I was trying to concentrate on a translation of Homer, when somebody plonked two glasses on the table and slumped onto a chair. A pint and a double whisky. Doctor Drummond.
He hooked a nicotine-stained forefinger over my book and lowered it so he could look in my face.
"Thought it was you," he said. "Quite the bad penny, are you not? Or perhaps it is I who should thus be dubbed?"
He chuckled and took a sip of whisky followed by a gulp of beer.
"Don't let me interrupt your studies, just pretend I'm not here."
Easier said than done. He had a large sticking plaster above his left eye, partly magnified by his glasses, and it seemed to draw my gaze.
"Honestly, you won't know I'm here."
He pulled a paperback from the inside pocket of his tweed jacket, 'The Innocence of Father Brown', and started reading.
I put pen to paper.
'The Homeric elements provide a consistency that...'
"Ha, ha!" gurgled Drummond, "Brown is such a choice character. 'Was it a very long cigar?' Marvellous! Have you read them?"
"Not lately."
"Oh. Well, quite. Don't mind me, don't mind me. Not another word, not a squeak! Promise."

He managed to keep reasonably quiet for a while but couldn't resist certain audible reactions to the short stories, and these were as incompatible with concentration as any actual remarks. I closed the books.

"Finished?" asked Drummond, peering at me over his glasses.

"Not exactly."

"Not exactly. Is there, indeed, ever anything exact about a piece of literary criticism?"

"Certainly not about mine."

He drained his drinks.

"Look, here's a fiver, why don't you get us another round, and after I've nipped off to witness the transubstantiation of beer into piss, I could take a look, if you want."

Gert, as he took my drinks order, nodded towards the departing figure of Drummond.

"Too old for you," he said.

"Oh, we're not, I mean…"

"Ooh, hear that, Floss? There's hope for me yet."

"Stop teasing the kid. Don't pay him no mind, son, he's got a one-track mind."

Gert laughed.

"At least I've got a mind. That's one pound fifteen, please."

When I returned to the table, Drummond was already into my essay, quietly reading. I dipped into Father Brown, and was nearing the conclusion of an investigation, when my companion slapped his palm on the arm of his chair, causing a little explosion of dust to disperse in the wintry sunlight.

"I see where you're stuck," he said, "and if you'll permit me, I think I can see how to proceed."

"Thanks."

He took a gulp from his pint.

"Not at all. You see, seems to me you underestimate the connection between Dedalus and Bloom…"

By the time we strayed out into the late afternoon air, the essay was almost done.

"Good-day, undergraduate," intoned Doctor Drummond, swaying slightly.

"And the best of luck."

"Thanks for your help."

"Not at all," he said, "It's what I do."

And then, as he turned and began to walk away,

"I still have it, still have it."

I wrote up the essay in the library and took it straight to Doctor Brooks. She looked a little surprised, and after a cursory glance at the pages, she placed them between us on her desk and looked into my eyes.
"You know, Timothy," she said, "it would be such a waste if you were to disregard your studies. I'm not saying the literary world would be shaken to its very foundations, but I hate to see an opportunity squandered. Tell me, do you usually consume alcohol in the day?"
"Sometimes. Maybe a lunchtime pint."
"I see. And during your studies?"
"Not really."
"Yet lunch falls between periods of academic endeavour, does it not?"
"Well, I don't really have any in the week."
"Pints or periods? Forgive me for pressing the issue, but today is Tuesday, and you have just handed in an essay while clearly under the influence of alcohol. You can tell me it's none of my business, and you might be right, but I would hate to see your degree go down the toilet, as it were, because of a predilection for intoxicating beverages."
"No."
"Meaning?"
"I don't think that will happen."
She smiled and sat back in her leather chair.
"I'm not a killjoy," she remarked. "Not entirely strait laced. Quite enjoy a spot of vino myself from time to time. Leave it with me."
"Sorry?"
"The essay."

Pipe dream

Peter and I met up with another boy, Justin, one Saturday afternoon, and as we were strolling along, Peter and he paused with an air of conspiratorial pride. Justin drew from his trouser pocket a small pipe, and Peter helped him to fill it with some shreds of tobacco. Peter smiled at my astonishment, and, as he took a few puffs, and blew out smoke, his eyes took on a challenging darkness.
My pride bit in.
Justin laughed,
"Have a go, Tim, it's great."

"It's a bad habit."
"Oh well, more for us then."
He passed the pipe back to Peter, and I walked beside them as they puffed with serious brows, exhaling extravagantly through ringed lips.
I just knew I was right, but it hurt to be there. I felt like a Christian being taunted by heathens. But I would not allow myself to be drawn by osmosis into naughtiness.
Strait laced at thirteen. Principled.
"You'll end up with a habit," I said.
Justin scoffed.
"So what?"
Peter grinned, but I could tell he was torn. He wanted in on Justin's rebelliousness, but he could see it was testing his friendship with me. I seethed with a jealousy that my priggish stance would not let me fully acknowledge.
A couple of puffs on a pipe. So what?
Nowadays I see kids peddling dope.

"When?" asked Simone.
"What?"
"When have you seen kids selling smack?"
"I never said smack."
"I'm sure you did."
"Not as sure as I am that I didn't."
She took a long drag on her cigarette, eyes closed.
"I think you're losing your memory."
"Maybe it's you losing your mind."
"Who could blame me? Anyway, at least I've got one to lose."
"I seem to remember hearing that before."
"Well I'm sorry I can't be more original."
She stubbed out her butt.
"Come on, Tim, what's the point of this?"
"What's the point of anything?"
"God, you are so…"
She stood up and kicked a copy of the T.V. times so hard that several pages were ripped from their staples. Leaving the room, she slammed the door, but carefully, so as not to dislodge the plaster-moulded figurine of 'Pedro the Mexican' that her grandmother had given her. I went over and made a

face at him, but he went on grinning from under his yellow sombrero, tiny black cheroot in the corner of his mouth.

Simone came back in.

"Sorry," she said. "Are you still coming?"

We were due to meet some friends at an 'American Style' restaurant, 'Dixie's Diner.'

"Suppose so. I don't know what there'll be for us to eat though. Who chose it?"

"Bob, I think. We can hardly expect people to be vegetarian."

"You do."

"What?"

"Nothing. Who's Bob, anyway? Don't bother, actually, I'll get ready."

The place was draped in stars and stripes, and the waitresses wore gingham skirts, and rolled around serving on skates. There was Meatloaf on the sound system. Loudly. On the menu, too. And Southern fried chicken. Rack o' ribs. Bar-b-cue steak. Charcoal grilled quarter-pounder. Home-style grill. Rawhide Chile. Beefy Buckaroo.

I had salad and chips.

Bob's plate was heaving with meat.

"Bit of a raw deal for you," he commented, waving a forkful of cow at me.

I still couldn't figure out who he was.

"Everything fine and dandy?" asked a waitress. Was there anything else we wanted?

I suggested they could maybe play some better music, and she smiled, cruised over to the amplifier, and turned up the volume.

I applauded, and felt Simone pinch my thigh.

Bob was having a great time.

"Don't you like a good bit of rock music?" he asked me.

"If it's good, I do."

"Hey, lighten up," he advised. "We're all here to enjoy ourselves."

Simone was getting cosy with a mate of hers from the Glamour called Anne, both laughing a lot with their hands over their mouths. Despite being, as someone once tactlessly remarked, like chalk and chocolate, they always got on really well, sharing gossip and mimicking each other's mannerisms. Reginald from my course was there too, quietly observing everyone, and jotting things down in a little notebook. He was widely expected to get a first. And John, who was leaving Uni because he predicted a coming property boom, and 'wanted in on it.'

These were the sorts of people Rose would have Simone and I associate with.

I started hoping Imelda might walk in. Better still, Wendy.

Relentless was the Meatloaf, and the suit jacket I had squeezed myself into was becoming uncomfortable, itchy at the collar. I would have removed it, but then the sweat patches under my arms would be revealed.

Bob was growing redder of visage with every carafe of plonk, beads of perspiration gathering on his large forehead. He waved his glass at me, sploshing a little red on the table.

"Cat got your tongue?" he asked, laughing, and glancing round the table to assure himself that no one had missed his quip.

"That's right, Bob, it has. Luckily, though, I've learned to talk through my arse."

"Hey, hey, steady! I don't think that would be very likely, would it?"

"I don't know; you seem to be managing it fairly well."

That snapped his sphincter shut.

But 'loaf' bellowed on regardless, pushing the blood through my heart until it throbbed against my rib cage.

I beckoned for a waitress, though I could see Simone was getting tense.

"Sir, what can I get you, please?"

"I'd like a bat out of hell, medium rare."

She lowered the notepad with attached pencil on a string, and smiled sourly, before returning to the sound system and increasing further the volume.

I thought of walking out, but something quite different happened. I don't exactly recall the decisive moment, but like Tippi Hedren in 'Marnie', I was suddenly seeing a lot of red. Maybe Bob's face had gone out of focus and he had become Blob, turning to jelly in the heat?

But for whatever reason, I found myself climbing onto the table, and clumsily attempting to dance among the plates of crappy food and tacky bowls of relish. A plastic ketchup container got under my shoes, and shot sauce like a miniature flame thrower, narrowly missing Bob.

Well, you can't have everything.

I slowed down as the crisis passed and saw that everyone round our table was looking at their feet. Everyone except Simone, who was firing contempt with everything her face and eyes could muster, and Reginald, scribbling in his book.

I stepped down, and the lull I had caused was relieved by the resumption of conversations at other tables. The music, though, had been turned off.
Bob was the first of our group to comment.
"Well done, mate, got any more tricks?"
I threw some cash on the table in front of Simone, who was now refusing to look at me.
Walking out before I was thrown, I almost broke into a trot, annoyed that politeness had obviated any support for my stance, but also regretful of the conspicuous way I had reacted. And since regret is useless, bitter irritation rose, and I bumped against anyone walking towards me, muttering under my breath.
It was as I turned into Brown Street that I realised Simone had caught up with me, pulling at my shoulder.
"How could you do that to me?" she shouted.
"It wasn't you. It was those idiot waiters."
"There was no need to act like a lunatic."
"Who was acting?"
"Well you said it."
"I tried to be reasonable, but they threw it in my face."
She sighed.
"They were probably just being playful."
"Playful?"
"Having a bit of fun with you."
I laughed.
"Tim, it wasn't such a big deal. You should learn to lighten up more."
"Christ! Now you're talking like Bob. Perhaps you'd prefer it if I was more like him?"
"Don't be ridiculous."
I felt suddenly the overwhelming need to commit some minor violent act that would also hurt me, so I kicked the nearest object. It was a shiny car door, and now it had a dent in it.
Simone grabbed my arm and hustled me along, swearing incoherently, but we hadn't got to the end of the street before we realized three young men, one of whom was wearing a dressing gown, were following us. We stopped, and so did they, an uneasy distance between us. At first no body spoke. It was like a small town standoff in a western, except the men were well-groomed Asians, and none of us had a gun.
Dressing-gown broke the silence.

"Why did you do that to my car?"
Simone made to answer, but I cut in.
"What are you talking about?"
"You were seen. My sister saw out of the window, and you damaged my car."
The other two nodded.
"The police will be here," said one of them, "so don't try anything."
"Oh, God," said Simone.
There was no siren, but the panda car did screech to a halt, blocking the street, and the one policeman it contained slowly opened the door, stepped out, brushed the front of his shirt, and adjusted his cap.
"Everybody stay calm and stay put," he said, ambling over.
He had a sotto voce confab with the aggrieved, then came up to me, looked me up and down, breathed in, and told me there was a witness to an act of vandalism on the property, being a motor vehicle, of the gentleman in the night attire.
"Let's all take a little walk and see what's been going on," he added.
"I've got nothing to do with this," said Simone.
"Oh, but you have, miss," replied the officer. "Because you were there."
I felt strangely calm.
"Come on," I said, "these people believe someone saw something, let's see what it's about."
To my surprise, as we returned to the scene of the incident, Simone started loudly screaming.
The copper raised his eyebrows at me.
"Sort her out, can you?" he said.
I don't know if it was her intention, but Simone's outburst briefly shifted the focus away from me. Then, with a warning that I should remain where I stood, the policeman went into a shop door with dressing-gown, presumably to interview the witness in the flat above. They returned quickly, the car owner looking displeased, and the cop came up to me.
"The witness is unwilling to testify," he said, ferreting a notebook from a pocket, "and therefore there is nothing to proceed with at present."
He took my details, and, as he made a few radio checks, the injured parties withdrew with a collective air of resigned disappointment. And as soon as the law allowed, Simone and I hurried along.
"That was deplorable, Tim," she said, walking fast beside me, "utterly deplorable! How could you collude with a sexist, racist pig like that? I can't believe it."

"I didn't collude. Would you have preferred I was arrested?"

"I don't know. But that was wrong. I wish that girl *had* agreed to testify! But look at what she sees, white bloke, short hair, laying into a car…"

"So what about the precious car! They didn't look exactly destitute."

"My God, Tim, it's not about the car! Can't you see that? Those people were frightened of you! And that copper, what does he see? Just a bunch of Pakis not worth his time. Nice one, Tim, I hope you're really proud of yourself."

"They'll be insured."

"Ha! So that makes it all right, does it? That woman was afraid to show her face in case of what you might do to her! Is she insured against that?"

"Come on, Simone, you should hear yourself."

"I can't believe you said that."

"Look, no one was hurt, I wasn't charged, I think that's pretty ok. Would you want a future with me if I had a criminal record?"

She bit her lip.

"I don't really know what I want anymore."

Although we were walking side by side, I felt suddenly quite alone.

"Tim, are you hearing what I'm saying?"

We arrived at the flat.

"I'm hearing," I answered. "But I'm trying not to listen."

The luckiest unlucky dog in Greater Manchester

Tawdry Christmas decorations were starting to appear in town. Artificial trees in shop windows. Spray-on snow.

Danny's corner shop, however, remained reassuringly unadorned.

"Waste of money," he told me, wrapping some ham in grease proof paper. "And it all starts far too early. When I was a lad, Christmas was a couple of days, and we were taught the meaning of it."

I noticed he had crackers and decorations among his stock, though, and he must have seen me glance at them.

"Ah, well, there's no harm in a bit of fun, don't get me wrong, but there's no need to go overboard. Are you in Manchester for the holidays, or will you be seeing your folks?"

"My Mum and Dad are separated, makes it a bit awkward. I think Simone's Mum'll probably come over."

"That's nice. I wanted our Gavin to have the day with me, but even that's too much to ask. Would you credit it? His mother passed away some years ago, rest her soul."

"I didn't know. Sorry."

"Did I not tell you? There's a thing. Oh, yes, I've had to cope on me own for a fair while now. Takes a bit of getting used to."

He pointed at the wrapped ham.

"Are you planning to make sandwiches for when you're at your studies?"

"Oh, yeah, probably will."

He patted the packet.

"Mum's the word," he said.

Later, walking to Uni, I strayed into the park, walking on the crisp, frosted grass. The sky was filling with the mottled grey that sometimes brings snow. A man walking his dog turned up his collar and threw a stick. As the hound chased it, I realised he had no hind legs, but he was strapped into a little two wheeled carriage that enabled him to propel himself forward. He returned with the stick, laying it down and making enthusiastic movements of his head to encourage his owner to throw again. And as soon as it was airborne, he was off again in pursuit, a joyful jumble of limbs and wheels.

"He'd do that all day, if I let him," said the man.

The snow did come, and when I arrived for my tutorial there was enough on the soles of my shoes that I should need to stomp them before going in. Doctor Skilbeck began as always by sitting with a book on his lap and staring up at the ceiling, moving his head in the manner of one listening to music. After a few minutes, he suddenly snapped open the volume, and started reading in a resonating voice, and when the poem was concluded, turned to face us.

"Now entertain me with your observations."

Today, as usual, Reginald sat forward to comment, but was silenced by the doctor's forefinger to the lips. His own, not Reginald's.

"Someone else, first," he said gently, "oh for someone else for once."

"It's banal rubbish, 'dulnesse' about sums it up," said Alan Haffenden, who wore make up and was in a band.

Doctor S smiled, stroking the pages of the volume he held.

"If only George Herbert were here to receive your splendid indifference."

Alan sneered at his feet.

"Who says I'm indifferent? I just think it's crap. I mean, 'Thou art my lovelinesse, my life, my light'. Sounds like fucking Perry Como."

"Indeed? I'm afraid, presuming he is a man, that I'm unfamiliar with the work of Mr Como, and I certainly can't imagine what auditory effect would be produced if one were to copulate with him. I am forced to defer to your superior knowledge in these matters. Would anyone else care to respond to Mr Haffenden's appraisal?"

Reginald did. At length.

Norman was hanging round the refectory at lunchtime. He sat watching me eat, a habit of his, which, if I was to enjoy my food, compelled me to share it with him.

"Cheers, Tim," he said, pie juice dribbling onto his chin.

"Don't mention it."

"I tell you, the grub here's miles better than at my college."

"Talking of which, are you ever going back there?"

"A blunt question. Trying to get rid of me?"

"I gave up on that some time ago."

"Well, no rush. Hey, it'll be Christmas soon. Maybe I should stick around for that. And New Year, we could have a party."

"I don't think so, somehow. Who would we invite?"

"Your mate Sage would come."

"Normally, yes."

"How do you mean, normally?"

"Nothing. He's just a bit…Let's just say thing's aren't straightforward."

"Then a party's what he needs. He can bring that girlfriend of his."

It was time to seek Sage.

"I have to go," I said. "Do you want the rest of those chips?"

Silly question.

But when I knocked on the purple door in Hulme there was no response. I called through the letterbox, but if Sage was there, he wasn't answering, so I turned and walked towards the stairs. A door opened as I passed, and a thin man in a vest peered out, squinting as if unused to natural light.

"They aint in, mate," he said, indicating with a nod Hilary's flat. "I aint seen either of 'em for yonks, apart from that bit of trouble the other day. You most probably heard about it."

I shook my head.

"I don't think I heard anything. What happened?"

He looked sideways at me, stroking his stubbly chin.

"You're not from the law, are you?"

"Do I look like it?"

He grinned.

"As it happens, you don't. Fancy a cup of tea?"

I didn't, but I wanted to hear about the trouble, so I followed him into a front room that had towels pinned up over the windows. He shuffled into the kitchen, talking as he made the brew.

"Yes, quite a spot of bother with the coloured lad, surprised you didn't hear about it. Mate of his aren't you?"

Although it was posed as a question, I could tell he didn't need an answer. He probably watched through the gap in the towels, day in, day out.

He brought through a dark brown teapot, cups, and a plate of garibaldi biscuits.

"Here, help yourself," he said, pouring. The tea was weak, and heavily sugared.

"Yes, not much goes on round here without my knowing about it. Quite a ruckus it was. Woke me up. So I looks out, and there's this bloke, can't have been much over five foot, hammering on their door. He keeps banging and shouting, and eventually your mate, the one with the turban, only he weren't wearing it as it happens, comes out. And stone me if the little bloke don't start laying into him! Gives your mate a right walloping, he does. Someone must've called an ambulance, the little bloke hears the sirens, he legs it, and your mate, poor beggar, gets a free ride to the hospital. Go on, have a biscuit, don't be polite."

I wanted to go and see him, but I guessed he would be in the same hospital as Hilary, and if he was, I wasn't sure I wanted to be there. I wanted to be a normal student, attend to my studies, go home to Mum and Dad for the Christmas holidays. But Mum was living with Arthur, and I didn't fancy seeing them under the mistletoe. And Dad hated Christmas these days. Anyway, we were having Rose to stay, and maybe even Simone's so-called Dad.

When I got home I found Simone standing in the kitchen, swaying slightly and smoking a spliff. She waved it in front of her, like a priest with the censer, coming unsteadily towards me with a lopsided smile.

I had never seen her so something-or-other before. I felt simultaneously jealous and protective. The spliff went out, and she started groping about her person for a match. Failing to find one, she almost wept, and then broke into a dry, hacking laugh.

"Fuck! Just one fucking match. I always have matches."

There was a box of 'Safety Impregnated' ones on the table. I lit her up, and she slumped onto a chair, and took a long drag.

"Jordan's turned up," she said.
"Is he ok?"
"Oh, he's ok. They roughed him up him a bit, but he got away. Always does."
"What happened?"
"Seems fly guy Jordan was peddling small amounts of dope for them, only he neglected to share the profits, and then he had the bright idea of stealing some much bigger amounts off them."
"Ok, hang on, who are we talking about exactly?"
"Jordan didn't let on, but I'm pretty sure one of the other bouncers at the 'Glamour' is involved."
"How come?"
"I've seen him with Jordan, and he looks shifty. Name's Gavin, and he's one of those types I've never really taken to."
"Doesn't necessarily make him a criminal."
"It wouldn't surprise me."
"And you think he's trying to get Jordan to tell them what he's done with the stuff?"
"Gold star, Tim. They really want him to tell them where it is. And J says, supposing he does still have it, for the future of his family he cannot return it, plus he hasn't got the dosh to pay them back either. That's why he's lying low at Mums' until he can work out what to do about Crystal and Jackson."
"Who?"
"His wife and kid. My nephew?"
"Oh, yeah."
She blew smoke across the table, where it coiled around the condiments like horror movie mist in a graveyard.
"I suppose he can't risk going home?"
"No. And I told him he better get out of Mum's place an' all."
"He better not come here again."
"Er, he's not likely to do that is he? Even Jordan wouldn't be that dumb."
She picked a shred of tobacco off her lip.
"What is it with my little bro, Tim? I mean, do you think it could be something genetic, you know, me and him having different fathers?"
"You got the good one."
She smiled in a sad way.
"I never really got to know him, and then he was gone."

She came over and sank onto my lap, holding on for balance. The joint was filling her head, her eyes getting squinty, expression vague. She started to say something, but the words fell over one another, and she became heavy upon me, breathing steadily.

I carried her into the bedroom, noticing en route how narrow her shoulders were, how skinny she was. It was some time since my hands had held her body. She flopped onto the mattress, oblivious, and a furtive thought crossed my mind.

She was wearing a man's white shirt, or, as she put it, a white man's shirt. She got them from charity shops. I loosened it, exposing her collarbones, prominent beneath her smooth, brown skin. She sighed, murmured something like, 'you jacket lost', and moved an arm up, framing her head on the pillow. Her chest rose and fell regularly beneath the cotton of her shirt. I drew the sheet up from its resting place at the foot of the bed and covered her.

I wanted to talk to someone about the mess that was Hilary, Sage and Bardolino, and I don't know why but I chose Wendy. She met me in the park, and we sat side by side on the swings.

"Come on, Timothy, spill the beans," she said.

"How do you know there are any to spill?"

"Feminine intuition."

We started in unison to back up our swings but kept our feet on the ground. It was as if neither us wanted to set ourselves in motion until I had broached the subject.

"You know Sage?" I began.

"Quite tall, loud voice, fairly dishy, shame about the beard."

"He's shaved it off, actually."

"You've never dragged me all the way here to discuss Sage's facial hair?"

We were swinging now, but out of synch, so we had to keep turning our heads.

"Not the beard, no. It's a bit weird, really…"

I wasn't sure how far I wanted to confide in her.

"Sage has got into a bit of bother, and now I think he's in hospital, but I'm not sure where, and I know the person who put him there."

Wendy slowed her swing.

"That's quite a mouthful. Sage is a mate, right?"

"Yes."

"Is the other party?"
"Not exactly."
"So, what's the problem? Ring the hossies, find Sage, go see him."
She made it sound simple, easy, trouble-free. To her, not really knowing the people involved, I suppose it was. Especially since I hadn't mentioned Hilary. It was fairly likely she would be be home by now, and I realised I should go and see her too.
"Timmy, you're fading," called Wendy. She had stopped swinging altogether and was dabbing her nose with a powder puff.
I was about to reply, when a woman with a pushchair pointedly remarked to its' occupant,
"I'm sure the nice man and lady will let you have a turn soon."
Neither of us had noticed them arrive. We repaired to the roundabout.
"Not too fast," said Wendy, "I get nauseous."
We rotated slowly in silence for a moment, passing little almost melted patches of snow, woman pushing the swings, pigeons, trees, climbing frame, man spiking litter, and above us the circling sunlit clouds in the blue, winter sky.
I looked at Wendy, who was lying back and gazing up.
"Is it permanent, then?" I asked.
She sat up to look at me.
"I presume you are referring to my gender?"
I nodded.
"Well, you know what the song says, 'always a woman'. Actually, one can chop and change, if you'll pardon the expression."
"I don't think I'll dwell on that."
"Don't be soft! I know someone who's changed sex so many times he can't remember what he came out as at birth. Has to ask his mother."
"Really?"
"Well, I may be exaggerating a tinsy bit, woman's prerogative. But, as they say, 'once, twice'…"
"Three times a lady?"
She laughed.
"Don't, I'll wet meself. And slow this bloody thing down, you'll have me throwing up."
"So, now that you're sort of female…"
"Sort of, cheeky mare!"

"Sorry, you know what I mean. What I was thinking was, the sort of blokes that notice you now will be, you know, heterosexuals."
"And?"
"Well, I just wondered how that would be for you."
"Think about it, sugar, as long as men fancy me, I couldn't give a toss if they're gay, straight or undecided. I don't think I'm going to be lonely."
She stepped off the roundabout and adjusted the line of her stockings.
"No, I'm sure you won't be. It's just, what I was thinking, say I met you, and I didn't know anything about you, would it be feasible for me to, you know, go for you?"
"Go for me?"
"Well, you know. I don't quite know how to put it."
"Or where, by the sound of it! Listen, I can assure you that you would not be disappointed. But it would depend on whether I'm your type, I suppose."
I felt a bit like I had been holding a paper bag full of air and someone had punched a hole in it. A bit like the first time you realise your parents are still sexually active. Unique smell of the master bedroom, somewhere between talcum and Brylcreem. Condoms under the double bed.
"Er, ground control to Major Tim, can you hear me? God, I've never known anyone daydream the way you do!"
We wandered out onto the street, where a passing cabbie whistled at us. Wendy laughed, kissed my cheek and said she had to go, someone to meet in town.
I walked towards home, still undecided about what to do about Sage and Hilary.
Simone was home alone, lying on the floor listening to Rod Stewart. She kept putting the needle back on to 'Sailing'. Irritating, but for once I managed to bear it well without comment.
Nevertheless, as I sat silently on the settee, Simone gave me one of her looks.
"Ok," she sighed, "what's so funny?"
"What?"
She thumped the carpet, disturbing some dust.
"You're grinning like an idiot."
"Am I? Actually I was just thinking, the more appropriate artist to record this song would surely be Brian Ferry."
"Ha, ha. Can you go away now please?"

I went and sat on the bed, and a sudden memory of my father and our home life popped into my mind.

He was watching 'Jim'll Fix It', while I sat staring at the wall, resentfully trying to ignore the cigar-sucking freak-in-a-tracksuit. It annoyed Dad that I didn't share the pleasure he felt at seeing people have their wish come true. "Why can't you be happy for him? That little boy has always longed to fly a helicopter."
"Boring. Anyway he's not really flying it."
"You've become so cynical, do you know that? I can't think where you get it from."
"And who's a lucky young man, then?" said Jim.
Not me. I hated everything I owned and most of the people I knew.
'Dear Jim, can you fix it for me to have a less crap life? And a girlfriend.'
Now I did have one and was starting to hate myself. In moments of stress and conflict, I would rend the already threadbare strands of empathy. Simone's opinion of me was surely plummeting, but still I couldn't resist biting the hand she held out to me.

Occupation

Imelda was friendly with a foreign student named Immy. He was rumoured to be a member of the P.L.O. and seemed always to wear a frown. Imelda dragged me into a café I was passing so she could introduce us. Immy held out a hand backed with dark hairs.
"Hello," he said. "You are a good friend to Imelda?"
She scoffed,
"That's a laugh!"
He looked puzzled.
"Don't listen to her," I said, "she likes to tease."
He nodded for about eight seconds.
"Immy's organising an occupation of the Poly building," said Imelda. "Foreign students having trouble with their fees are just being chucked out, it's really unfair."
I was sitting on a full grant. I'd never really thought about it.
Immy took a sip of coffee.
"It's short sighted," he said. "I think they don't want new blood in this country, but let's be honest, it needs it."
"Of course it does," said Imelda. "Will you take part, Tim?"

Immy scrutinised my face.

"Well, I'm not really much of a one for demos."

"Oh come on," protested Imelda, "how would you feel if they threatened to throw you off your course?"

Immy sighed.

"Don't bother, Imelda, you can't change him."

But he passed across the table a photocopied flyer detailing the proposed poly sit-in, and I slipped it in my pocket before leaving.

I strolled aimlessly towards town, wondering why, when anything took a political turn, I immediately felt my brain turn into guacamole. Also I was jealous of Imelda and Immy's friendship, and this irritated me. I found his serious eloquence and brooding good looks intimidating. Maybe I would take part in the occupation.

My introspection was popped by the sound of someone cheerily calling my name.

There was Hilary, all smiles and less bruises, waving and hurrying towards me.

"Tim, am I glad I've run into you!" she said, slightly breathless.

"They let you out then! How are you?"

"Better now I've got you. I've been trying your 'phone, aren't you ever going to get it fixed?"

"It's not broken, just cut off."

"You silly splitter of hairs."

We sat on a bench, wind whipping round our ankles, and Hilary hooked her arm onto mine.

"So tell me," she said, wiping her steamed up glasses, "has Sage left me?"

"What makes you say that?" I replied, evasive.

"Well, he fails to visit me in hospital, and when I get home, most of his stuff has gone and he's not there. I think that says something, don't you?"

If anyone ever deserved an explanation...

I did my best, and was quite surprised when, as I got to the part where Bardolino was seen to administer his own personal brand of justice, she burst into laughter.

"Oh, God, I shouldn't laugh," she spluttered, wiping her eyes. "It's just such a relief to know he's still around. I thought I'd lost him. I mean, he'll be alright, won't he?"

"Well, I..."

"Of course he will. Tim, I can't wait to tell him!"

"What?"

"You say 'what' an awful lot, you know? About my accident. The other day, when I got home, I was standing in the kitchen, and, like that, it came back to me about how I got injured. I'd been on the table changing a light bulb and must have come a cropper. So stupid. That kitchen table has got to go, it's on its' last legs. Like I nearly was. Listen, I have to go and find Sage. He really needs taking under my wing. Thanks, Tim, I love you."

She planted a wet one on my forehead and charged off up the pavement.

Arrows

Back at the flat, I found Norman throwing darts at a newspaper picture of Norman Tebbit taped to the kitchen door.

He paused until I was safely out of range, if such a haven is possible in the vicinity of a dart-flinging Norman, and took aim.

"Watch this, Tim," he said. "I'm going for double top."

"Which is?"

"Right between the eyes."

He released three in quick succession, of which the first glanced off the door handle, the second impaled the politician's lip, and the third nailed his eyebrow.

Norman scowled.

"Shit! First he takes my name, and now he takes the match!"

"You don't seriously think he stole your name?"

"Don't I?"

"Come off it! Take that to its' logical conclusion and you'll be accusing Wisdom, Collier, Bates..."

"All right, point taken."

"Greenbaum..."

"All right!"

Simone emerged from our bedroom, rubbing her eyes.

"What's going on?" she said. "I try to have a kip, and all I hear is these weird thudding sounds."

"Dunno," said Norman, trying to keep himself between her and Tebbit.

"Really? Sounded to me a bit like some body throwing things at the door. Pointy things."

She pushed past and scrutinised the perforated picture.

"Oh look," she remarked. "There seems to be a photograph here with a lot of dart-sized holes in it. And darts."

"Ah," said Norman. "I suppose I was sort of brushing up on my skills."
"Whilst also satisfying a desire to attack and disfigure a Tory?"
"Couldn't have put it better."
"Well, play is suspended."
She ripped down the picture, scrunched it into a ball, and tossed it into the kitchen bin.
"I'm going to make myself a cocoa and then I'm going back to bed. For a quiet sleep."
Norman looked at me.
"Pub?" he said.
The Coach and Horses, early doors, smoke from the afternoon session still hanging in the air.
As we sat with our pints, Norman became pensive. He took a long sup, looking at me sideways.
"So, Tim," he said. "Which way are you going?"
"What?"
"It's not a hard question. The thing is, to decide which way you're going."
"Straight to the bar if you keep this up."
"There you go! Prevaricating. There comes a time when you have to focus. It's all about direction. You can't just amble through the next couple of years waiting to see what happens."
"You're starting to sound like my tutor."
"Doctor Brooks?"
"How do you know that?"
He smiled smugly.
"I know a lot more than you think. But anyway, you should listen to her. She diagnoses correctly."
"Diagnoses?"
"She's a doctor, isn't she? And she can see that you're wavering."
"Wavering, not drowning."
"Oh, I get it. A literary allusion to get you off the hook."
"Something like that. Very like."
"Was that another one?"
"Maybe."
"There you are, see? Avoiding the issue. You could be in danger of chucking away a fine education."
"And you couldn't, I suppose?"
"Never mind me, I'm borderline. You have a real chance. A future."

Next morning, Simone was sorting through the post.
"Bills, rubbish, more rubbish, oh, a letter. For you."
I recognised Hilary's handwriting.
Simone looked at her feet.
"Aren't you going to open it?"
I did.
"From Hilary."
"That's nice. Can't seem to leave you alone, can she?"
I had recently told Simone as much as I thought she needed to know about the kitchen table fiasco, but she was clearly still puzzled about my role in it all.
"No, she just, you know, she just wants to tell me how it went."
"How what went?"
"Her visit to Sage in the hospital."
"Well you'd better go and see her then, hadn't you?"
She lit a cigarette.
"And meanwhile I'm finally going to get the fucking 'phone connected."

Hilary let me in to her flat, and she could hardly wait till I had sat down before embarking on her story.
"Tim, honestly, you couldn't make it up. I got to the hospital, and there were these policemen standing round Sage's bed. He's lying there not exactly looking his best. Weird, also, without the beard. When did that happen? Never mind, the thing is, the officers start going on to me about how they are investigating an assault, and advising me to back off because, as they put it, 'the patient is helping us with our enquiries.' And Sage keeps trying to say 'Hello', and they're going 'this is not helping, Sir.'
And what was so funny, as the senior officer was going on about an 'alleged assault on a woman', the younger copper was obviously starting to twig that I was that woman. So finally they let me get a word in, and I let them know there never was an assault. Except there was. On Sage! Now the cops got really interested, and the upshot was, I'm afraid, Sage dropped your chum Stan Bardsome, or whatever he's called, right in the proverbial. The officers scooted off, and I got to tell Sage that he wasn't murderer-material after all, and we can all live happily ever after."
"Except for Mr Bardolino. Come to think of it, how does Sage know him?"

"Ah. Further problems for Stan. Turns out he's a dealer, from whom Sage has frequently purchased."
"And I suppose he told the cops about that as well?"
She nodded.
"They left Sage with a caution, and while he and I had a nice cosy bedside reconciliation, they legged it in search of your man Stan. Sorry, Tim"
"Hardly your fault. Good to hear Sage is ok. You too. But I think I'd better go and bring Stanley up to speed."
The problem being, how to locate him.
Fortunately I had, no Hilary-related pun intended, a light bulb moment. I went to the hospital and managed to strike up a bit of banter with one of the porters, a friendly Australian called Robert. I pretended to be interested in driving for one of the courier companies who deliver to the hospital, and gained enough information to enable me to track down the one for whom Mr Bardolino sometimes works. They were not keen to divulge any personal information, but assured me they would pass on a message, and before long I got a note in the post.
Stan was waiting for me in the venue he had suggested, funnily enough the Hot Pot in Moss Side.
He was pacing the bar as I entered, puffing on a rancid cigar. Spotting me, he pointed at his empty glass, and sat down at a table.
Gert was serving.
"Evening, flower," he said. "Long time no see! Got yourself a date?"
I bought pints and joined Stan.
"Ok, Timmy-boy," he said. "What's occurring?"
I took a gulp of beer.
"Thing is, Stan…"
"Why do I not like it when people start a sentence like that?"
"I mean, it's like this…"
He glared.
"What it is…"
"Spit it out, Tim, I'm not getting any younger."
"It's Sage."
"And?"
"He's grassed you to the law."
He smiled. And laughed.
"The face on you! I thought you were gonna tell me he'd pegged it."
"No. He seems to have survived."

"Lived to tell the tale, eh? G.B.H?"

"And dealing."

"Fucking charming. Look, d'you fancy going somewhere less up-market? That twat behind the bar's been giving me funny looks."

Gert winked at me when we left.

"Don't do anything I wouldn't do," he shouted, giving a twiddly-fingered wave.

"Christ, Tim," muttered Stan, as he scanned the street for a cab, "I wonder about you, I really do. Come on, here we go."

He took me to a club I had never heard of, where he was a member. It was called The Barn, but resembled more closely a shed. A classy joint, with topless girls and legless lads.

Stan was obviously a regular, greeted familiarly by the bar staff.

"Evening, folks," he said. "I think my credit's good, and I'm in the mood for Scotch."

He ushered me to a table and set the bottle down between us.

"Tim, you and I are going to toast my departure. You've done me a favour; you didn't have to tell me, but you did it anyway. So the least I can do is stand you a good drink, before making myself as scarce as an honest copper. Cheers!"

He swallowed his shot in one and kept a beady eye on me that I should do likewise.

And so it went on, although whenever Stan went for a leak, I managed to decant a few of mine back into the bottle.

"Is it just me," he asked, returning from one of these comfort breaks, "or am I pissing a fuck-of-a-lot more than I used to?"

"I wouldn't know."

"No, I suppose you wouldn't. Have another."

He filled my glass to the brim and took a slug straight from the bottle.

"Cheers," I said, toying with the glass.

"Weird," he murmured, peering at the bottle. "Never seems to empty."

Back 'ome

I was shattered awake later that morning after a couple of hours of fitful sleep.

I got myself a cup of tea and sat in bed trying to remember how my meeting with Bardolino had ended, and how I had got home. Simone was snoring beside me, oblivious; I couldn't recall if we had talked when I got in.

What I did remember was that I had to get up and go on some visits.
Mr Eastwood looked even less cheerful than he did the last time I saw him.
"You know, Tim," he mused. "I sometimes feel my life is a film that's run out of plot."
"Sorry to hear that."
"Cue the end credits!"
"I suppose, in a way, we're all writing our own screenplay."
"Lovely thought. If only we had that much control over all the other characters and events. Over our own outcome, for that matter. I don't think I would have written myself into that loony bin where I stayed for so long. But then again, I'm sure I would have written you in to come along and save me. Forgive my whimsy. Cup of coffee?"
He did the honours.
"Talking of other characters," I said, "how did it go with the social worker?"
"Oh God. Can't seem to take to that woman. Full of herself. She's 'looking to scale down the service', I think that's how she put it."
"The agency still sent me round."
"Yes, but I think it's a sort of swan-song affair. Letting me down gently. And to be fair, even if I am a lonely old so-and-so, I am pretty independent now. Do drop by sometimes, won't you?"
I nodded but knew I probably wouldn't.
Mr Kahn was next, and I was running late.
Pinned to his front door was a note, scrawled in biro.
"Waiting, waiting, waiting, always waiting. Gone to buy fried fish."
'How can the agency afford to send me to a client to buy fried fish,' I thought, 'especially one who goes out to buy fried fish.'
I turned towards home.
As I was passing through Fallowfield, I noticed filming was in progress of a scene intended for 'Coronation Street.'
The reason I knew this was the red jag, from which emerged the small suave figure of Johnny Briggs, a.k.a. Mike Baldwin.
Having driven into the forecourt of a small hotel, he was required to exit his vehicle, open the passenger door, and escort his young female companion into the lobby.
Meanwhile the extras, a man carrying a suitcase, and an old woman with a Jack Russel, crossed the scene.
Cameras and lights surrounded this set up, and extra shrubbery on tripods overhung the shot.

I watched this scene being acted and re-enacted for as long as I could stand it, and they were still at it when I, possessed of a newfound respect for the actors of soap, moved on.

I told Simone about it when I got in.

"Thrilling," she said. "A fruitful day, looking in on old codgers, and gawping at Granada telly in action."

"I'm going to a lecture in a minute."

"So why are you here? I don't get your logic, Tim. Sometimes, actually quite a lot of times, you just seem, I don't know, so sort of out there."

"Funny that, because, as soon as I've made a sandwich, that's exactly where I will be. Happy?"

"Not particularly. And also, where were you half the night?"

"I have to hurry. Later."

The lecture was on Milton, and I fell asleep.

Simone was pacing the floor when I returned.

"Finally!" she said.

"What? You're always going on about me and my studies, and now you're annoyed coz I went to a lecture."

"Not annoyed. You just buzzed off as if you didn't want to talk about last night. I heard you come in, you know? How could I not, state you were in? Must've been after four at least."

"I know, I didn't mean to be so long."

"So where were you? The pubs don't stay open that late! I suppose you were round at Hilary's, or maybe you were with that skanky Irish girl you're always hanging around with?"

"There wasn't any girl. There's this bloke…"

"Oh, this just gets better and better!"

"Don't be daft. He's a sort of mate, and he's had a bit of a rough time."

"Ah. So he needed a shoulder to cry on. Sweet."

"Well I'm sorry."

"You should be. I was worried. If I'd got round to getting the phone fixed, would you have called?

"Course I would."

"Well, I'd better get it fixed."

"Re-connected, I don't think it's broken."

"Pedant."

"It won't happen again."

She managed a smile.

129

"It better not. Why is it you know so many needy people anyway? I'd have thought you'd had enough of that with the agency work."

"Just an all round good guy, I guess."

"Ha! Sucker, more like. I'm nipping out to Danny's for a bottle of vino."

I went into the living room and picked up a notebook, and, a little later, Norman came in and sat watching me scribble.

"Ah," he observed. "So this is how essays get written, is it?"

"No, I'm just trying out a few ideas."

"Such as?"

"I've been thinking of compiling a book of misery. A sort of Who's Who of Boo Hoo."

"A what?"

"A miscellany of misfortune. An unlucky dip. Unhappy happenings throughout history."

"A treasury of teardrops? The perfect gift."

"Why not? The antidote to Christmas cheer."

Simone joined us.

"What's this?" she asked. "Creative writing?"

"Destructive," said Norman.

I shook my head.

"Not really. It's my disappointment digest. A catalogue of the topsy turvy. Some people's lives are simply more remarkable for mis-hap than others."

Simone looked doubtful.

"Mmm. Not really that straight forward though, is it? I mean nothings black and white."

"Some things are," said Norman. "There's photographs, for instance. Some of 'em. And televisions. Old films…"

Simone clenched her fist.

"I'm surprised you don't mention the Minstrel Show."

"Ah, well, so far as I know, that's actually in colour. But I suppose the make-up is, you know…"

"Black and white?"

He nodded.

"Well thanks, Norman, for making that clear. Are there any other phenomena you'd like to include, be they photographic, televisual, cinematic, or just plain old-fashioned racist light entertainment?"

He shrugged his shoulders.

"Well thank the baby Jesus! Now maybe I can continue with the point I was trying to make. Trying to make to Tim, Norman. Only, guess what? I can no longer be arsed to bother."

"Haven't we rather strayed from the point?" I suggested.

"I don't think so," said Simone. "You're wasting your time on whimsy when you've got Uni work piling up. Add that to your list of disappointments."

She swept out, and when he was sure she had gone, Norman closed the door.

"You know what?" he said. "I forgot to include dominoes."

Simone was on her way out when I went to have a chat.

"You shouldn't get so worked up by him," I said.

"Worked up? By Norman? You must be joking."

"Well, he seems to be getting on your nerves."

"I've got other things on my nerves worse than that waste of space."

"I know."

"Do you, though? You realise I've heard zilch from Jordan? I've no idea what the fuck's happening, or what he plans to do"

"Have you spoken to Gavin?"

"Are you kidding? I wouldn't trust him with a barge pole."

"Touch him."

"What?"

"Nothing."

"Well, if that's all you've got to add, I'm off to work."

Next day so was I.

But not to my studies.

First was Mr Battyball.

"Oh, hello, son," he greeted me, "how's tricks?"

"They're ok. And you?"

"On the mend, on the old mend, son. Been getting out a bit, as it happens. Scaring the ladies!"

"Eh?"

"Oh, I dunno. A couple of whiskies and I'm talking rubbish. Don't bear me no never mind."

"Anything I can help with?"

"Truth is, I don't reckon there is now. On your way, old son. I'll maybe see you when you're older."

Next was Mr Bennett, except he wasn't at home. Just some of his cronies, sipping beer and smoking.

"Francis aint here," said one.

"Fact is," added another, "he pegged it."

I rang the agency and they sent me straight on to a new client.

When he answered the door, I was surprised by how young he was.

His name was Mr Maloney, and was perhaps in his mid twenties. He had fixed braces on his teeth and was hobbling with the aid of a pair of crutches.

"Accident!" he said, grinning. "What my Mum always calls me, accident waiting to happen."

He swung a crutch in the direction of an armchair.

"Take a pew, I'll make a brew."

He appeared to converse in note-form.

"Don't worry," I said. "I can do it."

He shook his head.

"No, no. Up to me. Keep active."

He headed for the kitchen, and I sat down, pondering why I was there.

As if reading this, he poked his head through a serving hatch.

"Social said I'm entitled to help. What with? Managing!"

He handed through two mugs of greyish tea and joined me.

"Name's Dennis," he said, propping one of his crutches against the wall, and extending a hand.

We shook.

"Thing is," he continued, "not to be ungrateful, but I don't see why they sent you. Don't need my hand holding."

I noticed he had the most bitten fingernails I had ever witnessed.

"Cigarette?" he said, nudging a pack across the coffee table.

We sat for a moment in silence, interrupted suddenly by the ringing of his telephone.

He picked up.

"Hello," he began. "Oh, Steve. How do? Eh? Hang on mate."

He put his hand over the receiver.

"A mate," he said. "Not so good. Needs a chat."

I made myself scarce.

As I walked home, Norman sidled up and fell into pace beside me.

"Are you stalking me?" I asked.

"Now why would I do that?"

He was eating pork scratchings, and when he opened his mouth to speak I got a whiff of their savoury aroma.

"Want one?" he said, proffering the cellophane packet.

"Thanks, but I prefer snacks that don't have bristles."

"Fuck off! These are a proper snack."

"Proper?"

"Yeah, like biltong. Proper bloke's stuff. I s'pose you'd prefer a muesli bar?"

"I'd settle for a Quaver, or Wotsit. Anything that's not the deep-fried epidermis of an animal."

He laughed.

"Typical English student! Swallowed a dictionary and can't stop regurgitating."

"Which is what you'll be doing if you keep scoffing that crap."

"No, not me, mate. Cast-iron constitution."

And so, apart from the brittle sound of crunching, we continued in silence. At the flat we spotted Simone in the window doing a spot of curtain twitching.

Norman turned on his heel.

"Pub for me, I reckon," he said. "I feel suddenly quite thirsty. And I don't think I'm exactly flavour of the month with the S word."

I went in.

"Saw your useless chum slope off," said Simone. "I suppose it's too much to hope that you told him to sling his hook at last?"

"Not exactly."

"Well, look, I don't want to say it's him or me."

"So don't. You don't seriously think that would be a choice?"

"I don't know, Tim."

"I mean, I know he's a catch, but he's not in your league."

"Funny."

We left it at that. Our conversations never seemed to get us anywhere anymore.

I got out my A4 lined pad and sat staring at how little of my overdue essay on Donne I had done.

The telephone rang, which surprised me as it hadn't done so for ages.

It was Imelda.

"Tim, no excuses, now, you need to get your arse down here."

"Down where?"

"The Union building. It's the start of the occupation."

"I don't know. I've got this essay."

"Always an essay! Anyways, it'll be the perfect place for you to do it."

"I'll have to see…"

She rang off.

"Who was that?" shouted Simone from the kitchen.

"Sage, wanting a beer."

"I hope you put him off."

"I did."

Back to Johnny D and "The Flea."

I felt like I had one in my ear.

So it's the start of the occupation. None of my business. Not dwelling on it at all. Especially not about Imelda over-nighting with Immy.

Why does he have to have a name that sounds like a pet version of hers?

No. Not thinking about her at all.

'The flea is you and I, and this

Our marriage bed…'

Sod it.

I donned my best Poly Occupation garb and, with a vague shout to Simone about going to the library, went to join the squatters.

Once they accepted I wasn't some sort of bailiff, I was cautiously admitted.

"Get you in your overalls!" said Imelda, prodding me in the ribs. "Proper proletariat, so you are."

"They're Simone's. I didn't have…"

"A stitch to wear? I hope you aren't in her undies?"

"That's where I draws the line."

"Come again?"

"Drawers."

"Oh. Fairly poor if I may say so. D'you fancy some wine?"

"Really? Drinking during a political protest?"

"All the best politicians were drunks. That right, Immy?"

He had silently loomed, placing a hand on her shoulder.

"You ask me," he replied, "and yet I am what you call tea total. How are you, Tim? So glad you decided to join us."

He had a very clean-cut smile, a tidy-toothed split in a face that otherwise showed

signs on wariness.

"Remember," he continued, "if anyone comes to the door with any writ or paper, crucial that nobody accepts it."

"Too right," added Imelda. "They can't evict us if they haven't properly served notice."

"Well that's a comfort," I remarked.

Immy frowned me another smile.

"Ah, Tim! Always the joker."

"That's me. And you perhaps are the Riddler?"

"Making me Cat Woman, I suppose?" said Imelda.

Immy raised his palms in a gesture of confused supplication, but I couldn't muster the generosity to let him in.

Imelda found her bottle of plonk, and since there were no glasses, we both took a swig.

Immy folded his arms.

"Sorry," said Imelda.

Immy shrugged his shoulders.

"Is no problem. You drink, I hope it makes you happy."

"Usually does. Until it wears off."

"All things wear off I think."

"You are so deep sometimes!"

She draped her arm around him.

"Not really," he remarked. "Maybe I should drink too. Maybe I am too boring."

She laughed.

"Someone with your looks has every right to be dull. And anyway, you're not."

I looked around me. Huddled under thin sleeping bags were several pale-faced students, smoking roll-ups and trying to look like they really wanted to be there.

I too was wondering why I had come, but when I watched Imelda wander away, still hooked up to Immy, and saw her spare hand move towards his bottom, I knew.

And it was not my sympathy and concern for the way the Poly was treating its' foreign students.

In fact most of me wanted to leave, but the Imelda and Immy show compelled a perverse part of me to remain.

I sat down on the brown acrylic carpet and studied its' stains.

Time drags when you're sitting alone at night in a dingy student building. Everyone else had somehow managed to fall asleep, regular breathing and snoring all around. The smell of stale cigarette smoke.

No sign of Imelda and Immy, but she had left the bottle of wine.
I took a few slugs, but it tasted sour.
Joyless juice.
Nobody would notice if I slipped out.
As I was passing the student's union office, there came from within some peculiar sounds, and then, through the partly poster-covered window in the door, I caught a glimpse of Immy. He was hunched over a desk, nether garments round his ankles, and Imelda was under him.
Face down.

Back home, I slunk in as quietly as I could, but Simone was waiting.
"What time do you call this?" she asked.
I didn't think people actually ever said that.
"I dunno. Sorry, I got waylaid."
"Got laid, don't you mean?"
"Don't be daft."
"I'm trying not to. So tell me, am I really supposed to believe you've been in the library all this time?"
"Well..."
"Because if it opens that late, I really take my hat off to the staff."
"No. You know, I was there, and then I ran into someone."
"Oh. And what's her name?"
"Nothing. I mean, there's this tutor I sometimes bump into. I think he's an alcoholic."
"Well he keeps good company. I can smell it on you."
"Just a bit of wine."
"Since when did you drink wine?"
"I don't know..."
"Neither do I, Tim. I hope you're not starting to lie to me? Don't you think I deserve better?"
"Of course. And I'm not. You don't have to worry."
"No? I really hope not, baby, coz I've got enough on my plate without that."
I nodded.
Didn't we all worry? But mine were petty things, furtive secrets, whereas she had family issues, an errant brother, circumstances that made my guilt seem sordid.
She did deserve better.
"Tim, you've zoned out."

It was true. I was having trouble concentrating. Simone's face seemed to recede into the middle distance, to blend and morph itself into the roomscape.

"Sorry. I must be tired."

"What do you expect, if you choose to stay out half the night with some old professor? It's like something out of a bad novel."

My pulp fiction life.

Simone shrugged her narrow shoulders.

"I can see I'm not getting through to you, so we may as well grab what little sleep we can."

"Funny, but now I actually don't feel all that sleepy after all."

"Well you look it."

We crawled into bed, and she turned aside and went quickly to sleep.

I lay watching the room getting light, an image etched on the ceiling of Immy and Imelda.

But when I finally dozed, they at least had the good grace to stay out of my dreams.

I woke at midday to an empty bed, the impression of Simone's head on her pillow. An ear plug squashed on the sheet.

I had already managed to miss a tutorial on Yeats.

"I hate you, William Butler!"

Actually, I quite liked him, and longed to ask him one question.

"Where has Maud gone?"

Surely that would provoke a poem?

No chance of that, though, so it was up, a shit and a shave, and off to my afternoon psychology lecture. (First year subsidiary subject.)

The theme was perception. How, based on the information conveyed to our brain, we make sense of the world around us. What we recognise as reliable, we believe to be true. When we see a person running, we know it is them moving and not the background, which is generally stable. But we've all been fooled, sitting on a train, when the other train we can see out the window starts to move, and we think it must be us that are off. The background we see cannot be moving. Can it?

This psychology lark was starting to do my head in.

"Pay attention, you muppet!"

No, not the lecturer, but Sage.

"What are you doing here?" I whispered.

"It's a free country, isn't it?"

"I'm not even sure if I know what that means."

"Really? Actually, neither am I. But I do know I can pass myself off as a student and sneak into lectures."

"Pass yourself off?"

"Not the best of phrases. I am attempting to self-educate."

"It gets worse."

The lecturer coughed like Jeeves doing his sheep impersonation, and suggested that, "if I perceive correctly that there are elements of the group who would rather be elsewhere, I suggest they go there."

We did.

A Guinness for Sage and a half of bitter for me.

"Half?" remarked Sage. "Halves are for poofs."

"Are you seriously suggesting gay people are incapable of pints?"

"Fuck off."

"Nicely reasoned. Anyway, poof or not, I'm trying to cut down on the booze."

"Laudable."

He drank off half his pint, and held up his glass.

"There you go. In solidarity I am also only drinking halves. One half first, and then,"

he took a long gulp, "another."

"Funny."

"I try. Which reminds me, the stand-up material's really coming along."

"But does it stand up?"

"Ha! Actually, I think it does. After all that shit with Hilary, me and my scrambled brain, I'm not so sure getting a hiding from that little mate of yours' didn't blow away the cobwebs. I can see clearly now the brain has gone."

"What?"

"Well, not gone, maybe, but re-jigged. The fog has cleared. I haven't had a toke in ages."

"Well I'm glad."

"And I'm Sage."

"The one and only."

"Thank Christ. Anyhow, what's the state of play with you, amigo? Still with Simone?"

"I think so."

"That doesn't sound too good."

"Maybe it isn't."

"Really?"

"I don't know. What about you, would you say you were devoted to Hilary?"

"Totally, man."

"No window shopping?"

"Not even that. I'm a one woman man, me."

"I envy you."

"Hey, tell me you haven't been cheating on Simone? She's a brilliant girl. Kind, smart, and a flipping gorgeous…"

"Gorgeous what?"

"Nothing. I just mean she's nice looking."

"I think you were about to be a little more specific."

He adjusted an imaginary neck tie.

"Ok, ok. I may have seen her at the Glamour."

"May have? There surely can't be much doubt about whether you've watched your mate's girlfriend getting her kit off?"

"It's a free country."

"Not that again."

"Look, no offence, I went to see a film, all right? I didn't know she was going to come on."

"Come on?"

"On stage, you wazzock. Look, consider it a compliment."

"That you've ogled my girlfriend?"

"Not ogled. Appreciated."

"Yeah. Hang about, what were you doing watching those kind of films? What happened to the old one-woman-man shtick?"

"Ah, well, that's different, that's not real. And a bit of porn tides you over."

"That's one way of putting it."

"Yeah! Keeps the wolf from the door. Slays the dragon."

"Rouses it, more like. An exercise in frustration, surely?"

"Not if the film has a happy ending."

"What? In a cinema?"

He nodded, smiling.

"Why not, no harm done."

"Unless you get caught."

"No chance. For such occasions, I make sure I'm wearing my patented porn cinema trousers, baggy, with the pocket linings removed."

"I'll treasure the image. Oh, wait a minute, please tell me you weren't sporting your special trousers when Simone was on?"

He frowned at me.

"Tim, what do you take me for, some kind of pervert?"

Bad Penny

I was sitting with Simone over a cup of tea, when out of the blue she asked me if I remembered the first time we spent a whole day together.

"Of course I do. A perfect day. You made me forget myself; I thought I was someone else, someone good."

"Ah, that's actually quite sweet."

"Not mine, I'm afraid. One of Mr Reed's."

"One of your tutors?"

"Really? Don't you know anything?"

"Yes, actually. I know a lot of things. Just coz I'm not at Uni, it doesn't mean I don't know stuff."

"Yeah, I'm sorry. It's like I said, I thought I was someone good."

"You're not bad."

"Thanks."

"You know what I reckon? You over-think things."

"Maybe. Anyway I'll always remember our first day."

"I wonder."

"What?"

"Whether we always, always remember anything."

"Now who's over-thinking?"

Norman shuffled in, wearing only a baggy pair of greyish Y-fronts.

"Oh, sorry," he said, crossing his arms over his chest.

"Thought you were out."

"What you need," suggested Simone, "is a good dressing gown."

"Dressing down," I added.

"Ha!" retorted Norman. "Very droll. I did use to have one, as it happens."

"What happened to it?"

"Sort of fell to pieces."

He sat down, picked a ball of fluff from his navel, and yawned.

"I suppose you want a tea?" said Simone, filling the kettle.

Norman stretched, exposing gingerish underarm hair.

"You are too kind."

"You're right there, Normster."

"Normster? That's not bad. Sort of nomme de plume."
I laughed.
"A what? You're hardly an author."
"Am I not, Tim? Am I not?"
"What I reckon," said Simone, stirring sugar into Norman's tea, "is that, deep down we're maybe all writers."
"Could be," I said. "That novel, lurking in the subconscious. Shame most of us fail to drag it into the light."
"Enough," said Norman, grabbing his mug. "It's all getting a bit too philosophical round here for my liking. Give me a shout when banality returns."
Simone smiled.
"Norman, it comes and goes with you."
He paused in the doorway.
"A tad harsh. You'll miss me when I'm gone."
"You're going?"
"Yes, going to don the apparel, and see if I can remember the way to the pub."
She shook her head.
"See, Tim. A great influence he is."
"Don't worry, I won't be following him."
"Are you in school?"
"A study day."
"Oh, the good old study day!"
"What?"
"Oh, nothing. I just know what you're like. Too many distractions. You should go to the library."
"Just what I was planning."
"Yeah. If you actually get there! Anyway, I'm off to Mum's."
But I did get there. No Sage slipping by, no sign of Imelda, not even a whiff of Dr Drummond lurking in a pub doorway.
Silence, for the first time since I didn't know when. And a complete blank between my ears.
What was it with me and essays? At least I was trying. Try, that's what essay means. Attempt. An effort. A cup of coffee...
Compared with the library, the refectory seemed unusually noisy. I sat with my greyish beverage and thought about Simone. A brown study. Would

Jordan still be there, at her Mum's? What would he tell Simone? What did a bloke like him think of one like me? What did Simone think?

This wasn't getting me any closer to Paradise Lost.

Or was it?

Satan's fall. La chute, Camus. Mind wandering again. The Fall, repetition.

If I was to marshal my thoughts, I obviously needed guidance, and I remembered that Dr Brooks encouraged visits, what she called an "open door policy."

I went and knocked on that door, but there was no answer, and it was locked.

So I decided to try the Union Bar.

"What'll you have?" asked Big Mandy, a seemingly permanent fixture at the pumps.

"I'm in need of inspiration, Mandy."

She laughed.

"Aren't we all? Sorry, love, but after the shift I've had, about all I can offer is perspiration."

"I'll have to settle for Guinness."

Maybe this would shift my synapses?

But, drink or no drink, they appeared to be stubbornly fused.

I remembered Norman would probably be in the Coach and Horses, and what I wanted, surely, was some witty, stimulating repartee? None the less, I went to find him.

He was hunched over a flat-looking half of bitter.

Noticing my approach, he glanced up.

"It's a miracle," he said. "Just as the last of my money sinks to the bottom of a glass, my saviour appears."

"What makes you think that?"

"My faith in the likelihood that you'll take pity and bring forth the cup that cheers."

"Cheers."

We clinked glasses, and my essay on Milton continued its' inexorable descent into oblivion.

Walking home, not much later, we spotted Simone walking ahead. She was wearing a headscarf, probably one of her Mum's, and looked older than her years, stooped against the driving rain.

I quickened my pace, but Norman grabbed my arm.

"Let her go on," he advised. "Give you a chance to sober up, cook up a story."

"Sober up? I'll be lucky to even get near drunk when I have to subsidise the likes of you. And why should I want a story?"

"The essay, squire, the essay. The non-existent fruit of an afternoon's literary endeavour."

"She's probably forgotten it."

He laughed.

"Yeah, right! Listen, man, she's on to you like a, I dunno, like someone who's totally on to you."

"Such an apt analogy."

"There you go, analysing *my* output, but when it comes to the great blind poet, you're lost for words."

"How come you know he was blind?"

He sighed.

"Tim, you're forever underestimating me."

"Well..."

"Well what? In fact, tell you what, I'll write the flipping essay for you."

"What? Are you familiar with Paradise Lost?"

"I could probably answer that with a wry joke, but this is not the time. It's a poem, right?"

"Quite a long one."

"Really? And there was me expecting a nursery rhyme. Just give me paper and pen, and, barring acts of God, or my being taken suddenly drunk, I'll have that essay for you by tomorrow."

"And what's the catch?"

"Tim, please. We're mates. Mind you, if you did feel compelled to recompense me with the odd flagon of intoxicating liqour, I shouldn't complain."

When we arrived at the flat, we found Simone sitting at the kitchen table, still wearing the headscarf.

"Very fetching," I remarked.

She seemed at first not to notice us, and then smiled rather wanly, pulled the scarf aside and let it drop to the table.

"Got any fags, Norman?" she asked.

"I can do you a roll-up."

"Thanks."

"Are you ok?" I said.

"I dunno, Tim. It was weird at Mum's. Jordan's like a hat on a hot tin roof."
"Cat."
"Sorry?"
"Nothing."
"Yeah, well there's something up, I know it. He's trying to put on a show for Mum's sake, but I know him better."
"Well," said Norman, "looks like you two have stuff to discuss. And I've got work to do. If Tim can find me some paper."
"Work?" said Simone. "When did you last do any of that? And what's he want paper for, Tim?"
"Oh, you know, he's got a lot of catching up to do."
"You can say that again."
I found him some foolscap. Well, A4 actually, but the latter would have fitted.
"Give me the essay title, Tim. I can't just waffle aimlessly. And a copy of the epic would come in handy, for quotes and that."
"Are you sure about this?"
"Hundred per cent. Like I told you, I'll have it for you by tomorrow."
But events shifted unexpectedly the next morning, putting paid to his delivering the essay.
I was, surprisingly, up early. So, not so astoundingly, was Simone. And, almost startlingly, so also was Norman. Technically, he pointed out, he wasn't up in the sense of having risen, since, so he claimed, he had spent the night writing about Milton.
I was about to ask if this was true, when I heard knocking at our door. Not buzzing at the front door but already at the door to our flat.
I left Norman to ponder his efforts, and went to answer, and as I opened up, the door swung in, and Jordan almost stumbled into me. He had an odd look on his face, tossing back his head and rolling his eyes, and then I realised there was somebody behind him, gripping his arm. And behind him was another, shoving, until all three were in, and the last had slammed shut the door.
"Who's this?" he asked, but instead of answering, Jordan struggle free for a moment and asked me if Simone was in. When I nodded, he simply said, "Shit."
And then she appeared.
"Jordan," she said, "what the fuck's he doing here?"

She was referring to the last of them to enter, and she got her answer from him.

"Shut up," he shouted. "Not a word from any of you."

His cohort nodded.

"Better do as Gavin says."

"Shut it," said Gavin. "Not a dicky bird from any of you unless I say so. Let's all go sit down in the kitchen, and little sister here can make us a nice cup of tea."

"In your dreams," said Simone.

Gavin shook his head.

"What part of 'not a word from anyone' don't you understand? Now, chop chop, get the fucking kettle on, and I'll tell you how this is going to run."

So we all shuffled into the kitchen, and Simone did as she was told.

"I'm guessing this is the boyfriend," said Gavin, with a nod in my direction. "And is there anyone else I should know about?"

Silence.

"I said, is there anyone else!"

"Does this mean," I asked, "we *are* allowed to speak if you ask a question?"

"If I were you," he replied, "I would not try to be clever."

"It wouldn't take much trying," remarked Norman, appearing in the doorway.

"Fucking shit on me," said Gavin.

"They're coming out the woodwork," added his un-introduced companion.

Gavin drummed his fingers on the table.

"Where's that tea," he shouted. "I can't hear myself think."

He leaned closer to Jordan.

"I thought you told me your sister lived here. You never mentioned it was some sort of hostel."

Jordan stared at the table. I had never seen him quite so ill at ease.

"Right," said Gavin, "this is how it's going to be. As planned, my not-so-nice buddy here is going to take Simone for a little trip to her Mum's. And he's going to stay there and look after them while me and Jordan have a bit of a man to man chat. As soon as I find out what I want to know, we can all go home and forget it ever happened. Trouble is, I wasn't expecting Morecambe and Wise here. Can't have you losers wandering off and telling tales, so it looks like we're all here for as long as it takes."

He prodded Jordan in the chest.

"So you see, old chum, the sooner you start talking, the better for everyone. I'm not known for my patience, and my mate here is even worse. And we wouldn't want him to get too restless with little sister and her lovely old Mum."

He stood up.

"Get her out of here, Jim, and wait till you hear from me."

"Can't I have my tea first?"

"Jim, get moving, no fuck-ups. And as you go, disable the telephone."

Jim complied, except he forgot about the phone.

Which left me, Norman and Jordan sitting round the table looking into our cups of tea.

And Gavin, looking at Jordan.

He lit a cigarette, offering none, and exhaled in our faces.

Norman stood up.

"Right," he said, "cosy as this is, it strikes me it's nearly opening time."

"Funny!" said Gavin, with a slight shake of his head. "But I think I made it clear; nobody is going anywhere. I mean, granted, I could have done without the extra company, but since you two clowns are here, it looks like I'm stuck with you. Having said that, I'm quite keen to have a quiet little one to one chat with Jordan. So why don't you go and play with one another in your room? And stay there until I say otherwise."

Norman looked at me.

"He can't just barge in like this can he?" he asked. "Telling us what to do?"

I looked at Gavin.

"Yes, Norman, I think he can."

But instead of going to 'our room', we sneaked into the living room and sat on the old settee, straining our ears for any sound from the kitchen. There wasn't much, just a muffled drone, mostly from Gavin.

"D'you reckon he'll notice if we try to slip out?" whispered Norman.

The kitchen door was ajar, and I could see Gavin, sitting on a reversed kitchen chair, keeping an eye out.

"Yes," I said.

He paced the room.

"Shit, Tim. What's this all about?"

"Drugs and money."

"Oh, drugs and money! That old double act…"

He was cut off by a sudden clattering noise as Gavin overturned his chair and moved out of sight.

The sounds that followed were hard to identify, although Norman said they reminded him of a time when his father had tried, unsuccessfully, to strangle a puppy.
"This is fucking messed up," he said.
"You don't say?"
"We should do something."
"Like what?"
"I dunno, we can't just let him torture the bloke."
"You don't even like him. And how do you know he's being tortured?"
"Well I don't think he's getting a massage."
"Suppose so. Mind you, a massage can actually be quite painful, sometimes."
"Really? I'll sleep easier to know it. Meanwhile I still think we have to intervene. Or at least try to see what's going on."
"I don't know…"
"What's the worst he can do?"
"Again, I don't know."
"I'm doing it."
He sidled towards the kitchen door, and I found myself following. And as we peered into the room, Gavin let go of Jordan and spun round to face us.
"Hello, ladies," he said, breathing heavily. "Was there something you wanted?"
"Just wondering if you fancied another brew," said Norman.
Gavin took a drag on his cigarette, exhaled, and sat down.
"As it goes," he said, "that's not such a bad idea."
Jordan, I noticed, was slumped face down on the table.
"Looks like he could do with one," I suggested.
"Yes," said Gavin, "let's all have a nice cuppa. And then it's back to business."
He went over to Jordan and shoved him back in his chair, smacking his face.
"Wakey, wakey, old sport!" he said. "It's your tea break."
Jordan put his hand to his head, alternately screwing up his eyes, and staring around him.
"Must've blacked out," he murmured.
"Blacked out!" repeated Gavin. "That's good."
"Fuck you," said Jordan. "I've told you all along, I aint done nothing."
"In that case," said Gavin, "as my old Granny used to say, you must've done *something*."
"I don't know what you're on about."

"But you do. Selling stuff and being economical with the truth about the profits. Stuff going missing."

"I done everything legit."

Gavin laughed.

"There's nothing 'legit' about any of this. But there *are* rules, and there *are* things you don't do, and you broke 'em, and you did 'em."

Jordan shook his head.

"Oh dear," said Gavin. "Looks like we could all be stuck here for some time. And by the way, the door's locked and I've got the key, so don't any of you even think of trying to do a runner."

"This is mental," said Jordan.

"So it is," replied Gavin. "And so am I. Now, tea-time's over, and I wish to be alone. With Jordan."

Norman and I returned to the living room, and he closed the door.

"Listen," he said, "you and I are going to have to jump him."

"What? I've got no idea how to jump someone."

"Well, you just…jump them. Take them by surprise."

"It's too risky."

"There's two of us."

"And one of him."

"Yeah, see what you mean. Ok, how about this? Sooner or later he has to sleep, and then we get the key off him."

"Sleep! You really think he's going to take a nap?"

"Fair point."

"I just wish Jordan would spill the beans and Gavin would piss off. Hang on, I've just realised."

"What?"

"Gavin. I reckon he's Danny's son."

"What are you wittering on about?"

"You know, Danny. Corner shop?"

"Yes, corner shop Danny, but in what way is this relevant?"

"Probably isn't. I just realised, that's all."

"Well I can't tell you how much better it makes me feel to discover it's not just any old psycho in our kitchen, but none other than Gavin, son of corner shop Danny."

"I was only saying."

"I know, but I suggest we focus less on who Gavin's related to, and more on what we're going to do about him."

"Maybe we could alert the neighbours?"

"And how would we do that?"

"We could stick a notice in the window, 'call the police' or something. We just need pen and paper."

"Ah. Trouble is, I used up all the paper on that essay."

"What, you actually did it?"

"Yes. Like I said I would."

"And you used all the paper?"

"Yeah, what an idiot, eh? You'd have thought I'd have kept a few spare sheets just in case of a siege situation."

"Must be a pretty long essay."

"Not really. There wasn't all that much paper."

"So we're back to square one."

"Looks like it, unless you've got any more brilliant ideas, like semaphore, or mime."

"We could climb out of a window."

"Now that's actually not bad."

But when we tried them, we found the windows had been painted shut. I remembered Simone doing them and telling me not to close them until they were really dry. But it had been a cold day, and they seemed pretty dry to me…

"They won't budge," said Norman. "Some wally must have shut 'em before the paint was dry."

"You're kidding," I said. "Oh well, I suppose that's that."

"Seems like it."

"Unless…"

"Yes?"

"You know you mentioned semaphore?"

"I did?"

"Yeah, and what I was thinking, how about Morse code? We could switch the lights on and off for shorter and longer periods, and transmit an S.O.S." He laughed.

"Tim, what kind of world do you live in? Even if anyone noticed, they'd just think we were off our heads. A fair assumption in your case. And, anyway, do you actually know any Morse code?"

"We did it in the Scouts."

"I'm sure you did. And even though I don't think there's a snowball's chance in Hell of this working, I ask you again, do you actually know any Morse code?"

"Not really."

"In other words, no."

I nodded.

"And guess what," he said. "Neither do I."

We sat down on the settee and stared at the carpet.

Not a sound was coming from the kitchen. In fact the only sound in the flat was the ticking of a clock, marking a silence that seemed, none the less, to hang timelessly.

Until it was broken by a sudden rapping at the door.

Neither Norman nor I moved, but Gavin quickly appeared in the doorway, a forefinger to his lips like a teacher in class.

The knocking subsided, to be followed by the muffled sounds of somebody calling out.

"Sounds like a bloke," I remarked, "in the hallway."

"Shut up," said Gavin. "He'll go away."

But he was wrong.

"Come on, Tim," came the voice, clearer now, louder through the door.

"Open up, Tim, I know you're in there. Your downstairs neighbour told me he's heard you moving about. Also I saw you in the window."

Gavin swallowed a swift expletive, and I wondered why there was no shout for help from Jordan.

"Right," said Gavin, "since whoever the fuck it is aint going anywhere, here..."

He tossed over my key.

"You better go down and get rid of him. Make up some excuse, whatever, but make sure he goes, and make equally sure *you* don't."

I picked up the failed-to-catch key from the carpet and started down the stairs, and I hadn't got far before I recognised our visitor's voice.

Stan Bardolino.

But why?

I turned the key and opened up an inch or two.

"This isn't really a very good time..." I began, but he pushed straight past me and headed for the stairs.

Gavin was straddling the summit, and for some reason he seemed to relax when he saw Stan. He even began to smile, but his face changed fast as Stan B suddenly sped up, jumped him, and twisted his arm behind his back. Gavin tried to laugh.

"Steady on Stan," he said, "what the fuck?"

"Shut it," uttered Stan.

"Hang on," I said, "do you two know one another?"

Stan gave a sardonic smile.

"Tim, the less you know, the better. And if I were you and Norman, though thank Christ I'm neither, I would get the smartish fuck out of here while you can, no questions asked."

He released his grip on Gavin's arm, and gave him a meaningful nod.

I looked at Norman.

"What do you think?"

"You heard the man," he said, "time to go."

I was about to mention Jordan, when he appeared in the doorway.

He leaned against the frame, pinching his fingers and thumb over the bridge of his nose.

"Know what, brother," he said, "I wouldn't wait to be told twice."

I wondered why he didn't try to make a run for it. He seemed wearily resigned, and though we'd never exactly hit it off, I felt sorry.

Norman pulled me by the arm.

"Come on Tim."

And we left.

"The first thing to do," I said, as we walked quickly away, "is to go and check on Simone."

"Really?" answered Norman, "I thought straight to the pub."

I gave him a look.

"Joking, Tim. D'you think we should call the law? I'm not their greatest fan, but, you know…"

"Not sure I do. And anyway, seems like Stan's taken control."

"And that's a good thing?"

"A better thing than Gavin."

"Marginally. What gets me is, why did he turn up?"

"Who?"

"Stanley. The Bardster."

"I can't figure it either, but for now I just want to get to Rose's and make sure she and Simone are ok."

"What about that other bloke who's holding them?"

"That's why you're coming with me."

"No problem. I owe him a couple of punches from last time."

"And, I seem to recall, some money."

"Well he can whistle for that."

We trudged on until we arrived at Rose's street, at which point I realised I didn't know the number of the house where her flat was.

"Are you kidding?" said Norman.

"I've hardly ever been here. She usually comes to us. Hang on, this looks like it."

There was a familiar sticker on the door,

"OWNER FRIENDLY, DOG ISN'T"

"I'm not so keen on dogs," said Norman.

"Don't worry, there isn't one."

"Oh. In that case, what's the plan?"

"Plan?"

"For the geezer. How do we handle him?"

"I dunno. He'll probably hope we think there's nobody in, so we keep on ringing till he sends Rose to put us off, and then we do a Stan."

"Yes! Straight in and disable the fucker."

"Disable?"

"Well, you know, render him incapable."

"Are you capable of rendering somebody incapable?"

He clenched a fist and flexed his arm.

"I'm stronger than I look."

"I hope so."

I pressed the bell, and a shape quickly loomed behind the frosted glass. Then a voice at the letterbox.

Simone.

"It's ok," I said, "it's me and Norman. We've got a plan."

"What do you mean?"

"For the bloke."

"There isn't any bloke."

She opened the door, cast her eye up and down the street, and let us in. Despite her assertion about the bloke, Norman and I had a quick look around.

Rose glanced up from her knitting.

"Well, well," she said, "if it isn't the cavalry."

None needed. There never had been a bloke. Or geezer.

"Soon as he dumped me here, he split," said Simone. "But he told us the flat would be watched so we should sit tight. Nobody to leave, none to enter."

"Did he rip out the 'phone?" I asked.

"We told him we didn't have one."

"And he believed you?"

"I don't think he's the sharpest tool…hang on, why's Jordan not with you? Is he ok?"

"Thing is," I said, "Stan Bardolino turned up out of the blue and got us out."

"But not Jordan?"

"No. That was the odd thing, Jordan just sort of stood there."

"For fuck's sake, what's Stan up to?"

"I can't figure out why he's even there."

"Because I called him."

"What?"

"I found his number among a list Jordan had badly hidden, got hold of him and he promised to help."

"I suppose he has," suggested Norman.

"Helped *you*, yes, but what about my brother?"

"What he told us," I said, "is that he was going to deal with it."

"What does that mean?"

"It really is a bit odd. I mean, why does Jordan have Stan's number? And Stan seemed like he knew Gavin."

"Oh, well that's all right then!"

"Stan looked like he could deal with it," said Norman.

"You both keep saying that, 'deal with it', as if that makes it all ok."

"What's going on?" asked Rose.

Simone sighed.

"I don't know, Mum. Batman and Robin here don't seem to have a clue."

"We did what we could," said Norman.

"Yeah, like running away."

"Which one's Batman?" asked Rose.

There followed a brief discussion about how to proceed.

Simone was worried, but she agreed about not involving the police.

"I don't think Jordan would want them sniffing around," she said.

Rose's eyebrows went up at that.

"What you mean? Jordan's not a bad boy."

"Maybe not, but he is sometimes a fairly stupid one."
"You're unfair on him. He's been staying here, you know, looking after me."
Simone gave a short laugh,
"That what he said? And what about looking after his son?"
"Little Jackson wants for nothing."
"Except having his Daddy at home."
I nodded.
"He's not the only one."
Simone laughed again.
"Oh come on, Tim, it's hardly the same! You had yours' there for you when you were growing up."
"And then Mum had to go and replace him with Arthur."
"All right, poor you, but can we at least for now keep this about how we're gonna sort out my idiotic sibling?"
"Fair point," said Norman. Trouble is what *can* we do? I mean, how long before we venture back there?"
"Stan said he'd 'phone me," said Simone. "When it was sorted, that's what he said."
Rose sniffed.
"So we all got to just sit tight 'til we hear from the man Stan?"
"It shouldn't be too long, Mum. I mean he must have been there over an hour. How long can it take?"
"I don't like it, these kind of goings-on."
"I'm sure we'll hear something soon."
But as we sat there with little to add, and no call came, I think we all began to wonder.
Norman stood up, hands in his pockets.
"Not really much use in us all hanging around like this."
"True, really," I added.
Simone sighed.
"All right then, since you're both so keen…"
"We'll have a walk, have a think."
"A drink, more like."
"Sound idea," said Norman. "You'll find us in the Union bar, the upstairs one."
"The 'Solem' bar?"

This was a small area that had been designed, probably in the early seventies, to look 'space age'. Odd curvy seating covered in purple fabric, painted plywood over the windows with circles cut out.

"What made you choose this place?" I asked as we walked in.

"I think it's pretty groovy."

"Groovy?"

"It's also cheap."

"That's good, coz you owe me a pint."

"Since when?"

"Since always."

"Tim, you know I would, but I'm cash-poor. And I did write you that essay, remember?"

Luckily, as we left Rose's, Simone had slipped me a fiver. Even in times of crisis she retained that carry-matches-in-case-anyone-wants-a-light kindness.

"I think we deserve these," said Norman, as we sat down with our beers.

"You and me have been through a traumatic experience."

"You and *I*."

"Thank you. You and *I* and fucking me have been through..."

"Not half so much as Jordan."

"True. Don't like the geezer, but I wouldn't wish Gavin on anyone."

"Pretty shit for Simone, really. He's her brother after all."

"Yeah, know what you mean. Blood's thicker than water."

"Never really understood that."

"Me neither All them old sayings, always contradictory. 'Two's company', but 'the more the merrier', all that kind of shite."

"Too many cooks spoil the broth, but many hands make light work."

"There you go. Never much cared for broth, as it goes."

I think we were both probably trying not to think too much about what might be happening at the flat.

I was about to mention it, nonetheless, when who should saunter in on stiletto heels, and sporting a fuchsia-pink frock, than Wendy.

"Well just look at you two glum drops," she said. "You look like you've lost a pound and found a penny. Talking of which, I've just spent one, I know, too much info! Still can't quite get used to going in the ladies. Anyhoo, I'm feeling expansive, so let me buy you something expensive, well a couple of beers actually, I'm not that flush. Ha! 'flush', and I've just come from the toilets."

She came back with the pints and a cocktail with a straw and little paper parasol for herself.

"Pina Colada," she announced. "I just love pineapple, love a big prickly fruit, me. So, what's the horror story, boys? Simone ran off with a welder called Zelda? Norman moved in for good and you're both living over the brush in mortal sin? Let les haricots flow!"

"What?" said Norman and I.

"The beans, boys, spill 'em. Tell Mummy and she might kiss it better."

Norman shifted in his seat.

"Thanks for the pint, and all," he said, "but…"

Wendy patted his arm.

"Don't be daft," she said, "can't a gal buy a boy a beer these days? And anyway, you're not really my type, no offence."

"Cheers."

"Bottoms up."

Norman shook his head.

"You can't help it can you?"

She slapped his arm.

"The girl can't help it! Too right, I'm like champagne, naturally bubbly."

"Except," I said, "champagne isn't naturally fizzy. They put sugar and yeast in it…"

"Tim, you take pedantry to a new level. And there's no yeast in me, I can assure you. Oh, look, isn't that Simone?"

She came slowly over, her face giving nothing away.

"Hello, William," she said.

"Actually it's Wendy."

"Sorry, hello Wendy."

"Hello back. Actually, are you ok love? You look like you've seen a ghost."

She sat down.

"Anything?" I asked.

She shook her head.

"Nothing."

"No call?"

"Like I said, nothing. Not a thing, and I don't know about you, but I can't just sit around waiting. I'm going to the flat."

"You're right," I said, hoping I sounded convincing. "We have to face it."

"I'm in," said Norman.

"Is anyone going to tell a girl what's going on?" asked Wendy.

"Another time," I replied.

It felt strange to be returning to the flat, a place taken over by Gavin not so long ago. There, ahead, was the familiar street, but we were all aware of the significance of approaching a place that now held about it an unsettling air of potential peril.

At the front door it was Simone who stepped up first.

"Are we just going straight in?" I asked.

"It's our home, Tim, and it's my brother."

"What is?"

"I mean he could be in trouble. Are you coming?"

I hesitated.

"Come on," said Norman. "If Bardolino's in there we should be fine."

Simone let us into the hall, and, furtive and silent, we crept up the stairs. At the top Simone put a finger to her lips, slotted her key into our door, turned it very quietly, strode over and pushed open the kitchen door. The room was empty, as was the living room, as was the entire flat.

"Great!" said Simone, "I mean isn't this just great?"

"Could be a good sign," said Norman. "Could be Stan's sorted it out."

"Then why not let us know? And where's Jordan?"

"Probably lying low," I suggested.

She flashed me a look.

"What's that supposed to mean?"

"I don't know, I just, you know…"

"Yeah, sorry. It's just, I can't figure this out, this stuff, it's messing with my head."

"I'll stick the kettle on," said Norman.

As we sat around the table drinking tea, I realised that Simone was sitting on the chair recently occupied by her brother.

"He'll probably turn up at your Mum's," I said.

She went to the telephone and called Rose, but Jordan hadn't appeared.

"Try not to worry," said Norman. "If they've sorted out their beef he'll be off the hook. No more cloak and dagger stuff."

She scoffed.

"Beef? Cloak and dagger? You really do talk some shit sometimes."

"I was just trying…"

"Well don't."

"Ok, ok, sorry I spoke. I think it's time I got my shite together and hit the road, find myself somewhere to live that's a little less hostile. And a lot less eventful."

He sloped out, quietly shutting the kitchen door behind him.

"Well he had it coming," said Simone. "I mean, come on, Tim, you have to admit it."

I didn't answer.

"Oh, wonderful!" she said, trying to laugh, "have I upset your little playmate? Why not run after him and help him pack?"

"He won't need it, he's hardly got anything."

"Well boo-hoo."

"Yeah."

"Yeah."

She turned her back on me, and as she began to wash up the cups, the door opened a little and Norman stood in the gap.

"Here you go, Tim," he said.

"What?"

"That essay I wrote you."

He handed me the folder.

"Cheers," I said.

"Yeah, cheers. I'll see you around. Bye, Simone."

She busied herself with the cups.

"Oh well," he said, "I'll see you when you're older."

And his footsteps faded down the stairs.

"Good riddance," muttered Simone.

"This isn't like you." I said.

"No? Well maybe I'm *not* myself. I'm calling Stan flipping Bardolino."

But S flipping B wasn't answering.

"Shit!" said Simone, slamming down the receiver.

And even though I knew whatever it was would probably be annoying and unhelpful, I searched for something to say.

"Try not to worry," was the best I could come up with.

She sighed.

"That's what Norman said. You're right though, I'm sorry I didn't mean…I just don't know what to think."

"No need to apologise."

"I was mean to Norman."

"He'll get over it."

"All the same."

I suddenly remembered how late I was with 'my' essay, and asked Simone if she'd be ok if I nipped out and handed it in.

"It's way overdue, but at least I've got a pretty good excuse this time."

She managed a smile.

"And so plausible! Look, how about I come with you? I could wait for you in the union bar."

So that's where I left her, and this time Doctor Brooks' door was open.

"Timothy," she said, smiling up at me over her glasses, "to what do I owe the pleasure?"

I put the essay on her desk.

"Not sure it's a pleasure," I said, "but I thought I'd better hand this in."

"The Milton essay! My word, I'd sort of given that one up as a hopeless case. A fallen Angel."

"I know. Sorry. Had a bit of a tricky time lately, hard to explain. It was done in a bit of a hurry, so…"

"Never mind, I have it now. And I have a window just after lunch, so if you can come back in a couple of hours, we can discuss it."

"Thanks."

"Don't mention it. Is everything all right now?"

"Pardon?"

"Have things become less tricky?"

"Oh. I'm hoping so."

"Well if you ever want to talk about it, I'm here."

"Ok. I'll come back around three?"

"Perfect."

Back at the bar I found Simone had been joined by Sage and Hilary. Spotting me, Sage strode over and almost lifted me off the floor.

"Steady on," I said.

"Sorry, man! Just so good to clap eyes on you again, where've you been?"

"I could ask the same of you."

"Yeah, yeah I suppose you could. You know how it is, been sorting myself out and that. Hey, take a look at them two!"

He indicated with a sweep of his hand Simone and Hilary, seemingly deep in conversation.

"Talk about 'house on fire', they've really hit it off. I could start to get jealous. No, seriously, it's nice isn't it?"

"Really nice, actually. Things have been a bit tense."

"Yeah? Sorry to hear that, man. Not to wallow, but it's been the other way lately with me and Hil."

"I'm glad."

"Gladioli! Hey, Hilary, look who it isn't."

She grinned, that broad toothy one of hers', and came over for a hug.

Simone smiled over from her bar stool.

"Well this is cosy," said Sage.

And you could tell he meant it.

"We can all do with a bit of cosy," said Hilary. "And since I've just been promoted, as it were, the drinks are on me."

"And," added Sage, "they'll soon be in us. Deputy Head she is, folks, how about that?"

Hilary laughed, shaking her head.

"Sage, you are so prone to hyperbole, if that's the word I want."

"I wouldn't know."

"Well I'm nowhere near what you said I was, Silly Billy, it's just a small step up in responsibility."

"Good enough for me," he replied.

So a round of beers appeared, with shots to be chased.

"I can see the way this is going," said Simone.

I nodded.

"Me too. But I better watch it, I have to go and get Brooks' appraisal of Norman's essay, and she already has me down as a borderline alcoholic."

"*Norman's* essay?" queried Sage.

"It's a long story, and not a very funny one."

When I did return to Doc. Brooks, I was feeling just short of the insouciance associated with incipient inebriation.

Plus I remembered I hadn't even read the essay.

My tutor gave me a searching look.

"Sit down, Timothy," she said.

"Look, I did say I had to do it in a hurry."

She raised an eyebrow.

"You do yourself a disservice. This really is one of your best."

Tinsel

The days were getting shorter, or the darkness greater.

It was nearly a week since the Gavin incident, and still no sign or news of Jordan.

Simone had given up her job at the Glamour.

"It just reminds me of Gavin, even though he's not been in since…you know."

"Not surprised. He's lucky we haven't shopped him. It's not too late."

"No. No law. Not till Jordan surfaces, and then it's his call."

I was more or less back on track with my course work, hoping to match at least some of Norman's writing ability.

I was coming out of the library late one afternoon, and the Christmas lights were coming on. There was a man up a ladder fiddling with a flickering display.

It reminded me, all of a sudden, of a certain December years ago when we 'had the builders in.' It had been a good year for Dad, doing his travelling salesman thing.

(Come to think of it, maybe his frequent absences had eventually provoked Mum's infidelity?)

Anyway, with cash to spare, he rashly decided to get a lot of work done just before Christmas, and thus our home became the workplace of a three-man team of builders.

"Have this lot done by Crimbo," said their foreman. "No problem."

They were a genial crew, turning up early each morning, brewing up in our soon-to-be-modernised kitchen, and smoking cigarettes.

They were distinctive figures. One always wore a jersey top with a hood, another a lumberjack shirt, the boss a soiled vest, and very swarthy around the chops.

'The hood, the plaid and the stubbly,' my Dad called them, which made me laugh, even though I didn't get the reference.

I must have been about twelve.

Dad loved Christmas, and he kept saying how good this one was going to be, what with the smart kitchen, new wallpaper, (yellow sunflower pattern), stair carpet, and car port.

I didn't really know what that last one was, but it sounded vaguely exciting, like something out of 'Star Trek.'

Of course, as the 25th loomed, most of it was only half finished, but Dad had a way of making things like that not matter.

Even when Mum sat on the bare wooden stairs one afternoon, tears in her eyes.

"It's all a bloody mess, what are people going to think?"

He put his arm around her, I'm pretty sure he did, and told her it didn't bloody matter what people thought because Christmas was going to be great.

Easy to say, but he didn't have to contend with the malfunctioning electric hob and faulty flickering lights in the kitchen ceiling.

"It's like a flaming disco in here," Mum had complained.

"In that case," said Dad, "we'll need some music."

And the sound of the Andy Williams Christmas album was soon floating through from the living room, or 'lounge' as we were now supposed to call it.

Followed by Dad bearing schooners of Emva Cream.

He was like a kid at that time of year.

Nowadays he just tries to pretend it isn't happening.

Back at the flat I found Simone sitting in a smoke-filled kitchen.

"You shouldn't smoke so many," I said.

She stubbed one out and lit another.

"I know. Don't you think I know that? But it helps keep me calm."

"Maybe it's time to call the police after all."

"I don't know. I don't see what use they'd be. And what are they gonna care about one more black man going missing?"

"Wonder how Norman's getting on."

"Don't tell me you're missing him?"

"No, no, just, you know…"

"Yeah."

Next morning I was up fairly early, my new regime for cracking on with my studies.

But first a boiled egg, into the cold water, set the heat, now for the eggcup.

Not there.

Simone appeared, sleepy-eyed, wearing a white towelling bathrobe.

"Morning," she said, lighting a fag.

"Morning. Have you seen my eggcup?"

"Eh?"

"My Batman egg cup. Have you seen it?"

She yawned.

"I suppose I must have done at some point. You use it enough. Why, do you want to show me it?"

The toast popped up and that meant the egg would soon be done.

"No I don't want to show you it, I want to know where it is."

She went to the cupboard and brought over an eggcup shaped like a chicken.

"There."

"That's no good," I said, turning off the gas. "I need my Batman one, you know, the one that says 'Good Morning Batman' on it."

I spooned the egg out of the water and laid it on the table.

Simone sat down.

"Tim, I can't believe you have to have your egg in the Batman cup, which I think is silly anyway."

"I always have that one. And what's silly about it?"

"Well, 'Good Morning Batman!' It's got a picture of Batman, so is he supposed to be greeting himself? Surely it should be 'Good morning Alfred'? Unless of course you are actually Bruce Wayne."

"I don't see why you're being so obdurate about it. Do you know where it is?"

"No. And I don't know what obdurate is either, and, no, please don't tell me. How about taking a crazy swerve and having a go at the chicken one?"

She went back to the bathroom, and I left the egg and went for the bus.

In the library I sat with my work in front of me and fought for some twenty minutes the urge to shout 'Batman!"

And then I did, loudly.

Scowls of opprobrium sent me on my way…

…to the Solem Bar, where, once again, I encountered Sage and Hilary.

"Not so long time no see," bellowed Sage. "And guess who else is here?"

"Elvis?"

He punched me quite hard in the chest and was about to elucidate when the lad in question came out from the gents and wandered over.

"Howdy, Tim?" said Norman.

"You didn't get far then?"

He smiled.

"Well, you're a hard man to walk away from."

"He is a top chap," said Hilary.

"I am, really, and so are you. Well, not chap, obviously, but it's nice of you to put me up for a bit."

"Put up with you," said Sage. "Hey, hang on, what's this?"

It was Wendy, tottering over on heels and waving a copy of the Evening News.

"Have you seen this?" she asked. "I mean this you have to see!"

We saw it, a headline.

'Rubber Man is University Don.'

Wendy sat down and proceeded to read aloud.

"University of Manchester lecturer Dr. Donald Drummond has been arrested in relation to the recent aggravated assaults on women in the vicinity of Oxford road. Items of attire found at his home suggest a link to the attacks perpetrated by a person clad in a rubber outfit and mask."

She laughed.

"Oh my God, Tim, this is one of your teachers! Talk about dark horses."

"Well, he's not actually one of mine."

"All the same, weirdos like that on the loose with impressionable students…"

"It's just allegations though," said Sage.

Wendy tutted.

"No smoke without fire. What do you think, Tim?"

"I hardly know him."

"So you do know him then?"

"I've had the odd drink with him."

"Odd's the flipping word!"

"Hold on," said Sage, "I mean *you're* not exactly…"

"What?"

"Well, no offence, Wendy, but some people might describe you as a bit out of the ordinary."

"*Extraordinary* if you don't mind. I am what I am, and it don't make me a weirdo."

"I wasn't saying that…"

"It's fine, don't get your knickers in a twist. And, by the way, he had a go at me."

"Who?"

"Who d'ya think, Doctor Rubbery!"

Sage laughed,

"Not bad that, daylight rubbery."

"Well I soon saw him off, remember Tim?"

"Yeah. Bit weird to think of him leading a sort of double life. He helped me with an essay once."

"Did he now?" said Norman. "What was he wearing?"

"Tweed."

"Isn't that a fragrance?" asked Hilary. "I hope he had more than that on."

"Talking of essays," said Norman, "he wasn't the only one to help you out in that department."
"Oh yeah," I said, "meant to tell you, it got the Doc Brooks seal of approval."
"See? Wasted, I am."
"Yeah," said Sage, "fairly frequently, so I've heard."
Norman smiled.
"Vicious rumours! Lies and flippin' slander."
"Like this story," I said, "I mean, are they allowed to print stuff that might not be true?"
"Depends on the wording," said Hilary. "And, trouble is, mud sticks."
Norman nodded.
"I bet Drummond wishes that little friend hadn't dropped in on him."
"What friend?" said Hilary.
"Keep up, Hil." said Sage. "Evening News, 'a friend dropping in'."
"Unlike you, Norman," I suggested, "who is one dropping out."
"Ha, ha. Another slur! I'll get by without a degree, I'm resourceful. I could offer a ghost-written essay service…"
"Spot of shop lifting?"
"Piss off, Tim. Next time you're stuck on Milton you can stuff him where the sun don't shine."
"Not that he'd really notice."
"Jesus H Christ," said Wendy, "this is all gerrin' far too eyebrow for me. Love you and leave you."
And off she trolled, soon to be followed by the rest of us.
On my way back to the library I spotted Imelda, but she pretended not to see me and crossed the road.
Later, Simone was at home, pacing the kitchen.
"I feel like shit," she said. "I'm hardly sleeping. Mum keeps phoning, we have the same conversations, Jordan this, Jordan that, I don't know what I'm supposed to say."
"She's worried."
"No shit! Jesus, I could do with a glass of wine. Run out of weed."
"I'll get you some from Danny's."
"Wine?"
"Well, yeah. I don't think he stocks marijuana. Red?"
"Please. Though I don't know how you can face Danny, what with all that's happened. I've a good mind to tell him about his precious son."
"Danny's an old bloke, and none of it's his fault."

"You're soft."

"I'll get the wine."

Danny did not look pleased to see me.

"Tim," he said, "I think you better find another place to shop."

"What?"

"Listen, I don't like it, but my Gavin's told me some things about your Simone and her brother. Drugs. And now he's been arrested."

"Jordan?"

"No, my Gavin. They haven't let me see him."

"I'm sorry. Look, I'll go to Ayub's."

"I think that might be best, for now."

Ayub didn't look all that happy to see me either. Probably knew I usually shopped at Danny's. Or maybe just my paranoia.

I found a slightly dusty bottle of plonk, and as I headed back I saw two police officers coming out of our flat. I watched them get into their car, and once they had driven away, went over to our front door. Simone opened it and stood staring down the street.

"Are you ok?" I said.

She smiled, saying nothing.

"Was it about the drugs?"

She shook her head.

"It was about Jordan."

"They found him?"

"Yes. His body was fished out of a canal. He's dead. I have to go to Mum's; they want her to formally identify…she can't do it alone. I'll be staying there for a bit. Can you help me pack some things?"

"Yeah, but how long are you going for?"

"I don't know. We'll see."

Alone again. Family sticks together, but I wished it was me who was helping Simone. I actually felt sorry for myself, and also surprised and guilty at how little impact the death of her brother was having on me. Maybe it was delayed reaction. Shock. But I couldn't help thinking that it wasn't.

I tried to knuckle down to some course work, but after a few days of isolation, reading and writing, I cracked and met Sage for an afternoon pint.

"Hey, man," he said, "awful about Simone's brother."

I realised I hadn't told anybody, but it had obviously made the news.

"Yeah."

Hilary came in then, followed by Norman.

"We can leave you two alone if you prefer," said Hilary. "Can't we Norman?"

"Eh? Oh, yeah."

"It's ok," I said. "The more the merrier."

"That's the spirit," said Norman. "Life goes on."

"I'll get 'em in," said Sage, pulling out a wad of notes.

"Wow," exclaimed Hilary, "where'd all that come from?"

"Had a bit of luck on the horses."

"Sage, I thought you said you weren't betting."

"Don't bet on it."

He went up to the bar.

"Sorry about the news," said Hilary. "How's Simone?"

"She hasn't said much really. We've talked on the phone a bit. Hard to know what to say."

"She not with you?" said Norman.

"At her Mum's.'

"Ah, right. She'll be back."

"I'm beginning to wonder."

After what seemed like a decent exchange of comments about Jordan, the conversation eased on to lighter matters.

"Doing anything for Christmas?" said Hilary. "Me and Sage are holing up chez-nous with a whole lot of food and drink."

Norman shifted in his seat.

"I'll be out of your hair, don't fret."

She laughed.

"Oh, don't be daft, we've rather got used to you, haven't we Sage."

"Yeah, can't turn you out into the blizzard."

"Cheers. Maybe I could do the cooking."

"Well, we'll see," said Hilary.

"We were going to have Rose over," I said. "Simone's Mum. But now…"

"Oh, crikey, Tim," said Hilary. "Come to us!"

"Nice of you, but I don't know. Since Mum and Dad split up Christmas has sort of lost its' appeal. Anyway, hopefully Simone'll be back by then."

"It's over rated," said Norman. "I prefer New Years' Eve. Hey, here's an idea, we should have a party, bit of a knees up."

"Knees up?" I repeated. "Where?"

"Yours' maybe. Perfect antidote to Christmas with the mother-in-law!"

"Might be nice," said Hilary, "nice little get-together. See in the New Year."

I was about to answer, when I noticed Stan Bardolino had walked in and was heading our way. Sage suddenly decided he needed the toilet.
Stan nodded and eyed me sideways.
"I'm not here," he said. "Really, I'm not, Tim, but I want you to come along somewhere else, man, where I will be. I have something to tell you."
He had the air of a man not about to take no for an answer, so we walked. Hastening me along, Stan kept glancing all around. I'd never seem him so ill at ease.
Once ensconced in a bar, he set down double shots and eyed me squarely.
"Tim, this is probably one of the hardest things I've had to do, and I've done some fucking hard things. But I like you, and I want you to know. It's about what happened to Jordan. Gavin is what happened. On my life, Tim, I tried to stop it, it was never supposed to go that far…"
"Are you saying?"
"I'm saying Gavin lost it, man, totally lost control. Fucking psycho went over the top, next minute the poor fucker was dead. I never touched him We were supposed to scare him, not fucking waste him. Jesus man, I wouldn't have got involved. I never touched him. All I did was help move him, and we put him in the water."
"Thanks, then. For telling me."
"You had a right." He knocked back his whisky. "That's it, you won't be seeing me in the near future. They got Gavin and I would be very surprised if he's kept me out of it, so it's not healthy for me to hang around. So long, kid."
I sat staring at my drink. What would I tell Simone? It'll bound to be in the papers, eventually. And then there's Danny, though he's already more or less banned me.
And then I became aware of a figure leaning over me.
"Thought it was you," said Dr. Drummond. "Mind if I sit?"
He did anyway, unsteadily placing his pint and shot on the table.
"Listen, old chap," he said, "I expect you've heard certain things about me, and I wanted you to know I'm innocent. Well, in so far as anyone really is. I've developed rather a regard for you, and this chance meeting seems like a gift for me to set it straight. About those assaults, I never had anything to do with them. All the police have on me is finding some rather idiosyncratic novelty garments in my digs. Nothing to be proud of, but they are strictly for my own personal use. Wouldn't think of going abroad in them, as it were. I think I may have been 'stitched up', as the expression goes. Somewhat

appropriate! I hope you believe me, old fellow. Oh, by the way this wasn't really a chance meeting. Saw you walking with your little chum, and followed you in."

He stood up, swaying, tossed off his drinks, and shambled out.

I went home, and as I climbed the stairs I heard some body moving around in the flat.

Cautiously I let myself in, and there was Simone, putting some things into a bag.

"Oh," She said.

I went towards her, but she shook her head.

"Don't think I'm back," she stated, zipping up her bag. "Although, know what? I did actually think about it, you know, just maybe we could make it work. And then *she* comes round."

"Who?"

"Miss Ulster 1978."

"What?"

"Oh, wake up, Tim, who do you think? Imelda, bloody Imelda! And it wasn't me she was looking for. Just can't leave you alone, can she? Well you're welcome."

And she was gone before I could think of an answer. No chance of a 'fresh start' and possibly progressing to the revelation of what had actually happened to Jordan.

I decided I should really try to cut down on the time wasting and the alcohol, and maybe eventually Simone would consider it worth giving us another try.

And for a few days I stuck at it, actually getting some reading done.

I found the best place to concentrate, now that it was just me, was the kitchen.

The Llandudno ashtray on the table contained some of Simone's cigarette butts.

Had any of us ever been to Llandudno?

I popped a tea bag in the 1977 Jubilee mug.

I wished it was 1977. Relatively carefree teenaged times.

I'd just discovered the Ramones.

'Swallow my Pride' on a pub juke box sandwiched between 'In the Navy' and 'Love Don't Live Here Anymore.'

A-levels looming, but not too daunting. A spot of revision and then, at ten o'clock in the evening, the John Peel show in stereo on radio two. If you had a stereo radio. Mine was mono, shaped like a ball, red plastic, with silver-effect dials and hanging from a chain. A pressie from my God Mother, Peggy. She somehow knew what to buy for a trashy teenager. None of the 'here's some money, but don't waste it on records,' or 'I thought you'd like this smart belt.'

A 'Pop Radio.'

Peggy just got it.

In a rare moment of ale-assisted candour, Dad once claimed she also tried to get him.

"Couldn't do that to your Mum," he told me.

And then she did it to him.

A school friend borrowed that radio and it never came back.

Simone's little transistor was still on the windowsill. I switched it on, and the lyrics of a dusty old song came crooning through the fluff-clogged speaker, 'I'm a rich man living a poor man's life…'

And I'm a poor man living it.

I switched it off, poured the remains of my tea down the sink, and headed off for the Union bar.

On the way I heard my name called, or rather, hissed.

It was Wendy, beckoning me over.

"Tim," she said, a little breathless. "I was going to call you, but I didn't have your number, and now here you are. It's fate, that's what it is. Come with me to the park, I've got something I have to tell you. We can talk like we did that time before, swings and roundabouts."

As we walked, there hung between us a sense of bated breath, conversation paused.

The play area was empty, wind agitating the swings, the light fading. We sat on the roundabout, static, and Wendy looked at her shoes for several minutes, before turning her wide tearful eyes to me.

"Tim, you've always been decent to me, sweet boy you are, so I've got to tell you, coz you're bound to hear about it anyway, and I want you to have it from me. I've been stupid and I've been a liar, and that's not really me. What it is, you know the so-called 'rubber man' thing?"

"Yes, and I also know it wasn't Doctor Drummond, or so he told me."

"He told you right, it bloody wasn't him."

"How do you know?"

"Because it was me."

"What?"

"I know. Please, Tim, try not to judge me. I don't know what I was thinking, all confused about myself. But I'm over it, promise. Fact is I got arrested. Plain clothes lady officer."
"You mean you…"
"Walked into a trap? Not half. Classic really! But I'm glad, coz it's the kick I need to sort myself out. I'll probably get a warning, suspended sentence maybe. It's bound to be in the papers, not looking forward to that. I might have to revert to William for a while."
"You told me he once had a go at you, and you punched him."
"I know, I'm really sorry. Sort of a smoke screen I suppose, trying to shift the blame. The guilt. God, Tim, I've been carrying such guilt for so long. I really am glad I got caught. And I feel better coming clean to you, though I don't suppose you do."
I didn't know what to say. I felt as if the roundabout had started to spin beneath me.
Wendy stood up.
"Tim, please don't be angry."
"I'm not, actually. But you think you know someone…"
"You do, Tim, you do! That stuff wasn't me, you have to believe me, and it's not gonna be ever again. I've been a very silly girl…Still friends?"
Were we friends?
I nodded and gave her a smile, and there were tears in her eyes once more.
"I was going to have a drink in the Union," I said. "You fancy one?"
She shook her head.
"No, I don't think so, dead nice of you to ask though. I think I'm going on the waggon for a bit."
By now I'd gone off the idea anyway, so we parted company and I walked back home.
On the way an Evening News banner,
'RUBBER MAN IS CROSS-DRESSING PERVERT.'
I bought a copy, but the item on Wendy was underwhelmingly vague and speculative, though it did confirm that Drummond was no longer a suspect. More interesting was a piece headlined 'Son of Local Shopkeeper under Suspicion of Murder.'
They nailed Gavin then.

Weary blues from waiting

I was sitting one afternoon looking at a blank piece of paper and wondering if I should try calling Simone. I'd been holding out, let her be the one to call, but the days since she left were stacking up.
I hadn't seen or heard from anyone in ages.
Nonetheless, I decided it was best I got on with some course work and just wait and see if Simone would reach out. She hadn't even let me know anything about Jordan's funeral. For all I knew it could have come and gone. Or maybe she expected that I should make enquiries? No. If they didn't want me there, I told myself, then too bad. I didn't care.
Who would be there, for that matter? He can't have been the most popular of men.
Probably just Mum, sister, wife and poor little Jackson. In spite of everything, I found it hard not to envisage the occasion, and it hurt not to see myself at Simone's side.
I turned again to the blank sheet of paper.
I was meant to be writing a sort of 'open essay' and the given title was 'The Medium is the Message.'
What was that supposed to mean?
My mind was as blank as the page in front of me, so I got up and walked around, jumped up and down, hoping to agitate my brain into action.
And then the intercom buzzed, and any possible ideas I might have had were dispelled by the dawning hope it would be Simone. I went down, opened up, and saw Sage.
"All right, man?" he said. "No need to look so pleased to see me."
He followed me up the stairs and we went on into the kitchen.
"Tea?" I said.
"Actually," he replied, putting a carrier bag on the table, "I brought some beers."
"I don't know really. Beer seems to keep getting in the way of work, and everything really."
"Blimey! You do need cheering up."
He opened a couple of cans and handed one my way.
"Here, can't hurt to give it a go."
"Probably can actually."
But I took it anyway, and within the hour, the medium and the message seemed even more like the irrelevant bollocks they were.

"Last soldier," said Sage, shaking his empty can.

"Coach and Horses?" I said.

As we went in I noticed the old man with the terrier was sitting in his usual spot.

But this time there was no terrier.

"Hello, mate," said Sage. "What happened to the yapper?"

The man took a sip of his bitter.

"I aint your mate, and anyway, what's it to you?"

"Only asking."

"Well you can piss off."

Sage laughed, lifted the man's cap, patted his bald head, and replaced the head-gear.

By now I had the pints and we found a corner table.

"What a miserable git!" said Sage.

"Maybe his dog died."

"Yeah, and I was trying to be sympathetic. What makes old people get so bitter?"

"I reckon they're just people who always have been. But maybe when you're getting on a bit it's harder not to be."

"Yeah, my old man is definitely griping more than he used to. Banging on about the Monarchy and privilege."

"He's not badly off is he?"

"That's the thing, he refuses to talk about money."

"Same with mine. Though in my case I don't think there is any to talk about."

"Better off probably. Root of all evil."

"The love of it."

"What's not to love? All that shit about money can't buy you happiness."

"Yeah, probably a lot easier to be a miserable rich bastard than a poor one."

"Exactly!"

He drained his glass.

"Drink up," he said, "my shout."

And so ensued yet another overslept morning, and lessons lost.

Or learned.

I made a cup of coffee, straight from the hot tap. Simone had always told me I shouldn't, something about the toxicity of the water pipes. But ever since seeing "Sunday, Bloody Sunday" on telly, I had been meaning to try the idea, and now I could, even though I wasn't a bohemian in a hurry. Or in a complex love triangle. Or love anything.

The instant powder refused completely to dissolve, scum floating on the surface.

I went into the living room and whacked on "Fun House" by the Stooges. The bloke in the flat below began almost immediately to bang on the ceiling, probably with a broom. I turned up the volume as high as it would go, and stomped and jumped around, whooping and yelling along with Iggy.

"Fuck you and fuck everything," I shouted. Three times.

"Mr Pop," I assured myself, "would approve."

And then I remembered that Sage, the night before, had slipped a little something in my trouser pocket. The substance and paraphernalia for making a reefer.

I spread it all out on the table and sat studying it for some minutes.

Then I called Sage.

"You're fucking kidding me," he said, laughing.

"I'm not. I really have no idea how to proceed."

"*Proceed?* You sound like Dibble, you frickin' twerp. Talk about sheltered! I'm on my way."

Well, I considered, most of the day's opportunities for education had already gone anyway, and here was the opportunity of one that might well prove to be of greater use.

By now my 'neighbour' had started repeatedly pressing the intercom, so I ripped it off the wall.

When I went down to admit Sage, he having alerted me to his arrival by lobbing stones at the window, the man of ire below stormed into the hallway and started to harangue me. But when Sage strode in, he shut up.

"Problem?" asked Sage, patting the bloke's shoulder.

"No, mate."

Sage laughed as we climbed the stairs.

"Presumably not a 'Stooges' fan?"

"Him? The Three Stooges maybe."

"Nice one. Anyway, what is a Stooge?"

"Sort of a foil."

"Well that wraps that one up. Come on Tim, time to roll one up."

And so we, well he, did, a big one, which we passed back and forth.

Before very long, so I thought, I began to get the feeling that either The Twilight Zone was on the T.V. or that I was living in an episode. Sage was there, though, and for both of us to appear in a broadcast of that fantasy drama seemed unlikely, especially as we were not in black and white. And yet it was also oddly plausible. Rod Serling was surely referring to me personally?

'A young man, confused, sitting alone. But is he alone? Or is he about to take a journey into…'

"Tim, pass the joint old boy," said Sage. He loomed close and his turban looked like a walnut whip.

"Is the telly on?" I asked.

"It was," he said, "but it went off."

"Where?"

"Wherever telly goes when it's not on, I suppose. How would I know?"

"I don't know."

"What?"

"How you would know."

He took a long drag and started coughing.

"That's your lot, Tim, down to the roach."

In my head was the response,

'Don't miss the coach, looks like I'm gonna be stuck here the whole Winter. With Harold Pinter.'

Pause.

Babbling Brooks

Sage was still there the next morning. I found him playing David Bowie records and singing loudly along.

'It's a God-awful small affair to the girl with the lousy hair…'

I yawned.

"I think you'll find it's mousey."

He turned down the volume and we heard muffled banging from below, which also ebbed away.

"Well, Tim, *you* look lousy. I trust you slept soundly?"

"I don't remember going to bed."

"You required assistance."

"Thanks. Sorry I didn't make you a bed."

"Such a construction, I think, would have been beyond either of us. Sleeping bag wouldn't have gone amiss."

"Yeah. Actually, I think Norman nicked it."

"Most likely. He does seem to have been dossing chez-nous inside some sort of unsavoury sack."

"Used to be mine."

"Norman?"

"Bag."

"Oh. And how about Simone?"

"I think it could be the end."

"The Doors, or Nico?"

"Crikey, Sage, you are so up with Western culture, man."

"Well I grew up in Salford, man."

"Yeah, man."

"Stop saying man, man."

"Ok, man."

Shortly after this weedy Sage-fest, much to mine and Doc. Brooks' surprise, I knuckled down, put my nose to the grindstone and worked my biros to the bone.

My tutor did really seem pleased.

"Particularly good on Yeats," she said.

"Thanks. Wild swans couldn't keep me away."

"Glad to hear it, although they can be quite fierce, so I believe! Glad to have you back, Timothy. When you put your mind to it, you have a certain…"

"Je ne sais quoi?"

She smiled.

"No, I was not about to employ that old cliché."

"So now I'm an old cliché?"

"Are you teasing me?"

"Would you like to have a drink with me?"

"Perhaps. But I won't."

"A soft one?"

"If I do, I prefer it hard."

I suddenly felt like I had jumped in the deep end, but I caught my breath.

"Then I could buy you a whisky, maybe?"

"My Achilles is brandy."

And there we were, off to the nearest boozer.

Watching her walk in, I realised she was actually pretty attractive. Boyish, gruff, and charming.

She ordered drinks, smiled, said "Chin, chin," and swallowed her double.

"Very good," she said, and ordered another. This also went down fast, while I was still on my first pint.

"Drink up, Tim," she said, "this place is awful, we can do a lot better."

She took me to a spot inhabited almost exclusively by women, quite a few of whom were snogging the gobs off one another.

My tutor gave me a wry smile.

"Sorry, Tim, perhaps a trifle sudden for you?"

"It's all right."

"Is it though? I've never done anything like this. With a student I mean. I shouldn't say this, but I think I have a thing for you. Which confuses me somewhat, as I've always been a lady's lady."

She sat down rather abruptly on a stool.

"Oops! Dear me. God, Tim, this is absurd. I don't suppose you'd like to fuck me?"

"I really like you."

"Ha! But not really fuck me?"

She leaned back, looking into my eyes for an answer, fell off her stool, and lay on the floor with her legs in the air, laughing and kicking. She was wearing small slip-on loafers with tassels.

I helped her up and she brushed her clothes and patted my cheek.

"Thank you, gallant Sir. Oh, you're kidding me!"

"What?"

"See that woman on the dance floor, the one in the hot pants?"

I nodded.

"Well take a good look, because that bitch was supposed to be mine."

"Oh."

"Oh, indeed. Oh dear, in fact. I do seem to have made a bit of a bloody fool of myself, don't I? I'm sorry, this is not fair. Maybe we can forget any of this happened? I need to gather myself. Shit, Timothy, I feel a bit dizzy. Really am sorry. Bright boy, you are, and rather sweet. Oh, God, I really do have to go to bed."

I called her a cab.

Walking home, having declined an offer of cab-share, I began sorely to wish I had someone to talk to about what had just happened. Maybe find a phone box and call Sage. But it was late.

I couldn't help laughing.

Personal tutor!

I felt coldly sober yet disinclined to duck into another bar. In fact, everywhere was closing. Doors slamming, bolts shot. Shops already shuttered.

A mild dreary night, pavements slushy and grey. Here and there a dog-end, bleeding nicotine.

Overhead, as I tramped on in my soaked plimsoles, the Christmas lights were going out.

Over the last few weeks, I found I had gradually developed an anticipation, each time I returned home, of finding Simone there. But it hadn't happened, and hope was beginning to wither into a sense of would-be cynical resignation.

Why should I care?

When my first proper girlfriend left me, (and it was partly because she was so proper), my Mum had assured me that there were plenty more fish in the sea.

"I'm not a very good swimmer," I replied. "But I'd settle for a mermaid."

She smiled and patted my shoulder.

"You're certainly original, I'll say that for you."

"Broke the mould," added my Dad.

I wondered if, actually, I was just plain weird.

Still do.

Here, alone. Messed up with Simone.

Tomfoolery with my personal tutor.

Studies gurgling down the drain.

My Dad in the lonesome dumps, and my Mum in the rank enseamed bed with Arthur.

Maybe I'm Hamlet? Except that my Dad's not dead and Arthur isn't my Uncle. Wouldn't mind killing him though.

Joke.

Would probably never get around to it.

Procrastinate.

To beer or not to beer?

Not much fun drinking alone. Norman could be a nuisance, but I felt his absence.

I went to the Coach and Horses and found, Norman not being there, that it was a big world after all.

I sat with a pint and started to imagine Sage wandering in and insulting the old bloke and his dog. But then I remembered that the dog died. And the bloke wasn't there.
When I went up for another beer, I asked about him. The barman frowned. "Old bloke? Oh, yeah, I know. Stopped coming in after the dog went. Came a few times, but he said it weren't the same without Terry. That were the dog's name. Anyway, I heard he died an' all, the old feller."
"Sad."
"Not really. Between thee and me he was a bit of a cunt."
"Really?"
"Well, bit harsh I suppose. Grumpy old so and so. Bit of a sod."
"A partial divot."
"Eh?"
"Nothing."
Time to drink up and go.

A letter arrived one morning from the University. What had I done this time? Or not done. Ripped it open; it was from Doctor Brooks.
'I think we should have you in,' she had typed. 'Clear the air.'
It was signed in ink, Olivia Brooks.
I realised I'd never known her first name. Given what had happened I felt oddly embarrassed. I suppose, if anything more had happened, we would at least have been on equal first name terms. I began to envisage a scenario in which it would have been inappropriate for me to continue to address her as Doctor Brooks. Unless she was fond of role play.
Banishing that thought, I re-read the letter. She had suggested a time and date, no need to reply unless I couldn't attend.
I was pondering this when the 'phone rang.
Imelda.
"So, Tim," she said, laughing, "I hear you got the elbow."
"Maybe."
"Maybe! Listen, you fancy doing something?"
"Like what?"
"I dunno! A drink, I suppose. Or maybe a film."
She pronounced that word with emphasis on the L.
"What film?"
"God, Tim, this is like pulling teeth, so it is. Just say if you're not up for it."
"No, I am. What's on at the moment?"

179

"There's that 'Midnight Express', but it does sound a bit bloody depressing, so it does."

"In that case, it's a drink."

"Hooray. Name the time and place."

"In twenty minutes at the Bowling Green."

"That old doss house? Oh well, any port in a storm."

"You and your propensity for port."

"Come again?"

"Nothing."

She was there when I walked in, looking rather fetching in an over-sized stripy jumper.

"See, she yelled, pointing at her glass, "I'm drinking port."

"And lemon?"

"Don't mind if I do. And will you get me some smoky bacon crisps?"

They didn't have any, so she settled for cheese and onion.

"Want one?" she offered.

"No thanks."

"Go on, at least these're vegetarian."

"Aren't all crisps?"

"Think about it, Tim. Bacon, roast chicken…"

"Yeah, that's what they're called, but none of them has any actual animal in them."

She scoffed a few and mused, peering at the bag.

"So it's all a sham?"

"I wouldn't go that far. They say, 'chicken flavour' and so on. Doesn't mean there's any real meat in there."

"What about pork scratchings, you're not telling me they're fake and all?"

"No, I think we can safely say they are a bit meaty."

"And going back to crisps, is there any potato in them?"

"Well what do you think?"

"I dunno! But I do think we've done talking about snacks. I'm starting to wonder if it was such a good idea asking you out."

"You didn't have to."

She blushed slightly.

"How do you know?"

"Telepathy. How's Immy, by the way."

"Ok, as far as I know. Haven't seen much of him lately."

"That why you called me?"

"Don't be silly. And stop asking so many questions."
"My Mum always said it was good to ask them. Show an interest."
"Boring. What did your Dad say?"
"Not much. He was away quite a lot."
"Bit lonely for your Mum."
"Not once she got friendly with the T.V. repair man."
"He fixed her, did he, turned her on?"
"Not funny."
"I thought it was quite good."
"Anyway, things have been on the blink ever since."
"And is he still on the scene, Mr Telly?"
"Oh yes."
"I suppose it's a bit like with window cleaners."
"What is?"
"You know, women home all day, nothing to do but housework. Blokes on the job, in and out."
"Can we talk about something else?"
"As long as it's not crisps."
"I'll get another round."
"You sure? It's my shout."
"Feeling generous."
When I returned I noticed she had removed her sweater.
"Suddenly felt hot," she said, smirking.
"Maybe it's the change," I suggested.
"The what?"
"You know, menopause."
"Fuck off, Tim, that stuff doesn't happen till you're old, like forty or something."
She did look warm, slight sheen to the forehead.
"Remember that wolf costume I had?" she asked.
"How could I forget?"
"Yeah, and you in that stupid Roman Emperor sheet! It was a good night though, wasn't it?"
"Suppose so."
"Jesus, you certainly know how to make a girl feel good about herself."
"You still got the costume?"
"Why, would I need it?"
"Eh?"

"Doesn't matter, little red riding hood. You fancy coming to my place?"
"I don't know. I'm not sure what's happening with Simone."
"Well it never bothered you before, and from where I'm standing it doesn't look like there's jack shit happening with Simone."
"It's just, I might still have a chance and I don't want to blow it."
"Well blow you in that case, I'm off."
She finished her drink and put on her jumper.
"See you, Tim. Let me know when you've sorted yourself out."
I sat staring at the remains of my pint, the head of froth disappearing, little bubbles wriggling to the surface and silently popping.
The barman came over, picked up Imelda's empty glass and pointed at mine.
"You finished?" he asked.
I nodded.
"I think I probably am."

Festive

As Christmas loomed ever closer, and no word from Simone, I began to wonder if it might not have been such a bad idea after all to have gone with Imelda.
Nothing seemed to work out favourably.
The meeting with Doctor Brooks had come and gone, and that, at least, had not been as awkward as anticipated.
She had even produced a bottle of sherry,
"Dry, I hope that's all right? Can't stand that Bristol Cream muck."
There were also shortbread biscuits, and we got by on small talk, and wished one another a happy Christmas.
"Spending mine with my aged Mater," she told me. "And you?"
I mumbled something about 'going home.'
What was home?
The one I grew up in, since Dad left, had become for me just a place of memories and nostalgia. Those I could keep in my head. No need to go there and endure the forced merriment of Mum and Arthur.
Should really stay with Dad, but his dingy bedsit, with its' portable telly and cheap hi-fi got me down. I felt guilty that I couldn't be more kind and just go to him.
I made a few Christmas cards, but there weren't many people to send them to.

A handful arrived for me. Mum and (of course) Arthur's played a tinny 'Jingle Bells' when you opened it. Dad's was silent. One from my brother in which he noted that he was going to spend Christmas and Boxing day with Dad.
'Welcome to join us. Can't imagine you're desperate to hang out with Arthur!'
But Dad's place was too small for the three of us.
I decided, or at least began to convince myself, that having Christmas alone for the first time might not be so bad.
Pubs would be open most of the time. I could do as I pleased, and be spared the usual stale bank holiday atmosphere, repeats on the telly, Billy Smart's flipping circus.
Also, since the intercom was still out of action, the twat in the flat below would have to deal with any Carol singers.
Scrooge came to mind, though it was unlikely I was going to be visited by any ghosts.
Not even the spectre of Simone's late Uncle Winston, although I might have entertained him if he'd brought along some rum.
More reliable to buy my own.
I went to Ayub's to get supplies, and, passing Danny's shop I noticed a hand-written notice taped in the window.
SHUT DUE TO FAMILY ILLNESS.
Things must have hit him hard; I couldn't recall him ever closing except on Christmas day.
At Ayub's, as I filled my basket with booze and mostly non-vegetarian grub, I was watched by the bearded proprietor, a morose expression on his face. I sensed he slightly resented me, surmising that I was usually a customer of Danny's.
"Danny shut shop," he said, as I set my basket on the counter.
"Good business for you?"
He held out his hands, palms upwards.
"Open again soon."
Since I'd started using his shop this was the longest conversation we'd had.
I handed over the cash, and he in return laboriously counted out the change.
"Merry Christmas," he murmured, as I turned to leave.
Baffled at how to respond, I kept walking.

Back home, as I put away my shopping, I realised I could have got twice as much for the price if I'd gone to the supermarket, but since being thrown out of there, I wasn't sure if I'd be welcomed back.

Was Ayub really all I had left?

I poured myself a large whisky and chased it with some cheap lager. Switched on the T.V. An old film, probably black and white, though on our telly so was everything. My telly.

I left it on with the sound down and started playing a few records. The Talking Heads went particularly well with some dance sequences featuring Fred Astaire and Ginger Rogers. After a couple more drinks, so did anything. Even the bloke in the flat below was on the beat with his broom. After a while I must have dozed off because I woke to a blank screen and a record that had reached the end and was cutting an extra groove at the centre.

The rest of Christmas panned out in much the same way. The record player still worked, albeit with impaired fidelity.

I didn't really care. In fact, it all struck me as rather grimly amusing.

Maybe next the T.V. would pack up, and then I could call Arthur and ask his advice.

Or maybe not.

I did no course work, hardly looked at a book.

Lots of music, lots of booze.

The only useful thing I achieved was to get the intercom working again.

I called both Mum and Dad on Christmas day.

Mum sounded tipsy. Dad didn't have much to say.

I was none too chatty either, until later in the day when I got into quite a lengthy conversation with myself.

Earlier that day I'd received a call from Hilary. She told me Sage had intended to ring but was already too "out of it" to dial. Ditto Norman.

"Come on Tim," she said, "you can't spend the day all alone."

"Can though," I replied.

I probably did want to go, but my stubborn notion of eschewing company held sway. I thanked her and declined.

"Shame," she said. "Given my present company you'd have been welcome. What I mean is, you'd have been welcome anyway…Sage and Norman started way too early on the squash, and all I've had is a small sherry! If you change your mind, you know where we are. If not, hope to see you soon."

To further enrich my day, I went to the Coach and Horses, and the old bloke with the dog, both of whom had died, was there with a new dog.
"I thought you said he died," I remarked to the barman as he handed me my pint.
He laughed.
"It's a Christmas fucking miracle."
As I headed for a table, I asked the old chap the name of his replacement dog.
"What's it to you?" came the reply.
Good will to all men.
Except me.
Maybe it's true, some people really are congenitally bad-tempered.
Lacking Sage's chutzpah, I refrained from any head-patting or peanut flicking, and merely smiled and stroked the dog's head.
At which, the man said, "Terry."
I went and sat alone, pondering the back-story to the other people in the bar.
There were not many, and none were in company.
Was this really preferable to sitting at home in genuine isolation?
There was a fiftyish man in a grey track suit, red-rimmed eyes and a permanent fag in the corner of his mouth.
A woman of maybe sixty, bone-thin, reddish-black dyed hair scraped back in a bun, talking continuously to herself.
Only chance of a decent conversation.
A bearded chap not much older than me who looked like he slept rough.
Probably begged the price of a few beers and had a wash in the bogs.
On the jukebox, the raucous voice of Noddy Holder,
"It's Kree-st-MAAAS!"
I decided to sup up, go home and ring Hilary, see if I was still welcome. But when I tried the 'phone was dead.
There was some whisky left, and a few lagers, and what I wanted to do was try leaving them alone and having a cup of tea, but I knew that wasn't really going to happen. I did at least make myself a sandwich, chicken paste with salad cream.
And then I switched on the T.V. and took my chances.
And that's how it came and went.
Boxing day was dark, wet and windy.

So was the rest of the week. By the time I got up, daylight seemed to have reluctantly turned up for a shift only to knock off early in the afternoon. My grant was quickly running out, funds low. I tried to read and write during those fleeting spells of natural light and then sit in the dark, thus saving a pittance on electricity. But I would almost always crack and head for the pub, swilling away any money saved.

One evening, to my considerable surprise, the old bloke with the dog bought me a pint. I was drinking at the bar when he shuffled up to order.

"Get you another?" he said.

"Oh, you don't have to."

"There's a lot I don't have to do. You want one or not?"

The dog at his feet looked up at me.

How could I refuse?

Later, walking home, I felt guilty that I hadn't returned the favour. Mind you, what I had done was listen to the entire history of the various dogs the man had ever owned since 1949. And I really was broke. Perhaps he had noticed? Written all over me, the impecunious student.

The next few days didn't seem to be getting any longer, yet time still somehow dragged.

I decided, Christmas having been such a damp squib, to avoid New Years' Eve. altogether.

And I was doing pretty well until, early evening on the thirty-first, there came a-calling on the intercom Sage and Hilary.

"We demand to be admitted," crackled the imposing tones of the turban-toting titan.

"What he means," added Hilary, "is that we thought you might like some company."

I pressed the button, and up they came, bottles and cans in tow.

Hilary gave me a tight hug.

"Hope you don't mind," she said. "We tried calling but the line was dead."

"Yeah," interjected Sage, "so here we are, and that's not all. You, my old mucker, are throwing a party."

"What?"

Sage glanced at Hilary.

"He's always saying that. 'What.' What not, old boy? We've invited a few over, is that ok?"

"I don't seem to have much choice."

"Tim, try not to over-do the enthusiasm."

"It's just one or two friends," said Hilary, "we thought you might need cheering up. You've been lying a bit too low for my liking."
We cracked some cans and I asked what to expect.
"The unexpected," said Sage, as he began to roll one up. "Wait and see, you never know, this could be your lucky night."
"Not sure I like the sound of that."
"Don't be daft! Anyway, it's out of your hands, so sit back and enjoy the ride."
Which gathered speed almost immediately. The first of the un-invited invited was Imelda.
"Hello, sexy" she said, "where've you been all my life?"
"Mostly in Philadelphia."
"Funny. You been avoiding me?"
"I've been avoiding everyone, except for one man and his dog."
"Still a weirdo then. Give us a kiss."
"We'll see."
"That we will! Who else is coming?"
"No idea, it's out of my hands."
"I should hope it bloody is."
"Have you been on the squash already?"
"Of course, it's New Years' Eve. You've got some catching up to do."
I got started by chasing down a couple of shots.
"That's the spirit," bellowed Sage. "Quite literally. Bung some sounds on, man, and if that twat downstairs kicks off he'll have me to answer to."
"No need to be a bully," said Hilary.
I dropped the stylus on some King Tubby's dub, and Imelda shimmied up behind me and put her hands over my eyes.
"Guess who?"
"Aint got a clue."
She turned my head and pulled me in for a kiss.
"There now, that wasn't so bad was it?"
The intercom intervened.
This time it was Norman.
"Crickey," I said, "you have a beard."
"Nothing gets past you Tim. Slight dearth of razors going on, I'm that fucking skint. Hence also my empty-handed-ness, partly caused by the crisis I'm currently undergoing."
"What's that?"

"My kleptomania confidence seems to have deserted me. I'm sort of a reformed character and it's messing with me mind. How've you been?"
"Better."
"That's good."
"I mean, *been* better."
"Oh, yeah, know what you're saying. I kept meaning to drop by, see if you fancied a bevvie, but I can't seem to get my arse in gear lately. Mind you, you've been pretty incommunicado yourself."
"Suppose I have. Been trying to sort myself out."
"Good luck with that! Mind if I help myself to a libation?"
I turned back to Imelda and took hold of her hand.
"Ah," she said, "you're a dote."
"A dolt?"
"Come again?"
"Don't tempt me."
"What if I can't help myself?"
"And what about Immy?"
She scoffed.
"God, Tim, what a pseud he turned out to be. You're ten times the man he is."
"Well, maybe five. He's out of the picture then?"
"Totally. And good riddance. He was deported, as it happens."
"Ah, the dear deported."
"You're wicked, so you are. Come on, let's have a dance."
We had a go and quickly realised that neither of us knew how to dance to dub reggae.
In the meantime, Bob, whom I hadn't seen since the American Diner fiasco, had appeared. He was wearing an acrylic reindeer-motif red jumper.
"Matches your face," I said shaking his hand.
"Eh?"
"Nothing."
"I see. Well, I brought this," he said, holding up a bottle.
"Red wine. You've really thought this through."
He frowned.
"Know what, Tim, I'm never sure whether or not you're just taking the mickey."
"Well, Bob, that makes two of us."
"Really. And will you be treating us to any table-dancing?"

A couple of others had followed him in.

"Friends of yours?" I asked.

"Can't say they are. Gate crashers probably, want me to chuck them out?"

"Bob, a bouncer we do not need. Relax, pour yourself some rouge."

He wandered into the kitchen, followed by the newcomers who quickly set about the bottle of Scotch.

Imelda sidled up beside me and slipped a hand in my trouser pocket.

"What have we here?" she whispered in my ear, her lips brushing my skin.

"Steady on," said Sage, exhaling a billowing cloud of dope haze. "Better pace yourselves, kids, it's only, hang on, my watch has stopped. Fucking cheap Seconda. Seconda's out, get it? Here Norman," he shouted, "that flipping watch you sold me…"

"Caveat emptor," said Norman.

"We'll see about that. But, anyway, point is, the night is but young, girls and boys."

"Says you," I replied, "as you make free with the wine and the weed."

He laughed.

"So speaks the nineteenth century. Here, have a puff."

I reached out, but Imelda beat me to it.

"Shit," she said after a couple of tokes, "what is this stuff?"

"Anyone's guess," said Sage.

I felt a tap on my shoulder, and there came a quiet voice.

"Hello, Tim."

It was Wendy, wearing a tight-fitting three-piece brown tweed suit, hair cropped and slicked back with gel.

"Am I welcome?"

I reached out my hand and we shook, a tear rolled down her cheek, and she put her arms around me.

"I'm a flamin' liability, Tim, that's what I am. Shoulda been drowned at birth."

"Don't be daft, stuff happens."

"You can say that again, kiddo. But thanks. Anything decent to drink?"

"I don't think we can stretch to Campari."

"Good, coz the last time I stretched to that stuff I realised I hated the muck. I brought wine, but I think I fancy a beer."

After she had taken a few gulps, I asked if she had returned to being William.

She shook her head and wagged a forefinger.

"What you see before you is Wendy through and through, but I'm in disguise."

"Sort of dragged up?"

"Which is exactly what I was. Me old man down the boozer and me Mam out working all hours. No wonder I'm such a nightmare. Anyway, I'm lying low while I'm on parole."

"What happened in the end?"

"No, Tim, don't want to talk about it, all in the past where it belongs. Happy New Year for when it comes."

"Not that long to go."

She raised her bottle, saluted, and wandered off.

"She's a queer one," said Imelda. "Or is it he?"

"Don't go there."

"I won't. I'm sticking with you. Wanna try another dance?"

Someone had put on Simone's Andy Williams L.P. and it was a slow tune.

"This is cosy," said Imelda, arms draped over my shoulders, mine around her waist.

And then Norman lifted the needle and spun some Joy Division.

"God," said Imelda, "d'you want us all topping ourselves or something?"

"Do what you like, but I can't stand easy-listening. Kenneth fucking Williams my arse!"

"Interesting sentence," I replied, to which he raised his middle finger.

"Charming," said Imelda. "Was that the intercom?"

I went and pressed, opened the door, and there down the stairs was Simone. She was in the hall struggling with two large bags.

"You can come down and help me if you want," she said.

I hurried down.

"Hello Tim," she said, glancing at the baggage. "Look, I guess this is a bit presumptuous, me turning up like this, but I couldn't get through on the 'phone, and, oh it's New Year and you're such a disaster and, God knows why, I've missed you."

"Look, Simone…"

"Hang on," she said, craning her neck, "have you got company?"

"Well, not really, I mean…"

"It's a party isn't it? After everything, you decide to throw a party?"

"No! It's just a few people…"

But then the door above was opened and the escaping noise said otherwise. Imelda started down the stairs, bottle in hand.

"Hey Tim," she slurred, "who is it, another of your idiot mates?"
Simone nodded.
"Not far wrong is she?"
"Simone," I said, "none of this was my idea."
She looked me in the eye.
"Lame, Tim. Look, here comes your girlfriend. And here goes your ex."
"Don't, please, where will you go? *Simone*."
But she kept on walking. I followed, found myself shouting her name, but she carried on and turned the corner without looking back.
I stood staring at the empty street, and then lights appeared above Danny's shop and he came out and hastened over.
"Dear me, Tim," he said, "I couldn't help but notice what just happened. Are you all right?"
"Don't know really."
He put his hand on my shoulder.
"Look, Tim, we've all been through the mill. I should never have blamed you, and I understand now about Gavin, tough though that is. I've disowned him, he's no son of mine. He's dug his own grave, if you'll pardon the expression."
I nodded.
"By the way," I said, "how come you're in the shop New Years'?"
"Ah, well, can't seem to settle at home, too many reminders. I'm stopping in the wee flat above the shop. Listen, wait there a minute."
He trotted off to the shop and came back with a bottle of whisky.
"You're a good customer, Tim, I hope you'll accept this. And you'll come back won't you? I'm re-opening tomorrow."
"Sure."
"Good man, and a happy New Year to you."
"And you Danny."
I stood a little longer, taking in the rain-darkened street. Simone would find a cab. Knew how to look after herself. Some people just do.
The lights went out at Danny's and I turned back to the flat.
Imelda was shivering in the doorway, a few people passing her on their way out.
"Rubbish party," I heard one of them say.
Imelda took me by the arm.
"Come on," she said, "what you need is cheering up, so you do."
"So people keep telling me."

We went up and joined the few who remained.

Norman handed me a can.

"You ok?" he said.

"Why shouldn't I be?"

"I dunno, you look a bit…"

"A bit what?"

"Forget it." He raised his can. "Cheers, anyway."

"Yeah, cheers."

Close to midnight, Sage and Hilary came up to me, arm in arm.

"Tim old sport," began Sage, "almost forgot to tell you…"

"What he's trying to say," interrupted Hilary, "is that we've decided to get married."

"Yeah," added Sage, "we're getting wed, man."

"That's nice, "said Imelda, "it's sweet, Tim, isn't it?"

I smiled, nodded, and went looking for where-ever I had left the Danny Scotch.

There was a bloke sitting and smoking at the kitchen table.

He looked up.

"All right," he said, "looks like the booze has run out."

I handed him the whisky.

"Here, knock yourself out."

"Cheers, you're a gent."

"Thanks. And who or what the fuck are you?"

He put down the bottle.

"Steady, mate, let's not spoil things."

"What things? What's to spoil? Go on, have a drink."

"Nah, you're all right."

"Am I?"

He got up, stubbed his fag, and walked out.

I unscrewed the cap and took a stinging slug from the bottle.

"That's right," said Imelda, standing in the doorway, "turn to the bottle."

"If you've come to give advice…"

"I have so, and it's for you to have another shot and pour one for me."

I sat down and she came over and sat across me.

"Know what Tim?" she said, warm whisky breath in my face, "I think I love you."

"And who wouldn't?"

"Quite a catch, so you are."

"The one that didn't get away."
Norman came in.
"Ah, state of you two," he said, "love's young dream or whatever it is. Come on, better join us, it's nearly time."
The countdown had just begun, led by Sage booming out the ten, nine, eight...
And there it was, from one split second to the next, a year past and another begun.
A lot of cheering, smiles, Simone walking away laden down by her possessions, Imelda hanging on my arm trying to kiss me, Norman lighting up a fat joint and Sage and Hilary trying to instigate a sing-along of Auld Lang Syne that never quite got off the ground.

1980

I woke late the next morning and it took me a few minutes to recall what had recently happened. When I did, my stomach sank, and when I sat up my brain seemed to shunt forward and hit bone. Every sound was nerve-tweakingly amplified, including the snoring that was emanating from Imelda's open mouth.
I looked under the covers and found that neither of us had undressed.
The last thing I could remember was something about Sage and Hilary and a wedding, but I wasn't entirely sure if that might not just have been a dream.
I went to the bathroom, put my head under the cold tap, carried on to the kitchen.
There were cans and bottles on the table, floor, in the sink, ditto dog ends.
I put the kettle on and began chucking some of the debris into a bin bag.
A young chap I didn't recognise came in yawning.
"Oh, hi," he said, "d'you live here?"
I nodded.
"Right. Yeah. Well, cheers for letting me kip on the sofa."
"Didn't realise I had."
"Right. Sorry about that. I'll be off then."
I went into the living room which contained a haze of stale smoke, opened the curtains.
The fall-out was similar to that in the kitchen, but at least there were no more bodies.

I took two mugs of tea to the bedroom, but the bed was empty. Then I heard retching sounds from the bathroom, shortly after which Imelda re-appeared looking almost translucently pale.

She picked up an almost empty bottle of Scotch from the foot of the bed.

"Jesus, did we drink all that?"

"Can't remember."

"That makes two of us. How're you feeling?"

"About how you look."

She smiled wanly.

"That tea for me?"

She sat on the bed, took a sip, and patted the space beside her.

"Coming back in?" she said, "coz I know a great cure for the hangover."

"Greasy fry-up?"

"That wasn't what I had in mind."

"Let's settle for toast."

Even that was hard to swallow.

Imelda went to the kitchen cupboard and started lifting cans and shifting boxes.

"I can't believe you," she protested, "no aspirins in the bathroom, none anywhere."

She remained standing with her back to me.

"Tim, will you tell me something?" Her voice was quiet. "Do you not fancy me?"

"I do."

"Then how come we sleep together and nothing happens?"

"We were drunk."

"And now we're hung over. What's happening?"

"I don't know. It's not you, I'm just, you know…"

"Do I? It's not like I'm asking you to marry me or anything."

"You did once."

"Oh, bring that up, won't you?"

"Just saying."

"Well don't. I'm beginning to wonder what I see in you, so I am."

"Not much to see."

"God, talk about maudlin. Know what, Tim, you can stuff your bloody tea and toast."

She strode past me and out the door.

"I'll maybe see you around," she yelled, as she went down the stairs.

I went back to bed, and later carried on clearing the flat.

My head was still banging, and I remembered Danny saying he was opening New Years' day.

I nipped over.

"Ah, Tim, good to see you," he said, turning the sign on the window to 'closed.' "You're just in the nick of time, early closing today."

"Oh, yeah. Well, it's just some aspirins."

He gave me an arch look.

"Took a few drams did we?"

"Something like that."

"Soluble?"

"What?"

"Which type of aspirin."

"Any type. It's nice to see you open again."

"Nice to be open. Onwards and upwards."

"Yes. See you Danny."

"I hope you will."

During the next few days I set about a proper tidy up, clear out some junk. I figured a bit of streamlining would help me sort myself out.

I started with the laundry pile on the bedroom floor, and found, among the shirts and pants, the hairy jumper Simone had given me. I'd hardly worn it, wasn't dirty. Maybe I'd sort of hidden it? I also uncovered a stripy odd sock of Simone's. I wondered if she had the other.

I was about to head out for a walk, when the intercom went.

It was Norman. He still had the beard and had rather carelessly dyed his hair.

"Come in, Norman," I said, "I'll run you a bath."

"There's no need."

Printed in Great Britain
by Amazon